**PRAISE FOR TAYLOR KEATING
WRITING AS CATHRYN FOX**

♦

"Sizzling, irresistible, wonderful."

—Lori Foster,
New York Times bestselling author

"Cathryn Fox is the next Queen of Steamy
Romance."

—Julianne MacLean,
USA Today bestselling author

"A Cathryn Fox book is a must-read great escape."

—S. J. Day,
author of *Eve of Destruction*

BOOKS BY TAYLOR KEATING

Game Over
Mind Games

MIND
GAMES

◆

TAYLOR KEATING

TOR®
paranormal romance

A TOM DOHERTY ASSOCIATES BOOK
NEW YORK

This is a work of fiction. All of the characters, organizations, and events portrayed in this novel are either products of the author's imagination or are used fictitiously.

MIND GAMES

Copyright © 2011 by Taylor Keating

A Tor Book
Published by Tom Doherty Associates, LLC
175 Fifth Avenue
New York, NY 10010

www.tor-forge.com

Tor® is a registered trademark of Tom Doherty Associates, LLC.

ISBN 978-0-7653-6548-4

First Edition: June 2011

Printed in the United States of America

0 9 8 7 6 5 4 3 2 1

For Simme, Hessel, and Gerjan. For always being there.

For Annie and Katie, who wanted so much to see me published but ran out of time. Totally my fault for not writing fast enough.

As always, for the members of Romance Writers of Atlantic Canada.

MIND
GAMES

CHAPTER ONE

♦

They were being watched.

Chase Hawkins, Guardian of the Fae—freezing his ass off on an unfamiliar world while trapped in another man's body—sprang into action. Even though Hawk knew better than anyone that this particular Fae, River Weston, was far from helpless, he could no more stop the instinctive reaction to protect her than he could stop breathing.

He didn't plan to cease either activity anytime soon.

He pushed her slight frame behind him, her usual lightning-fast reflexes dulled by shock and lack of sleep. Whatever watched them from the thick undergrowth of the forest had the advantage on them. They had nowhere to run. At their backs a wide river, its cold, late autumn waters gleaming in the afternoon sun, blocked their escape.

Hawk hated the limitations this foreign body placed on him. It was tall enough, but lacked his muscle. He felt awkward in it, not to mention he had no love for its previous owner. That meant he felt no need to look after it, which was good. He clenched his fists and took a combative stance. So what if it acquired a few extra scars?

"What is it?" River asked, immediately trying to slip past him to see for herself what had made him react with such aggression.

"I don't know," Hawk admitted, grimly pleased that River didn't brush off his concern. They'd been through too much together in the past few days for her to doubt him, but she wouldn't take kindly to his attempts to protect her either. "It's there. In the bushes. This is your world," he added. "What do you think it might be?"

She didn't get a chance to answer him.

An enormous brown bear, silver tipping its shaggy fur, lunged from the forest to their left and hurtled toward them. The attack was unexpected because it came from a different direction than where their watcher lurked in front of them.

River, who in Hawk's experience feared very little, drew in a sharp breath and grabbed his arm, dragging him to the water's edge with surprising strength. Awed by the sheer size and silent speed of the approaching monster, Hawk didn't resist.

He thanked the Great Lords of the Guardians that he'd been able to step into Nick Sutton's body—may he rot in his own special hell—before River's virtual video game had failed, because her reality held every bit as much danger as the virtual one she'd found herself trapped inside through her use of untutored magic. If Hawk had let his soul return to his own body in his Guardian world and left her with no one to watch over her here on earth, who knew what might happen to her now?

Not that he would ever willingly leave her alone. Guardians protected the Fae. Except this particular Fae liked to prove she could take care of herself, which meant he had to do something. Fast. The bear, anger gleaming from its beady eyes, was almost on top of them.

Hawk yanked his arm from River's grasp, pushed her into the water, and squared off against the snorting beast.

An arrow, accompanied by the low whine of whirling fletching, breezed past his cheek and embedded itself in the bear's head, piercing its brain and dropping it in its tracks. Hawk dodged as its lifeless body fell with a heavy thump, a death groan rattling from deep in its throat.

River, wet and angry, surfaced gasping from the cold water.

"What the *hell,* Nick?" she shouted at him, her dark hair streaming around her shoulders, her blue eyes shooting daggers of ice.

Hawk's heart froze in his chest. This wasn't the time to be sensitive about the fact she'd called him by another man's name, even though technically he was wearing that same man's body and she could be excused for the mistake. Somewhere nearby, someone was armed and Hawk didn't intend for his next target to be River.

"Get down!" he ordered her, and with a Fae's instinctive response to the command of a Guardian, she dropped back into the water without hesitation. She was going to be angry with him later for that.

Hawk crouched in front of her, shielding her as best he could, and scanned the forest's edge. He could detect no signs of movement and yet he knew someone was there.

"Show yourself!" he shouted in the direction he guessed the arrow had projected from.

"Step away from River!" came the equally determined response.

At first Hawk thought he'd misheard and that he was being ordered away from the river. Then he realized the owner of the voice, undoubtedly male, knew River's name. And that he sounded unusually young.

That didn't mean Hawk intended to let the faceless archer have a clear shot at her. He'd learned to trust no one.

River didn't share his concern.

"Jake!" she called out. The warm welcome in her voice wasn't lost on Hawk. She knew the identity of the watcher lurking in the undergrowth.

A boy, perhaps twelve or thirteen, gangly limbed and with shaggy blond hair, stepped warily from the woods. He held a crossbow in his hands, another arrow nocked and aimed steady at Hawk's heart. Hawk didn't doubt for a second the boy would shoot him if Hawk gave him a reason. What was going on in River's world?

And who was this kid?

"Put down that crossbow," River said to the boy she'd called Jake. She waded from the water, soaked and shivering and clearly as puzzled as Hawk. "What on earth do you think you're doing, wandering around the woods by yourself?"

Jake kept the crossbow trained on Hawk, and Hawk felt a twinge of respect for him. He might be a boy, but he was a damned good shot and an even better judge of character. Nick Sutton had been the biggest piece of crap Hawk had ever seen.

And Hawk was going to be seeing the piece of crap in the mirror every day unless he could get his consciousness back to his own cryonically frozen body before it was too late. If he'd known when he accepted the mission to search for missing Fae souls that his own was going to be shanghaied by a pissed-off Dark Lord, he'd have requested a better contingency plan and possibly more danger pay. Finding River had been the only good thing to come out of the whole mess.

"Who's he?" Jake asked River with a jerk of his chin in Hawk's direction.

Hawk would be damned if he'd show fear of a little kid. He stooped to examine the still-warm carcass of the bear—not that he had to stoop far. He gave a low whistle. Crisos. That was one mother of a bear. Perhaps he should show a little fear of the kid, at that. He doubted if he would have been able to make such a shot at the same age.

"This is—"

"Nick," Hawk interrupted River smoothly, glancing up at Jake. "Nick Sutton."

River looked at him strangely, and a fierce gladness surged through him in response. This situation was going to take some getting used to—on both their parts—but at least she knew him for who he really was.

That didn't mean Hawk wasn't going to do his damnedest to get back to his own body. Or get River off this shithole of a world and to where she really belonged. Her birth father had been a Guardian, but the magic tied to her soul meant she was 100 percent Fae.

"Did you have to kill it?" River was scolding the boy. She had a Fae's respect for life. She was a healer, a nurturer, a grower. She was not a killer, although she could kick ass when need be.

That was definitely the Guardian genes coming out.

Jake's face grew sullen. "I thought about letting it rip this guy to pieces. But I wasn't sure if he was a friend of yours or one of the people who've been looking for you, so I let him live."

Hawk's head shot up. "Someone's been looking for River?"

"Don't you watch the news?" Jake retorted.

River swayed on her feet and Hawk moved quickly to steady her. She had transported them from the Dark Lord's disintegrating virtual prison to the place she'd been born and raised. She'd done so instinctively because she'd always felt safe here. To find out that she wasn't—not anymore—had to come as a shock to her.

She was wet and shivering. He shrugged out of Nick's jacket, wincing at the bullet hole and the damp patch of congealing blood, and wrapped it around her. Something had happened to River in the final level of the game. She'd disappeared from it suddenly, only to reappear a few moments later with Nick's dying body in her arms. Hawk hadn't yet had a chance to ask her about it, although the bullet hole told him quite a bit, and he was willing to bet whatever it was, it had something—everything—to do with River.

Someone else out there in her adopted world was aware she was . . . special.

"I haven't seen the news recently," Hawk answered Jake. "I've been out of touch the last little while."

"You another gamer?" Jake demanded, a sneer of distaste curling his lip. The crossbow never wavered from its target.

Gee, Jake, tell me what you really think. Hawk turned to River and cocked an eyebrow. "Who's the kid?"

She ignored the question, all her attention on the juvenile delinquent. "Put the crossbow *down*," she ordered again.

When Jake finally lowered the weapon—grudgingly, Hawk noted with approval—River wrapped her arms around the boy and drew him close. He was tall for his age, although he hadn't yet filled out, and he returned her hug with all the embarrassed enthusiasm of any normal teenage boy. Still, it wasn't difficult to tell he was equally as fond of her as she seemed of him.

She turned her head to answer Hawk's question.

"This is Jake. My little brother."

♦ ♦

River couldn't get over how big Jake had grown. She hadn't realized how long it had been since she'd last seen him.

She'd also forgotten how much he looked like their father.

She sat uneasily on the edge of her chair in the sunny kitchen of the farmhouse where she'd grown up, although it hadn't been a true home to her for years. Her parents—the ones who'd raised her—were long gone and the blonde woman across the table from her was little more than a stranger.

River tried to get her head around all that had happened.

Hawk, and regardless of how he looked on the outside River would always know him, pulled his chair closer to hers as if he sensed her disorientation and wanted to shield her from it. River pretended she didn't notice. This particular battle was hers, not his. Melinda had never welcomed her presence in this house. River's father had showered too much of his love on her, and Melinda never forgave him for loving an adopted daughter as much as he'd loved the two natural sons she'd given him. It hadn't mattered that River loved the boys, too. Melinda wasn't big on female competition of any kind.

In all fairness, River didn't care much for Melinda either. She'd appeared in her father's life a little too close on the heels of her adoptive mother's death. River could accept that her father had needed a woman's companionship. She couldn't accept Melinda's need to erase her mother's existence from her father's life.

The flat palm of Hawk's hand went to the slight curve between her shoulders, resting in a casual but protective manner, and Melinda's pale eyes didn't miss

the intimate gesture. The room was too warm and
River was tired, mentally and physically. She stifled a
yawn and tried to focus on what Melinda was saying
to her.

"You can't stay here." Melinda widened her fingers
and pressed her hands atop the old oaken table as if to
brace herself for a fight. "I have children to think
about."

Jake, who'd taken up a watchful stance by the wood
stove, opened his mouth to protest. River held up a
hand to silence him, her eyes pleading with him not to
make things more difficult.

"I understand," she said to Melinda, and she did.
The friends River had worked with for months were
now dead, and River was wanted for questioning. That
was a polite way of saying she was the prime suspect.
Being the prime suspect meant River was guilty until
proven innocent, and anyone caught helping her would
be considered guilty as well. It wouldn't matter that
Jake and their other brother, Sam, were only thirteen
and eleven. She was lucky Melinda didn't take this
opportunity to plant a bullet between her eyes. She'd
be well within her rights to do so, and call it protecting her property. River would bet the only reason she
hadn't was because of Jake standing watch.

Jake couldn't watch over her forever, which meant
she and Hawk weren't safe here. They needed to go.
But go where?

"Well, I *don't* understand," Jake declared. His feet
were planted wide and he fixed his mother with a look
of such disapproval he again reminded River of their

father, and she would have laughed if she'd been able. "This is *River*. She's my sister. And I'm not a child," he added as an afterthought, suddenly picking up that his mother had included him in her reason for denying River a place to stay. He patted the strap of the cross-bow still slung across his shoulder. "Anyone else tries to come after her, they won't get close enough to the house to even know she's here."

Things might be settling down somewhat in the cities after the war but here in the mountains, vigilantism was alive and well. River hated this life for her brothers, and their father had, too, but Melinda seemed to accept it and River had no say.

"One night and all day tomorrow," Hawk said. "We'll be gone by tomorrow night, as soon as it's dark."

River wanted to leave immediately. "That's not a good idea," she said to him quietly. "If we stay, we put them all in danger."

"You need to sleep," he pointed out in return. His gaze went to Jake although he continued to address River. "You've gone too long without it. And if you're going to sleep, I want someone I trust standing guard over you."

That comment scored him major points with Jake. The boy glowed from the compliment and River tried not to roll her eyes. She looked at Melinda, stone-faced across the table from her, easily interpreting her step-mother's thoughts.

"I think we should leave now," River said.

Melinda bit her lip and looked at Jake. It occurred to River then that Melinda didn't want to alienate her son, and that she relied far more on the boy than she should. Jake had become her protection, and River felt fury rise in her that Melinda would put a child in such a position.

Her fury died as quickly as it rose, replaced by guilt. Melinda had never been able to look after herself. Therefore, had Melinda put Jake in that position, or by walking away from them after her father's death, had River?

"One night," Melinda said, and River could tell that it almost killed her to make the concession. "But I want you out of here as soon as the sun goes down tomorrow."

Another blond-headed boy, smaller than Jake and with baby fat still rounding out his cheeks, dashed through the door of the kitchen, banging it loudly behind him. He drew up short when he saw who sat at the table. His feet began moving again as soon as he recognized her.

"River!" he shouted, launching himself across the kitchen and into her arms. Laughing, he wrestled her from the chair and onto the floor.

She had him on his back with his shoulders pinned beneath her knees before Hawk could decide to take offense to the assault.

Hawk, however, seemed more amused than offended. He leaned back in his chair. "Another brother?" he guessed.

"This is Sam," she said, getting to her feet. "Sam, meet . . ." Again, she stumbled over the name. She found it difficult to look at Hawk in Nick's body. She couldn't quite meet his eyes and she felt his amusement fade when he realized it.

"Nick," Hawk said easily, holding out his hand for the eleven-year-old to shake.

River hoped Hawk pretending to be Nick wasn't a permanent situation. Nick had died because of her, and more than anything else she hated that reminder every time she looked at him.

At Hawk.

Supper was awkward, not that she'd expected it to be one big happy family reunion. They all sat at the round table, Sam and Hawk chatting easily, Jake sullen and silent, and Melinda and River trying to ignore each other's existence. Melinda kept looking at the drawn curtains as if worried someone might somehow be looking back.

Jake got up from the table and flipped on the television.

The news was on. River's picture filled the top right-hand corner of the screen as the story of the dead gamers scrolled across the bottom, over and over, while the anchor delivered the local weather in a nasal monotone.

Hawk's knife clattered to his plate. "Turn it off. River doesn't need to see that."

"Yes, she does," Melinda replied, delicately sliding a forkful of peas into her mouth.

Jake's hand hovered near the television's control and he looked at River, clearly not knowing what he should do.

"Leave it, Jake." River's eyes fixed on the words on

the screen as her dinner turned to ice in her stomach. She flinched when her picture was replaced with shots from the bloodstained crime scenes.

It was true. Her friends were dead. Johnny, Tanner, and Marcia, who'd never done anything bad to anyone. Okay, maybe Marcia had been a bit of a trashy bitch. That didn't mean she'd deserved to die. Especially not the way she had.

"Who do you think really killed them?" Sam asked with all the tact of an eleven-year-old, although River appreciated his assumption that it hadn't been her.

"On this world?" Hawk's lip curled. "It could have been their own mothers."

River had forgotten that Hawk—who looked like Nick—was Guardian, not human, and that his opinion of humans wasn't particularly high. His antagonism for anyone who might try to harm her, even with words, could push him too far. To him she was Fae, and Guardians protected the Fae at all cost. Being here was a bad idea, but when the virtual game they'd been trapped in had begun to collapse around them, all she'd been able to think about was her father, and home, and safety.

She rubbed her temples to ward off an impending headache. Her parents were gone and this wasn't home anymore, and she and Hawk were far from safe. Melinda was right. While they were here, neither were her brothers.

But where were she and Hawk supposed to go?

"I'll do the dishes," River said when the meal was over, pushing back from the table.

"No!" Melinda said sharply, and Sam and Jake both turned to look at her in surprise. She pulled herself together and smiled thinly. "I'm sure you both need some sleep. You look tired."

River was. She knew Hawk was tired as well. But River didn't need to read minds to know that Melinda wanted them out of sight.

"We'll sleep in the attic," River said. She had old clothes up there, and she'd be damned if she'd ask for permission to claim her own belongings.

"Come and wake me before you go to bed," Hawk said to Jake, who nodded.

Men. It saddened River to realize her brother was becoming one far too soon.

"You realize, don't you, that he won't go to bed?" she whispered to Hawk as they climbed the creaky, narrow flight of wooden stairs to the attic on the third floor.

"Just like he realizes I won't go to sleep," Hawk whispered in return. He smiled at her frown. "Don't worry. Nick had a bit of stamina left in him. One sleepless night won't hurt."

River bit her lip. There had been more than one sleepless night for Hawk. Physically, he'd be fine without it for a little while longer. Mentally, however, Hawk had been thrown more than most people could handle. He was strong, but she knew he worried about the state of his mind.

River worried about it, too. He'd spent months with his consciousness trapped in a virtual prison by an angry Dark Lord, and sleep hadn't been an option for him. To go to sleep would have meant losing touch with reality. Somewhere on the Guardian world Hawk's real body waited for him in stasis, and his soul was all that held his consciousness connected to it. River was the reason he hadn't returned to his body when the virtual prison she'd tapped into through her game collapsed, because as long as he believed River was in danger, he would never leave her.

"You have to sleep," she said to him.

"Tell you what," Hawk replied. He pushed open the attic door and felt for a light switch. The bare bulb dangling from the slanted ceiling flared to life, blinding River for a split second. "Why don't you grab a few hours first?" He touched her shoulder, just a light brush of his fingertips, before he drew his hand away. "I'll wake you."

She didn't believe him. He might look like Nick on the outside, but the stubborn light in his eyes was all Hawk. It was pointless to argue. She reached out to place her palm over where Nick had been shot, intending to pass on some of her natural healing energy so his body would at least have that, but Hawk backed away.

"Please, River," he said softly. "Let me get used to all this first. I promise you I'll sleep, but not right now. Okay?"

What more could she say or do? Hawk knew his limitations better than she did. She found a couple of old folding cots and two sleeping bags stored against one wall, pulled them to the center of the room, shook out the dust, and curled up on one of the thin, musty mattresses.

It felt like heaven.

Sleep, however, wasn't coming easily to River either. The video game she'd spent months developing in her adoptive mother's memory had ultimately failed, and worse, had only ever worked because of magic. Her friends were dead and she was wanted for questioning. Somewhere out there, in another world, Hawk's body waited for him to return to it. Her parents—her birth parents—were dead, too, their souls trapped in an unmarked grave she needed desperately to find.

And whenever her lids flickered shut, she saw the man with the crazy eyes aiming his gun at Nick and pulling the trigger. Something about that particular memory bothered her, but she was too tired to puzzle it out. She hadn't been able to save Nick. Nothing else mattered.

Hawk flipped off the attic light and River heard him settle onto the cot in the darkness beside her. The tips of the old maple tree next to the house, its branches naked now of leaves, scratched at the weathered siding with every slight nudge of the wind.

"We need to find Andy," River said.

Hawk's steady breathing stopped for a second, then resumed. "Forget about her. She has magic, River. That's why you chose her to be the Wizard in your game. The magic in you recognized the magic in her. I didn't trust her then and I won't trust her now. We need to find out what happened to your parents and then get the hell off this piece-of-shit world before anything more goes wrong."

"If Andy has magic," River replied, not liking the criticism of her friend, "then that's all the more reason to find her. Maybe she's Fae. Maybe she can help us find my parents. And it's not a 'piece-of-shit world,'" she added as an afterthought, not liking the criticism of her world either. "We've had a bit of a setback, but new technology is helping us to rebuild."

"Andy's not Fae. I guarantee it. And whatever she is, she's not going to help us." He sounded certain of that. The springs on his cot creaked as he shifted position. "I thought only the Fae and the Dark Lords had magic, but Dark Lords are male. I don't know how she can have it as well, but she does, and I don't trust her. Something's wrong on this world. Really wrong."

Fae souls, he'd told her, held the magic of life, and when the Fae passed on, their souls were reborn. Fae numbers were dwindling and no one knew why. Hawk had been sent to find out, and his drifting consciousness had been caught by a Dark Lord contained in a long-forgotten, Guardian-created virtual prison. River had tapped into that prison through her game and helped set Hawk free.

But he wasn't free. Not yet. Now he was trapped in Nick's body, refusing to leave her because he believed she was Fae, while River didn't know what to believe anymore except that she'd felt the unmistakable presence of her birth parents somewhere here on Earth, and they were far from at peace. She had to find them. After that, she would help Hawk get home.

She would not, however, be going with him. Her mind was made up. No matter who her birth parents might have been, or where they were from, this was River's world. She already knew she was good with technology. If she had magic as well then she owed it to the memory of the adoptive parents who'd loved her, and the brothers who needed her, to help her world recover after the devastation of a viral pandemic and the chaos of global war. Her ego wasn't so large as to think she could do it single-handedly, but her parents had brought her up to believe that everyone had to do his part, and no part was too small.

"Andy is my friend." River didn't doubt that, regardless of what Hawk might think. "That's the reason I copied the Wizard after her. She didn't steer us wrong in the game, and if she has magic, she'll help us now. Besides," she added, pointing out the obvious, "with my photograph splashed all over the news, where else can we go?"

Hawk grunted, clearly unhappy but without an alternative suggestion. River would have liked to crawl into his arms and pretend everything was normal, but it would be too weird. In her game he'd played the role of Sever, the character meant to watch her back. Now he was Nick, and that was going to take some getting used to.

No matter what role he played though, inside, he was Hawk. And she trusted him more than anyone.

"If she starts talking that cryptic shit again," Hawk complained, "I'm going to forget she's a woman." He reached over and nudged River's cot with his foot. His voice softened as he changed the subject.

"Why don't you tell me what happened to Nick?"

♦ ♦

Nick Sutton had always assumed death would be more . . . final.

He hadn't factored in the possibility of being hijacked by someone—something—with a bit more tenacity. Now Nick was trapped, without a body, on a world that looked like the ass end of hell, with some sort of psycho who thought of himself as a Dark Lord. And both of them were royally pissed.

He didn't care what happened to the nutjob clinging like a hemorrhoid to his consciousness. Nick wanted to get his body back. He worried about River, too. The jerkoff had better not touch her.

The wind lifted and tossed shimmering sheets of red sand, snapping them about like the covers of an unmade bed. A thick haze of heat made the skyline dance. Nick could feel nothing solid—not the heat, not the sting of the flailing sand. Hate, however, he felt just fine. And he hated that thieving video game character Sever even more than all the crazy-ass psycho killers in his life. The fact that he had more than one of them was a fleeting cause for alarm, but then Nick remembered that he was technically dead and therefore had no life. Alarm disappeared to be replaced by another fear.

What if Nick couldn't get his body back?

The raging homicidal maniac attached to him, hovering at the edge of his consciousness and mixing his thoughts with Nick's, wore at Nick's already frayed nerves. Regardless of what this other guy thought, he wasn't yet ready to accept the possibility that this might be his new home for all of eternity. Worse, that this might be his new soul mate. He'd always hoped Marilyn Monroe would be waiting for him on the other side. He kind of dug hot, older babes.

Carefully, not wanting to alert the nutjob that he was snooping, Nick probed the edges of the swirling storm of memories thinly attached to his own. This guy made General Amos Kaye, the mother of all human crazies, look like the Tooth Fairy. But mixed in with the images of the video game character Sever being torn limb from limb—which Nick enjoyed—and of River with glowing red eyeballs and a crushed Sever oozing from between her tightly clenched fingers—which Nick also enjoyed but found creepy—he managed to pluck out a few details regarding his current unpleasant predicament.

The Dark Lord had been around for so long that he couldn't remember his real name. He'd been trapped on this world in a virtual prison, which River had tapped into through her video game, by a race the Dark Lord called *Guardians*. The Dark Lord was held here now by the magic of another race he called *Fae*. And Nick, lucky bastard that he was, was held by the Dark Lord because the crazy fuck thought he might somehow be useful to him.

Nick was nothing if not an optimist. He'd survived life by doing what was necessary. He'd survive death the same way. Somewhere in all those random thoughts the Dark Lord couldn't quite control because of his anger, Nick caught the image of a bowl of stones, flickering and gleaming with light, and the impression that these stones were somehow important.

The rising wind whipped the sheets of sand into swirling dust devils, boring deep to bare the ground beneath. A flash of light uncovered by the shifting sand, then another, snagged Nick's attention.

Hey, Sandman, he thought, mentally shouting to catch the raving lunatic's attention. If he could be useful to the Dark Lord, then maybe the Dark Lord could be useful to him. He projected an image of the stones lying in the sand to the other consciousness, and felt it go still. *You got any use for these?*

CHAPTER TWO

◆

Hanging by his arms from a steel hook in the ceiling, the toes of his boots barely grazing the floor, blood dripping down his back and the smell driving him wild, Bane struggled to lift his head against the clawing pain in his neck and shoulders.

One of his shoulders popped, and he let out a low howl.

"More," he panted through the waves of pain. The man standing in front of him didn't so much as blink. Bane didn't know how General Amos Kaye had managed to track him down, but he had, and this was his punishment. He might as well enjoy it.

"You are a moron," Kaye replied without inflection.

"I told you to separate River Weston from her team members. I didn't tell you to tear them to pieces and scatter their remains over the entire city. That was several degrees of separation too many."

Bane had known at the time he was going too far, but once a Were got a taste of blood it was next to impossible to stop. Since Kaye had been the one to bio-engineer Weres he'd known that particular quirk about them, and in Bane's mind that made everything Kaye's fault, not his.

But while Bane might be a moron, he wasn't suicidal. He kept his opinion to himself. A few hours of torture were a small price to pay considering what Kaye normally did to the people who failed him.

He shook his head, tossing his sweat-soaked black hair away from his face, ignoring the white-hot pain in his dislocated shoulder. One good thing about being a Were—pain didn't stop them. It kept them going. Once he'd made his point, Kaye wouldn't waste a lot of time on torture.

Somewhere in the dim, dark recesses of Bane's brain, a thought shouted out that he should probably let Kaye know he'd gotten the point before it was too late.

"It won't happen again," he said through broken lips.

Kaye stared him hard in the eye, something Bane really hated, and worse, Kaye knew it. If he were any-one else Bane would have gone for his throat—even lashed to the ceiling as he was. Kaye, however, was es-tablishing dominance, and Bane let his own gaze drop to the floor in acceptance of it.

Kaye drew back a steel-toed boot and kicked Bane hard in one knee. Bane bit back a snarl in response.

"Cut him down," Kaye ordered. Someone who smelled of french fries and day-old grease stepped up from behind, out of Bane's line of vision, and seconds later Bane crumpled to the sawdust-covered floor at Kaye's feet. His shoulder snapped back into place and his eyes watered.

Kaye leaned over him, his boots close to Bane's face. "The next time I give you an order, you do exactly as you're told. Don't ever make me have to clean up after you again. Do you understand?"

Bane nodded, not yet able to catch his breath past the pulsating pain in his knee. His back, too, was on fire, and the scent of his own blood mixed with fresh sawdust made him drool. He wanted to hurt someone. Preferably someone else.

"Now," Kaye said, hunkering down on his heels and hauling Bane's head back by the hair. "I have another job for you, and this time I want it done right. I want River Weston. And I want her alive."

♦ ♦

Hawk listened to the soft sighs of River's breathing, slow and steady, in the darkness of the cold attic as she finally gave in to exhaustion.

She was the first ray of light to come into his life in a very long time. Protecting her gave him a purpose. She didn't take away the pain of losing his wife and daughter, but she made their loss bearable.

He rolled to his side on the small, creaking cot and

tucked his elbow under his head to use as a pillow. Hawk couldn't really fault River's stepmother for wanting to protect her children. If he could buy back that last moment with his daughter, he'd never let her leave the house.

He pondered what River had told him about Nick and those final moments in the compound before she had jumped. Sooner or later she was going to figure out that Nick had betrayed her. He'd sold her out and Hawk had to find out to whom, how much they knew about her, and if that knowledge could be contained, because River had no idea how valuable she was or the amount of danger she was really in. She might have been born on this world but she didn't belong here. That she was the result of a mating between a Fae and a Guardian—something both races forbade— didn't change the fact that she possessed a Fae's magical soul, or that she belonged with them.

But what had happened to River's birth parents?

Hawk frowned at the rafters. When he and River had been trapped in her game, fighting their way from level to level, she had sensed the presence of her birth parents in a graveyard outside of a laboratory she hadn't programmed. A lot of her game had been developed using the magic she hadn't known she possessed, and someone else had tapped into that magic to introduce elements she couldn't control. His money was on Andy, aka River's Wizard. River would never leave this world until she found out what had happened to her parents, and Andy would know that about her. Also, Andy had called him *Guardian* in the game. If she knew that much about him, she'd know that he would never leave here without River.

But if he didn't get back to his own body before it became unsustainable, he didn't know if he could get home again. He had no desire to stay in this borrowed body any longer than necessary. Looking in the mirror made him want to punch himself in the face.

Hawk waited patiently as the household below slowly settled into sleep. Somewhere down there, Jake was wide awake and worrying over what was going on with his sister. Hawk didn't intend to give the kid any reason to shoot him.

He swung his feet to the floor, wishing he dared take River in his arms and hold her while she slept, but he wouldn't do so. He didn't like the idea of holding her while he was in her former lover's body. If he were to touch her, he wanted her knowing exactly who he was and what he meant to her. There would be no mistaking him for Nick.

Besides, River was Fae. That, to Hawk, was more important than anything else. They had slept together as virtual characters, but now that they were back in reality, he had no excuse to touch her. Whatever circumstances had thrown River's Fae mother and Guardian father together, Hawk would not repeat their mistake because it had undoubtedly cost them their lives. His duty now was to guard River, to protect her, and to take her home where she belonged and could realize her full potential.

He was not, however, going to take her from a brother who loved her without at least trying to make him understand. What if Jake spent the rest of his life looking for a sister who couldn't be found?

Hawk would have torn the universe apart looking for his wife and daughter if he hadn't known for certain they were dead.

He cracked open the attic door and Jake tumbled through. Hawk grabbed him by the shoulder to keep him from rolling across the floor, hoisted him to his feet, and put a finger to his lips. Jake nodded in understanding and they quietly descended two flights of stairs, Jake pointing out for Hawk where the steps creaked.

They went into the kitchen. Hawk closed the door behind him, not wanting to wake anyone else in the house. This conversation was between him and Jake.

"Why were you sitting outside our door?" Hawk asked. "If anyone tried to break in, they'd come in through one of the downstairs doors or windows, not the attic."

Jake's chin edged up. "I wanted to be sure River was okay."

Fair enough. Jake had wanted to be sure River was safe with Hawk. He sat down across from Jake, resting his folded forearms on the table. "One thing you should understand," he said. "River is always going to be okay when she's with me."

"Unless she's being chased by a bear," Jake added.

Cheeky little bastard. "How often are people chased by bears?"

Jake met his gaze. "Usually just once."

Round one went to Jake.

The clock on the wall ticked off the seconds. Hawk drummed the table with his fingertips. "What if I told you River has the potential to outrun bears or anything else that might go after her?"

"I'd wonder why she'd bother to run," Jake said. "Who do you think taught me to use a crossbow?" He folded his arms, too, mimicking Hawk's posture. "What if I told you that bear wasn't after River? That it was only after you?"

Hawk liked the kid. He really did. He would have made a kickass Guardian. "I'd believe you. But I'd ask why you think so."

"I don't think so, I know so." Jake's tone was triumphant. "River's not afraid of animals and they aren't afraid of her. But they don't like everyone, and they don't like to be surprised, so she taught me to use a crossbow when I was six."

Interesting. River didn't like killing, but she knew the need for it sometimes. That had to be her mixed heritage coming out in her. Hawk sat back, thoughtful. "Do you think that's normal?"

Jake's young face instantly went wary. "It's normal for River."

Which meant Jake knew River wasn't normal. Hawk wondered how many more people in River's life knew she wasn't. His blood chilled just thinking about it.

An earsplitting scream rang out from the attic. Next came a loud crash as someone knocked something over upstairs, most likely as they were startled from sleep.

Hawk couldn't remember ever hearing River scream like that before, even though she'd had plenty of reason to do so. He rattled his chair back and took the steps two at a time, well ahead of Jake pounding behind him, registering the alarm on Melinda's face as he ran past her open bedroom door on the second floor on his way to the third.

"No, Jake!" she said sharply, and the footsteps behind Hawk skidded to a stop as Melinda grabbed her son by the arm.

Hawk raced up the second set of stairs, threw open the attic door, and flipped on the light.

The attic was empty.

Breathing hard, he looked around the room. River wasn't there. He heard Jake on the stairs and quickly stepped back, closing the door.

"She thought she saw a rat," Hawk said shortly. "Wouldn't you know it? The one animal she is afraid of. She's fine. She told me to get the hell out and shut off the light so she could go back to sleep. Women."

There was enough doubt on Jake's face for Hawk to breathe easier. River had a phobia about rats and her brother knew it. Seeing one of those might make her scream.

"Go calm your mother down," Hawk added, his hand on the doorknob. "I'll talk to River and in a few minutes you can come in and talk to her, too, if it makes you feel better. Just wait for me to call you, okay?"

"It was probably just a mouse," Jake said. He turned and went back down the stairs.

Hawk ducked into the attic and closed the door firmly behind him. He had a good idea where River had gone, but how was he supposed to get there?

High on the end wall, just under the peak of the rafters, was a small window, most likely meant to help keep the roof from sweating. Hawk thought he could probably squeeze through it with a minimal loss of flesh. Since it wasn't his flesh to begin with, it was no big deal to him.

He stood on some boxes and hoisted himself through the window, grunting as the rough frame scraped his ribs. He looked down and immediately wished he hadn't. He hated heights. He gritted his teeth. He wouldn't do this for anyone but River.

It was too far to jump to the ground, but a maple tree with sturdy branches was well within reach. Pushing farther out of the window, and hanging mostly from his hips, he seized hold of one rough branch and hauled himself the rest of the way. When his legs were free he let the branch take his full weight, swinging like a pendulum until he could hook his ankles around the base of the branch near the tree trunk. From there, it was an easy climb to the ground.

Hawk had a good sense of direction and even in the dark it didn't take him long to find his way to the river. He didn't try to be quiet as he half walked, half ran. If he startled any more bears they would just have to eat him.

Nick probably tasted like shit anyway.

"River?" he called, scanning the clearing as it came into view in the pale light of a spent full moon.

There she was, shivering near the water's edge, a sleeping bag still wrapped tightly around her.

"What the hell happened to me?" she demanded, sounding more pissed off than anything. "And how do I keep it from happening again?"

Hawk really liked that about her—she didn't waste time worrying about what was over and done with. She focused on the solution.

"You jumped," Hawk said. It was how the Fae traveled from world to world, but River was new to her talents and she had no idea how to control it. One of the ways beginners coordinated their jumps was by following a thread. She'd jumped to the river again, not because it was someplace she felt safe, but because it was a place she'd jumped to already and she'd instinctively known the way. She'd told him her adoptive father had found her here when she was a baby, which meant she'd probably jumped here with her birth mother. Hawk wondered why he hadn't figured that out before.

But what had made River jump here tonight? She'd been asleep when he'd left her alone in the attic.

"We won't know how to keep it from happening again until we know why you jumped in the first place," he said to her. "What was the screaming about?"

River tugged the sleeping bag tighter around her slender shoulders and Hawk caught a quick flash of distress on her face. He'd seen her wear a similar expression only once before, when she'd felt the souls of her parents trapped in a hidden graveyard. He hadn't liked it then and he didn't like it now.

"River," he prodded. "What was it?"

She waved her hand, trying to dismiss it as nothing. "Just a dream."

Fear of dreaming was what kept him awake. He was afraid he wouldn't be able to tell the difference between what was real and what wasn't, or worse, that there would be no difference.

He hid his concern in a Guardian command. "Tell me about it."

"I felt . . ." Her words trailed off as she tried to find the right words. "A soul. And I felt magic."

"Fae magic?"

"Yes. No. I don't know." She blinked up at him. "It felt like mine, only different. More like the magic back in the graveyard. It felt . . . twisted." She cleared her throat and the sound cut through the quiet of the night. "Damaged, somehow."

A breeze whispered in the forest behind him and Hawk turned, sweeping his gaze across the wide expanse of trees and shrubs, half expecting another bear attack or something even more dangerous. His months in a virtual prison had taught him to trust nothing. His hand went to his leg, only to come up empty.

He needed a weapon.

He turned back to River, who was watching him intently, and for her sake he tried to be calm. "How close did this soul get to you? Does it know where you are?"

"It looked at me. It didn't want to hurt me. It wants me to help it." Her chest rose and fell as she drew in a breath of frustration. "How am I supposed to help it when I don't even know what it is?"

"I'm not sure." He didn't care what it was or if it needed help. He wanted River safe. He scanned the woods a second time. "We need to go back to the house."

"You don't think I'm going crazy?"

They shared a similar fear. Not surprising, considering everything that had happened to them. He didn't dismiss or downplay it, but gave it the same careful consideration he would if he'd been the one with an unsettling dream.

"No, I don't," he said honestly. "It's entirely possible that something is here, trying to contact you through your dreams or your magic." His mouth tightened. "That doesn't mean I believe it's harmless."

Her glance drifted in the direction of the house. "You don't think anything's harmless. And you might not think I'm crazy, but right now Melinda probably does."

Self-doubt was foreign to the River he'd come to know, and Hawk refused to encourage it in her. She was a survivor. "If anything, she probably thinks you're a sissy. I told Jake you screamed because you saw a rat."

She brightened at that, and the fist of worry squeezing his heart loosened its grip. "Perfect. Melinda will hate the thought of rats in the house."

"For a Fae, you've got a real mean streak," Hawk pointed out, amused and relieved by the pettiness of her response.

The flash of her smile in the moonlight sucked the air from his chest, and he felt her soul reach out to his. "It must be the Guardian half coming out in me."

The subtle shift in her mood presented him with a different type of danger. River wanted to burn off tension, and while he liked her methods—liked them a lot—if he touched her, he would never be forgiven for it. Neither would she.

"Now we know why Guardians and Fae are forbidden to mix," he said lightly. "It makes for a bad combination."

She wasn't about to be put off so easily. The sleeping bag slipped from her shoulders. "The Guardians and the Fae don't know what they're missing. I don't think it's a bad combination at all."

Crisos. He was no longer even mildly amused. She was the most beautiful woman he'd ever met, and the touch of her soul never failed to make his skin tighten. They had been together in her game, but it was forbidden for them to be together in reality. She didn't understand that, nor did she care.

He did. Very much. He was the one who would have to be strong for both of them, and thanked all that was holy he was not in his own body right now. Nick's body, he could torment. If he were in his own Hawk doubted very much if he could find the will to resist her. Not when her flawless Fae beauty, her silky smooth skin and firm breasts, beckoned his touch, his mouth.

The memories alone were enough to bring him to his knees.

As if sensing him weaken River took a deliberate step closer, and he felt the warm waves of desire pouring off her. A low, tortured noise crawled out of his throat, a half groan, half growl, and there wasn't a damn thing he could do to stifle it. The sweet scent of her skin reached his nostrils and might have undone him if he hadn't spotted the smudges of fatigue beneath her eyes as her lids fluttered shut. Concern for her well-being overrode his own desire.

No matter how much he craved her, or knew that she wanted him, too, he had to fight the powerful pull between them. She could never be his. Fae produced one child only, and that one child had to be able to host a Fae soul. To the best of his knowledge, River was the only half-breed who could.

She was the only half-breed he'd ever even heard of.

"You have to take us back to the attic," he said to her. "Before we're discovered missing."

With a heavy, resigned sigh and a shrug of her shoulders, she gathered the sleeping bag she'd dropped to the ground and the mood was broken. "I don't know how to jump on purpose," she complained. "It sort of just happens."

Hawk's own knowledge was strictly secondhand. Before River, he'd never known a Fae in real life. His wife had been the traveler, the one who'd accompanied the Fae and aided in rebuilding troubled worlds. Hawk was military. He didn't rebuild worlds. He'd been trained to defuse them.

"Reach out with your soul," he instructed her. "Search for a thread, something that feels connected to you. Then follow it with your thoughts and see where it leads."

River closed her eyes and Hawk waited, trying not to rush her, but time was fast running out. Jake wouldn't wait long to knock on that attic door.

"I have it!" she cried, triumphant, her eyes flashing open.

Hawk wrapped his arms around her waist, hoping she'd picked the right thread and that they weren't about to find themselves back on the Dark Lord's dying planet. There was only one way to find out. "Pull on it," he ordered.

With a jerk, they were back in the attic.

Jake stood in the open doorway, jaw hanging open and shock etched in his face.

♦ ♦

Constable James Peters sat in the Premier's office, praying this meeting would be short and sweet, and hoping like hell he didn't slop espresso on his uniform. Dress was hellish hard to clean.

The smug bastard in the two-thousand-dollar suit—Peters read the papers just like everyone else—slid the file across the polished mahogany desk with the tip of a manicured finger.

"I don't need a visual image," Premier George L. Johnson said with distaste. "If General Kaye says River Weston is guilty, then she's guilty. I have no reason to question his findings."

Peters wished he dared remind Johnson of the good old days, before the virus and the war, when a person was presumed innocent until proven guilty. The premier, with his fancy law degree and years as a Supreme

Court judge, should remember those days. That thick thatch of white hair and the heavy bags under his eyes made him look older than God.

Peters hadn't wanted to come here today. He'd been summoned, and that fact alone left him unenthusiastic. But he'd seen a chance to plead River Weston's case and stupidly, he'd grabbed it. He didn't know her. He'd never even met her. But call him a softie, he couldn't shake her photograph from his mind. He'd believe in Santa Claus before he'd ever accept that the fresh-faced, innocent-eyed girl in the file photos had turned on her friends and torn them to shreds.

That two of the victims had outweighed her by at least a hundred pounds was another fact in her favor, and Jim Peters never argued with the facts. He was a cop because he believed in the inherent goodness of humanity, not because he liked all humans as individuals.

Johnson leaned forward, his cuff links clicking against the desk. "Kaye tells me you led security detail at Westmount."

Peters swallowed hard. This was a part of his past he'd hoped never to revisit. Westmount was one of the better areas of Montreal. During the war some of its wealthier residents had pooled their pocket change to turn Westmount into one giant, gated community and funded their own private army to police it. If Peters had fully understood what "private army" meant to them, he would have turned mall cop instead. He'd traveled as far west as he could to escape that particular chapter of his life.

The whole world should be ashamed of some of the things that had happened during the war. He knew he was, and late at night he sometimes still woke in a cold sweat. Being young and ambitious was no excuse, merely an explanation.

"That was a long time ago," Peters said. Most of the people in that community were long dead. It took a special kind of leader to keep an army of genetically modified mutants in check. A lot of them hadn't grasped the difference between the people at either end of their leash. They'd go after anything that moved.

"Kaye also tells me you were especially good at keeping the Westmount army under control."

The small pewter clock on the desk ticked into the silence as Peters pondered his options. He knew what had really killed those poor gamers, and Johnson knew he knew. Johnson probably also knew he wouldn't talk about it, since he'd kept his silence over Westmount. He'd never spoken of what had made the papers, let alone what hadn't.

What Peters didn't know was why those gamers had been killed, or why Kaye, and now Johnson, were trying to blame a skinny, innocent little girl for it. Neither did he want to know. He hadn't yet reached retirement age. He'd done all he could for her.

"This General Kaye seems to know a lot about me for someone I met once," Peters replied, trying to buy time and find out how much shit he was in.

Johnson tilted back in his executive chair, steepling his fingers, and stared off into space. Peters strongly suspected he was wondering how much information to reveal.

"General Amos Kaye," Johnson said finally, "is a genius. He's the man behind the research and development of the Bioengineered Military Program."

The room tilted for a few heartbeats before righting again. Peters worked hard to keep the fear from his expression. Shit had just piled up to chin level. Kaye was the Monster Man, and Peters had sat across from him at a table in the station's conference room while Kaye had pinned those murders on River Weston. Either Kaye was covering up for one of his monsters . . .

Or River Weston *was* the monster. Peters was no longer so certain she couldn't have killed those gamers.

Sweat trickled down his spine and pooled at his waistband. Ethics had been the first thing to go when the virus broke out and the world went to hell, but the so-called "army" he'd once overseen hadn't been so difficult to control as long as he'd remembered what he was dealing with. Kaye—the crazy bastard—had taken animal and human DNA and combined it. The result was a human with animal strength and instincts, but that wasn't especially intelligent. Peters had established his dominance and played the pack leader, so he'd been okay, but he hadn't slept very well at night wondering when he'd be challenged for the position. When he noticed the first subtle shifts in pack dynamics he'd quit his post and gotten as far away from their territory as he could. He'd heard his replacement hadn't been as observant. When the pack had turned on him and the community they were supposed to protect, it had been impossible to keep it out of the news. People preferred to believe in mythical fairy-tale monsters come to life rather than that their military had manufactured them. With a loss of ethics went common sense.

"The BMP was shut down a long time ago," Peters said.

"Yes. Well." Johnson cleared his throat, for the first time looking uncomfortable. "It wasn't so much shut down as put on hiatus for lack of funding. Funding has since been restored."

He didn't want to hear any more, although it wasn't exactly a surprise. Particularly not after the gamer deaths. "This has nothing to do with me."

"It does now." Johnson's face went grim. "River is part of Kaye's latest research and he wants her back."

Peters hadn't been born in a cabbage patch. He hadn't fallen off a turnip truck, or any of the other clichés that meant he was stupid. And he was sick to frigging death of how far society's so-called leaders—the country's supposed moral fiber—had sunk. He still believed that people were basically good. He also believed that absolute power corrupted absolutely. The Johnsons and Kayes of the world did not represent humanity. They represented power.

If River Weston was a monster, she was the highest functioning one Peters had ever been exposed to. She was smart—she hadn't become a software engineer and video game designer by ripping the arms and legs off her coworkers. She'd have had to dupe her boyfriend,

Nick Sutton, too, and that boy was no fool. "I still don't see how this has anything to do with me."

"Kaye has a soldier who can track her down and contain her, but he's proved a little difficult to . . . control." Again, Johnson looked uncomfortable. Peters didn't miss the way his glance shifted to the file folder still on his desk. Inside were the pictures of the crime scenes and the tattered remains of the dead gamers. "He wants you to work with this soldier to bring River Weston in."

Peters placed his half-empty cup of espresso on the desk, stood, and for the first time in twenty-some years found his backbone. "Tell Kaye he can go fuck himself."

"You misunderstand." Johnson's eyes went cold. "I'm not asking. You either work with Kaye or you work against him. If you're working against him, you can expect that what happened here"—he tapped the file—"will look like a mercy killing compared to what happens to you. There's nothing I can do to help you."

Peters wasn't yet ready to put his service revolver into his mouth and pull the trigger. If he'd been so inclined he would have done it twenty years ago. So that was option B.

But, Jesus, he hated being ordered around by dickheads who refused to get their own hands dirty. He snatched up the file.

"I'll think about it," he said, and wiped his dress shoes on the thick cream carpet before he walked from the room.

CHAPTER THREE

♦

Spencer Jennings, Spence to his friends, walked the long marble corridor leading to the meeting chamber of the Great Lords of the Guardians with all the enthusiasm of a man condemned.

As the lead cryogenicist in the current research program, he might as well be condemned. The Great Lords' pet project, Lieutenant Colonel Chase Hawkins, was turning into an enormous scientific snafu and no one wanted to admit it.

Spence was about to. He had a real soft spot for Hawk. They'd become good friends in the months leading up to Hawk's current cryonic state, and Spence didn't like the way the research project was now heading. In theory, a frozen mortal body should last for a thousand years. In practice, the variables dropped that number to a matter of months. The mortal body was far too complex. Intracellular damage from water condensation was its biggest threat.

The fact that Spence was being yanked from the project and assigned to another lab didn't give him much hope for long-term success either. The Great Lords wanted him teaching his research findings. Spence wouldn't mind doing so, again in theory, except it meant turning over the safety of his volunteer and friend to a former student more concerned with status than with stasis.

Spence relied on gut instincts when it came to

mortal health and welfare, and his gut was telling him the tiny fraction of change in temperature he'd noted—even though it barely registered on the monitoring system and almost immediately dropped back to normal—had put Hawk's life in grave danger.

Spence wanted to bring him out of his cryonically frozen state. His former student wanted to leave him there in the hope Hawk would return on his own with the information the Guardians needed on what was happening to the missing Fae souls. Spence was about to put his case in front of the Great Lords. So was his former student.

Spence's white robes, acceptable formal attire for hearings in the meeting chamber, swirled around his ankles as he walked and threatened to trip him. He wiped the palms of his hands in the folds of the crisp fabric as surreptitiously as possible. He took a deep breath and entered the chamber through the intricately carved arch doorway.

Robert Jess had gotten there before him and already stood in front of the panel of Great Lords, who were seated at a long table at the far end of the room. Spence felt like a bug under a microscope as he made his way forward, fighting a nervous urge to scratch his chin under his neat, gray beard. He'd delivered lectures to the greatest minds of his world. He was considered a leading expert on cryonics and his intellectual abilities were second to none. He was a genius.

And the thought of making a presentation to the Great Lords made him sweat like a scolded schoolboy. He might be a genius at cryonics, but his social skills could use a lot more attention. These people weren't interested in his scientific research. They were interested in politics.

The First Lord, a bald man of advanced years with mild eyes and a round physique, looked up from the palm reader in his hand. "I see we have a disagreement as to the future of the current cryonics project you have been leading, Dr. Jennings," he said. "You wish to shut it down. Dr. Jess wishes for it to continue. Who would like to speak first?"

Spence conceded the floor to his colleague. It might seem like a polite gesture, but in reality, Spence wanted to know exactly what he was up against. The little shit had always been a suck-up, but a brilliant one.

"Colonel Hawkins was a brave and dedicated man," Jess began.

Is, you bastard, Spence corrected him silently.

"He would be the first to stand here and tell you the fate of the Fae is our primary concern. Cryonics holds the potential to keep him in stasis for up to a thousand years. If there is any chance whatsoever for him to find the information he was sent for, then we owe it to him to give him the time required."

Simple enough, Spence thought, relaxing somewhat.

"Dr. Jennings?"

Spence cleared his throat. "My colleague is correct in theory. Cryonics does offer the possibility of stasis for up to a thousand years. However, that is a possibility only and cannot be applied to the complex mortal form. Freezing and thawing occur at the cellular level and must be carefully monitored. A recent flicker of temperature in Colonel Hawkins' brain indicates to me that stasis is failing. If we don't retrieve him immediately, permanent damage or even death will undoubtedly occur. In fact, I cannot guarantee that irreversible damage has not happened already. Colonel Hawkins is a highly decorated and valuable member of our military. His loss would be a blow to the Guardians."

The First Lord again consulted his palm reader. "Is it true that Colonel Hawkins was handpicked by you for this project?"

Spence nodded, swallowing past a throat made dry with nervous worry.

"Can you tell us why?"

He wouldn't lie. Not in this room, not to these people who had the ability to destroy his career and all of his research if they chose.

"Colonel Hawkins approached me privately. He indicated he had nothing worth living for. He felt he had little left in him to offer his people. He wanted to participate in a study that held a great deal of meaning for his late wife. Since he had the training and the mental fortitude required for the program, I was more than willing to accept him."

The First Lord clasped his hands, tapping his index fingers together in thought. "How is Colonel Hawkins supposed to return on his own if his body is in a frozen state? How would you know he was back?"

"We have a separate monitor hooked up to his brain," Jess leapt in to explain. "It records the activity surrounding it, not inside it. Simply put, Colonel Hawkins' consciousness will knock on the door and we'll let him in."

"The flicker in temperature I noted may be the 'knock on the door,'" Spence added, afraid to look at Jess for fear he'd punch him. He hoped the flicker really was a sign Hawk was trying to return, because he was seriously afraid of what else it might mean. The fact that he stood before the Great Lords to admit that a project worth millions was most likely a failure was a good indication of the magnitude of his fear.

"We'll reconvene in twenty minutes," the First Lord said.

Spence waited with Jess in the hall outside the meeting chamber.

"I understand how much this project means to you," Jess said to him.

Spence looked him in the eye. "The project means nothing to me. Life means far more. What happened to Hawk's wife and daughter was a terrible tragedy and he deserves a chance to find a new life with meaning. I'd hoped to give him that. Instead, I'm afraid he's been damaged beyond repair."

"You've become idealistic." Jess looked back at him with something akin to pity. "Colonel Hawkins was a soldier, and a damned good one. He understood duty and the risks involved."

Spence remembered Jess as a gifted student, far too ambitious, but when had he grown so cold? "If you keep referring to him in the past tense, I'll have you removed from future research projects involving mortal life."

Spence could do it. He had enough influence, and Jess knew it. They waited the remaining moments in silence.

They were called back in after exactly twenty-one minutes. The First Lord addressed them.

"Dr. Jennings, in two weeks' time you are to bring Colonel Hawkins out of stasis. Until then, he is to be closely monitored by you. In three weeks you are to present yourself to your new position at the School for Scientific Advancement."

It was more than Spence had hoped for, yet still, he worried it would not be enough. He could bring Hawk's body out of stasis, but when he did, would Hawk's mind remain intact?

♦ ♦

River stretched, the springs in the foldout cot creaking loudly in the empty attic. Thin fingers of morning light filtered in through the high window on the end wall and fanned out across the dusty plank floor.

Despite the thinness of the mattress and her worries over everything that had gone wrong with her life, and the unsettling dream and ensuing jumps, she'd finally crashed. She'd needed the sleep. Her body had spent a number of days flat out on the gaming room floor while her mind had been trapped inside her video game.

The remainder of the night had been dreamless.

The air in the attic was so cold, River could see her breath. It wouldn't be long now before snow fell in the mountains. She blinked her eyes into better focus and

slowly angled her head to take in Hawk's empty cot
and neatly folded sleeping bag. He hadn't woken her.
That meant he hadn't slept. Anxious for him, she
wriggled from the warmth of the sleeping bag, rolled
from the cot, and planted her sock-clad feet on the icy
wooden floor. Maybe Hawk would go to sleep now
that it was daylight. He needed rest, too, mentally and
physically, and if he didn't soon get it, she was afraid
of what might happen to him. He might be able to
handle the lack of sleep in his own body, but as much
as she'd liked Nick, Nick had been lazy.

River didn't want to think about Nick.

She heard muffled movements in the kitchen two
stories below, then a door closing. Hawk's and Jake's
voices drifted up from the yard and she wondered what
they were up to. She frowned. Judging by the dim light
it was still early, but Jake should be getting ready for
school.

From the stack of old clothes she'd collected the
night before and haphazardly tossed at the foot of her
cot, she tugged on a pair of snug, skinny jeans, an old
T-shirt with a frayed neckline, and a thick, navy wool
sweater she'd knitted as a teenager while sitting in the
evenings with her dying mother. She'd needed to keep
busy and it was a project her mother had been able to
help instruct her on. She also scrounged up an old pair
of hiking boots and she set them aside for later. Luckily for her, Melinda hadn't thrown anything out.

She'd buried River's family in the attic instead.

River padded in her socks across the floor to the
single small window, but it was too high. She could

run downstairs to the bay window in the living room but the stairs creaked and she thought it best not to wake Melinda too early and piss her off even more.

Stacked crates and packed boxes allowed her to climb up and peer out. She cupped her hands around her face and pressed her nose against the glass to scan the ground below. Wind shivered the threadbare treetops, knocking free the few colored leaves still clinging to life. Squirrels darted through the under-brush, collecting food in preparation for the upcoming winter. Beneath the dark blue sky, long columns of smoky white fog radiated off nearby fields of flattened dead grass.

She caught a quick glimpse of Hawk and Jake before they were swallowed by the forest. They were up to something, and whatever it was, she didn't like being excluded. Wistfulness welled up inside her. She and Hawk were still getting to know each other and circumstances weren't aligning themselves in their favor. He wasn't planning to cooperate either, if his rejection last night was any indication.

What a shame. Sex with Hawk was an excellent energizer.

She considered following them but decided against it. It had been too long since there'd been a man in Jake's life and a little male bonding wouldn't hurt either of them. She grinned, wondering if Hawk had managed to explain to Jake's satisfaction how they'd appeared like magic right before his eyes. Jake was a hard kid to bullshit.

She shifted her weight on the stack of boxes and

crates, accidentally bumping into some metal storage shelving with her shoulder. She reached out to steady it to keep it from tipping over. As she did, she noticed the portable fireproof safe her parents had once kept under their bed now hidden behind some old cans of paint.

She climbed off the stack of boxes and crates and slid the safe off the shelf. It was heavier than it looked. *Weston,* her family name, had been scratched into the bottom. The key had been left in the lock.

She'd never been allowed to touch this safe. Her father told her he kept valuable legal papers in it, like the deed to the property and his will, and he didn't want anyone messing with them.

If it contained important legal papers, why had it been relegated to the attic?

Perhaps Melinda had removed the papers and moved them to a safe-deposit box at the bank now that the banks were again stable, but hadn't bothered to discard the old fire safe. Or perhaps her father had hidden it up here to keep the boys out of it.

The key in the lock suggested whoever had put the safe here didn't believe it held anything of any real value.

The safe wasn't big enough to hold more than a few papers and maybe some jewelry. River had already been given her mother's engagement and wedding rings so she doubted it held any of that. But what if it contained other things belonging to her mother?

If so, River wanted them.

She blew a layer of dust off the top and let loose a

loud sneeze when the particles tickled her nose. Half expecting to find Melinda standing behind her, catching her snooping, she blinked watering eyes and shot a glance over her shoulder at the closed door for reassurance she was still alone.

She perched on the edge of her cot, and balancing the safe on her knees, she turned the key and popped the lid.

Inside she found a hefty stack of photos. She pulled the pictures out and began flipping through them. Most were of the river, the woods, and of an old cave she used to explore when she was a child. Toward the end of the pile her flipping slowed, and she tilted her head, unsure of what she was looking at.

Confused, she held one of the photos up to the bare bulb suspended over her head and examined the image. She turned the photo in her hands, looking at it from all angles until her brain finally processed what she was viewing and came to its own horrifying conclusions.

Sweat broke out on her skin and she had the unsettling sense of being watched, that the damaged soul she'd felt in the night was again hovering nearby, attempting to touch her thoughts, desperate to tell her something.

A shiver moved through her as she swept her gaze around the room, peering into the dark, dusty corners and trying not to make monsters out of shadows. When she saw nothing she pushed the unease aside and turned her attention back to the pictures. Fingers fumbling, she rifled through the rest of the stack, and when she came across photos of the crest of a hill with a blurred, unidentifiable image in the background, her heart stuttered in her chest. Memories, not her own, danced at the edge of her thoughts.

River returned the photos gently to the safe, closed her eyes, and rubbed her temples with the tips of her fingers. She'd been touched by souls before. She'd felt those of her birth parents, trapped in a graveyard she now needed to find. A few souls she suspected she'd unconsciously touched, unaware she could do so, and only then because they belonged to people she loved. Hawk's was the only soul she'd ever deliberately touched. His had called out to hers, and she had claimed it. With that claiming had come memories, things he'd shared with no one but her.

If she accepted the memories this new soul needed desperately to share with her, was she accepting a link to the soul of a creature so damaged it teetered at the brink of insanity?

But didn't this poor, tortured soul deserve a chance to find peace?

She thought of the souls that had been trapped by the Dark Lord in his virtual prison. Hawk's had been one of them. She'd almost lost her own soul as well. Could she live with herself if she didn't do all that she could to set this soul free?

Hawk had said she needed to learn to keep her thoughts better protected, but she didn't know how to do so, and besides, this soul wanted to give, not to take. Perhaps it was better for both of them for her to accept what it offered rather than fight against it.

Hello, River invited, relaxing her guard and opening her thoughts just a little. *What is it you'd like to show me?*

With that, the floodgates opened.

♦ ♦

Jake wanted to show him something but he wouldn't come right out and say what it was.

Instead, he'd said he wanted to check rabbit snares before school and told Hawk he could come along if he liked. Since they hadn't yet seen any snares, either Jake had something to show him or he was choosing a spot to hide Hawk's body.

Hawk hadn't liked leaving River alone in the house, but finding out what was up with Jake was equally important. The boy hadn't asked Hawk any questions last night, and he hadn't yet this morning. That didn't mean he wasn't going to. People didn't simply appear out of nowhere like that.

Hawk strongly suspected Jake wanted to blame him for the trick.

Dried leaves, slippery with frost, crunched beneath Hawk's boots as Jake led him deeper and deeper into the forest. Gray, intertwined branches above their heads blocked out much of the light and made it harder and harder for him to see the beaten trail before them through the trees.

Jake, however, wasn't hindered by the lack of light. Even with those gangly teenage limbs he easily dodged grasping branches and sidestepped twisted roots blocking his path. Here in the forest he was in his comfort zone and seemed to know the area extremely well.

Hawk admired the kid but felt a little sad for him just the same. A teenage boy should be hanging out with his friends, not constantly scouring the woods for danger.

With the back of his hand Jake brushed his fair hair off his face and glanced up at him. "Nick?"

Question time.

"Yeah?" Hawk turned to him. He owed him an explanation. He just wasn't sure how much of an explanation to give him. People were looking for River, and giving anyone—especially a thirteen-year-old boy—too much information could be dangerous for them all.

"Is River okay?" Jake asked, dancing around his real question.

Hawk braced himself. "She's fine. Just a little different. But you already knew that about her," he reminded him.

"She's not *weird* different," Jake said, his eyes defiant. "She's special."

"She's definitely special," Hawk agreed. He waited a heartbeat before introducing their next point of discussion. "Did you know she was adopted?"

Jake kicked at a fallen log blocking the trail, shattering the moss-coated, rotten wood into long splinters. "Yeah. I knew it."

"Her biological parents were different, too. They gave River the ability to do things most people can't."

Jake's next words were more deliberate, as if he were testing Hawk. "I once saw her pull a fish out of the water with her bare hands."

Hawk tried to sound only mildly interested in that, as if it were nothing unusual. "So?"

Jake shot his hand out and snatched it back to demonstrate. "That fish didn't stand a chance. Not with her speed. Dad called it 'tickling fish' and said it was a trick the local native tribes used to use. Maybe her real parents were native." His tone dared Hawk to challenge his explanation.

"Maybe they were." Hawk relaxed. Jake's justification of River's unique talents meant her secrets were safe with him. To Jake, she was special. He wasn't about to let anyone think anything less of her.

Of course, what people thought of Hawk was another matter entirely.

"How much trouble is River really in?" Jake asked.

Now there was the loaded question. Hawk took the time to choose his words carefully. "She's wanted for questioning. That doesn't mean the police think she's guilty of anything, only that they think she might know something that could help in their investigation."

Jake frowned at that and looked down at his tattered sneakers, a dark sock poking out of one where the upper had separated from the sole.

"Come on, Jake, be serious," Hawk added. "Just look at her. How could anyone really believe a midget like that could murder three people?"

Jake peeled a leaf off a tree and began slapping it against his palm. He looked at Hawk as if sizing him up and deciding whether or not he could trust him. "Are you special, too?"

"No."

"Didn't think so." Jake sniffed dismissively. "Not the way you handled that bear attack." He hesitated a few more moments, then said, "I want to show you something."

Hawk hadn't survived months of mental torture in the Dark Lord's prison by being careless. Jake was protective of his family. If he thought Hawk posed a threat to River, Jake wouldn't hesitate to nail him to a tree with that crossbow he carried.

"What is it?" he asked, trying for casual.

Jake gestured with a nod to the side of the trail. "It's right over there. In that cave."

Hawk hadn't noticed the rock cave at first because of the poor light. Dry, broken ferns and dead, leafless vines covered its entrance. He had a bad feeling about this. His jaw clenched as he braced himself for what was coming next.

Jake stepped ahead and dragged the brush away from the mouth of the cave.

"You wanna see?" he asked Hawk, pulling a flashlight out of his coat pocket.

Behind the question in Jake's eyes, Hawk read a different expression. He'd seen it before in young soldiers' eyes, and he knew what it meant.

There was something dead in that cave.

"Do you want to?" Jake asked again.

It wasn't so much that Hawk wanted to, but deep in his gut he knew he needed to. He didn't believe in coincidence. Whatever was in that cave was linked to River and what she'd experienced the night before.

He took the flashlight from Jake's hand, shouldered him aside, and directed the light into the narrow opening. "Wait out here."

"Why?" Jake demanded. He squared his shoulders, clearly offended and ready to argue. "I've seen it before."

Hawk ran his hand along the jagged rocks as he shone the light inside. Toward the back of the cave he could see something, but from this distance it looked like nothing more than a mound of dirt. "What *is* that?"

"It's a body," Jake said. "Sort of."

"There's no such thing as 'sort of.' It either is, or it isn't. How long has it been here?" Hawk pressed his mouth and nose into the crook of his elbow, cautious about breathing in the damp cave air. Whatever it was, he had no way of knowing what killed it. He wanted to say something to Jake about the danger of airborne diseases—after all, a virus had nearly wiped out this world's population—but it was too late to warn him. If it was airborne, Jake had already been exposed.

"Here, use this."

Hawk glanced over his shoulder and accepted a handkerchief from Jake. *Smart kid.* He was glad he'd kept his warnings to himself. After tying it around his nose and mouth he moved in deeper, Jake tight on his heels, his own handkerchief in place.

"It's been here awhile, I think," Jake said, his voice echoing off the rock walls.

"When did you find it?"

"A few years back."

Hawk twisted to look at him. "That long ago?"

"It might have been here longer. When Dad was

alive he said I was too young to go into the woods so I never got a chance to look around."

Which made Hawk wonder if his father had stumbled upon this as well, or maybe even had something to do with it. He wished he knew more about him, but River had loved him so Hawk was going to give him the benefit of the doubt. For the moment. "Have the police ever been here?"

Jake gave him an *Are you crazy?* look. "No. I haven't told anyone." He shrugged his thin shoulders. "If Mom knew, she might not let me come into the woods anymore."

If Melinda had an ounce of self-respect she wouldn't allow it anyway. Jake was just a kid, and these woods held predators—some natural, and some maybe not so much.

Something scratched against the rock wall and Hawk stiffened. He fanned his flashlight along the jagged crevice in time to catch a rat as it scurried away from the beam of light. When he turned his light back on the corpse, a second rat crawled out of its skull. Air rushed from Hawk's lungs in a whoosh, and his feet scuffled backward.

"Crisos," he swore.

Jake mistook his reaction and fixed him with a look of teenage disdain, as if Hawk had just failed a manliness test. "You're not afraid of rats, too, are you?"

No. He was afraid of rotted corpses that looked less like a man and more like man-made. This planet was even more fucked up than he'd imagined, and his opinion hadn't been high to begin with. He stuffed the handkerchief into his pocket. Disease hadn't killed this creature. Primitive bioengineering and a lack of understanding of biomechanics had.

"You were right," Hawk admitted, rubbing the back of his neck. "That's sort of a body."

He stared at it, clinically analyzing what he saw. The basic structure had human elements, but the muzzle on the face indicated someone had tampered with human and animal DNA. The body was too large, the back hunched between the shoulders as if meant to support a greater muscle mass than a human's, more like a dog's or possibly a wolf's.

The long, humanoid limbs, however, were purely mechanical. They would have to be, since naturally occurring limbs couldn't possibly have supported the greater mass of that torso. Scarring along the natural bone where it had been fused to the mechanical limbs suggested prolonged tissue rejection, although the living flesh and muscle were long gone.

Pity and horror filled him. Whatever this creature had been, it wouldn't have survived for long outside of a lab. And if it had possessed any sort of human intelligence whatsoever, its years in a lab to reach this level of maturity would have been nothing short of hell.

Even Guardians, with all their technical knowledge, did not manufacture mortal life. Life was a gift from the Fae. If River's Guardian father had known of this, he would have moved heaven and earth to get this information back to the Great Lords.

Then again, perhaps he had known. Perhaps he'd tried to do so. Something terrible had happened to him. Hawk remembered the unknown lab from the game and the graveyard outside it where River had sensed the presence of her birth parents. He'd assumed it was part of the game—based somewhat on reality, true, but a twisted reality. Not until now had he thought it might have been more real than imaginary.

Hawk crouched down for a closer examination of the remains, bracing one knee on the hard ground. He surfed around in the dirt with his fingers until he found a stick, then used it to nudge at the corpse. An arm fell off. Attached to that arm was what looked to be a Guardian transporter, the kind they usually wore beneath the skin at the small of their backs so they could travel with the Fae. Hawk had one implanted in his own body, but that body was frozen in stasis so it wasn't much good to him at the moment.

He retrieved the handkerchief from his pocket and wrapped it around his hand before picking the transporter from the mechanical bones. He handed Jake the light. "Here. Hold this for me."

Jake kept the light trained on Hawk's hands as Hawk tapped the transporter. He guessed he knew who it had originally belonged to, and he wondered if he should tell River. "GPS is broken," he murmured to himself. "I wonder how this thing got hold of it. Or if it knew how to use it."

This was bad shit. Really, really bad. This was more than likely the presence River had felt hovering around her last night, and while Hawk felt truly fucking sorry for it, his duty was to River. He didn't want any of this anywhere near her.

He didn't want it near her brothers either.

"You keep Sam away from here," he ordered Jake. "Do you understand me?"

Jake nodded.

"I mean it," Hawk warned. "This isn't something you want anyone to know about. Someone will have been looking for it, likely still is, and it's not going to be someone you want knocking on your door. If anyone ever asks any questions, you pretend you don't know anything. You've never seen this. Got it?"

Jake nodded again, and Hawk was satisfied with the fear he saw in the boy's eyes. Jake wasn't stupid. He'd already known this wasn't something to talk about. He'd taken a big chance in showing it to Hawk—but he probably knew that, too.

Hawk didn't want to leave the transporter behind, but he didn't dare take it with him on the off chance someone who knew what they were looking for eventually found the remains. They'd probably already stripped it apart and analyzed it anyway.

Instead, Hawk slipped the transporter back in place and tried to arrange things so it looked as if nothing more than animals had been at the carcass. He flashed the light around the floor and carefully wiped out their footprints with his hand.

Back on the path outside the cave, the sun was now up and birds were singing. A fat gray squirrel, its bushy tail curled in a question mark, scurried up a nearby ash. The mountain air was crisp and clean and smelled of the earth, and Hawk breathed it in deeply.

He was tired. Mentally and physically. He couldn't

remember ever being this tired before, not even in the Dark Lord's prison.

He wanted River. He wanted to know she was okay. He wanted to hold her, and be damned with the inappropriateness of that desire. He wanted to feel her strength, to have her touch his soul with her Fae magic, and to rid himself of this awful sense that more evil than good inhabited the universe. For the first time, even after losing his family, he felt like life wasn't worth fighting for.

If it had only been River's birth father she'd sensed in that lab's graveyard, Hawk might have had less of a problem walking away from this mess. Her father had been a Guardian. He'd known what he was getting into.

But River's Fae mother's soul was also at stake, and Hawk could no more walk away from that than he could walk away from River. He had to find that graveyard and he had to set her parents' souls free.

Then he had to get River off this shithole world before it imploded.

"Let's go," he said to Jake, and started back down the path to the house.

CHAPTER **FOUR**

♦

Sandman wasn't so much crazy as he was a mean, evil son of a bitch. To Nick, that made him less scary but a whole lot more dangerous.

Dangerous, but predictable. Since he needed Nick, and Nick had a direct line to his thoughts—although granted, that was a two-way street because Sandman also had a direct line to his—Nick felt he could live with the danger. They now had a common goal, and that goal was to get back into Nick's body.

As Nick understood it, his consciousness was the key. It was what connected a body to its soul. The thieving bastard who had stepped into his body had done so a little too quick, and voilà, Nick's consciousness, body, and soul hadn't had a chance to completely separate. That meant his consciousness still had a direct line back to his body.

The problem was the mental hemorrhoid. Sandman had a grip on Nick's family jewels and he wouldn't let go because he was trapped on this dust bowl by some sort of magic and hoped to escape it through Nick.

Sandman needed to fine-tune his evil master plan. He wasn't making much progress and Nick was growing more than a little impatient.

The glowing stones he'd found in the sand helped ease the boredom. Once Nick had figured out how to navigate through the swirling sandstorms with his consciousness, it no longer mattered if the stones were buried or exposed. He could access the images contained in the stones by using his thoughts, and the image he was most interested in watching was his own.

Damn, but he was a handsome man. That bastard video game character Sever had better take care of his body. Sever wasn't going to have it for long, not if Nick could help it, but it wouldn't take long for him to damage it. Nick didn't doubt the jerkoff would take pleasure in doing it, too.

Along with the ever-present rage tugged a twinge of jealousy. River had to know by now that the person she was with wasn't really Nick. Did it matter to her?

Did it matter to him if it didn't?

Damn straight it did. He'd taken a bullet for her. That should be worth something. She owed him. He wanted her to miss him, at least a little. It stung more than he'd expected to think that she didn't.

He watched with distaste as he—or Sever, or whoever—and some skinny kid found the mutant in the cave. Some weird shit went on in the universe and Nick now had firsthand experience with a lot of it. He'd known about Kaye's experiments, but he hadn't realized he'd had any success with them. Nick examined the remains more closely through the images in the stones. On second thought he didn't think it accurate to call that lump of metal and dried-out flesh a success. It looked more like Dr. Frankenstein's monster gone seriously wrong, which was probably why Kaye had kept it so secret. If it had worked out he would have put it to use, and the stories would have leaked out—just as they had about his Weres.

Sandman was trying to get his attention. Nick felt the equivalent of an inner head slap. *Ouch.*

Irritated, Nick delivered one of his own in return and felt Sandman recoil in surprise. Good enough. He wasn't interested in a bitch-slapping contest, but he'd been having a really bad time lately and didn't feel like bending over and taking it anymore. Dark Lord or Lord Almighty, right now they were on equal footing.

Sandman was pissed with him but ignored it in favor of barking out orders. Nick half listened at first, more interested in watching what was happening with the fake Nick, but then a few bits and pieces of ramblings caught his attention.

Sandman, it would seem, could transport himself much as River did when she jumped, but not while he was imprisoned by magic. He thought he might have found a way to work around the restriction, but in order to do so he needed Nick's cooperation. Cooperating meant practicing some sort of self-meditation/hypnosis, which in turn would help Nick create a trail, or a link, back to his body. Nick then had to follow that trail, which was how River could jump—except she could do it physically by using her magic. Because Nick's body was currently occupied by Sever's consciousness, Nick had to strike while that consciousness was weak—that meant in its sleep. Once Nick was in, he had to make Sever believe what was happening in his dream was reality. The more Sever accepted it as reality, the more real it would become. The more real it became, the more magic Nick could siphon off Sandman. And once Nick had more magic than Sandman, he could draw Sandman over and let Sandman finish off Sever.

Nick was more than willing to cooperate if it got him his body back. He could worry about shaking the hemorrhoid later.

Back up a bit and explain it again, he interrupted. *I'm listening.*

♦ ♦

River had paid close attention to what the shadowy figure in the photos had told her, and to the memories it wanted to share. She now had a clear understanding. She wished she didn't.

She wrapped her arms around her legs and propped her chin on her knees. The photographs had fallen to the floor beside the cot, and with a flutter and a sigh of what seemed like relief, the poor, tortured soul had finally let go of this life.

The creature in the photos had been born in the laboratory that had made its way into her game. That laboratory and the graveyard outside it were linked to the deaths of her birth parents. She remembered their touch.

She had to find them.

She heard Hawk's steps on the stairs, then him calling to her.

"River?" He blew into the room, smelling like fresh air and frozen sunshine.

"How long do you think a person can go without blinking?" she asked him.

Hawk crossed the room and gathered her into his

arms. His warm touch pushed back some of the chill, his brow furrowed in concern for her. His keen glance moved over her eyes, her face, her body, assessing her well-being before scanning the room.

"You okay?" he asked, sounding breathless and annoyed by it. He must hate the restrictions Nick's body put on him. Nick was fit enough, but in a weekend-warrior kind of way.

River smiled into the front of his shirt. Hawk would have him whipped into true warrior shape in no time. "I'm fine," she lied. Pressed against his chest, she could feel the erratic pounding of his heart. "Are you?"

"I think I'm having a heart attack," Hawk complained. "Nick was a lazy bastard. And I'm pretty sure he drank too much."

That might be true, but if they were going to move forward, both of them needed to get past what had happened to Nick—River because thinking about it made her crazy wishing she'd been able to save him, and Hawk because he hadn't liked or trusted him. A bit of jealousy might be mixed in there as well.

She wrapped her arms around Hawk's waist and opened her soul to him. She'd always been able to touch souls, but she'd never known what she was doing before she'd met Hawk. Now that she did, she knew his was the soul meant for hers. The packaging didn't matter. He had no reason to be jealous of Nick, or of anyone else.

When the time came to let him go, it was going to rip her apart. A piece of her soul would go with him.

She let her strength flow from her to him until the beating of his heart steadied to normal.

"Cut it out," he said when he realized what she was doing, but there was no real force to his words. A lot of his tension had eased.

She frowned. Something had unsettled him. It didn't take long for her to pry a few images from his thoughts and figure out what. He wasn't trying very hard to guard his thoughts from her.

He gripped her shoulders and inched back until their eyes met. "There's this cave in the woods," he began.

River started to shake. "I know about the body."

He didn't seem surprised. "This is bad shit, River. I have to do something about it. I can't leave here until I do."

She agreed with him. It was bad, and something did need to be done. She wanted her parents to find peace. She couldn't bear the thought of them suffering.

One of the pictures on the floor stuck to the heel of Hawk's shoe and made a dry, scraping sound as he dragged his foot backward. He glanced down, then looked again as he realized what the photos scattered on the floor contained.

He bent, grabbed a fistful of the pictures, then straightened to his full height. His worried glance moved back to her face. "Where did you get these?"

"On the shelving, hidden behind some old cans of paint."

Hawk scrubbed his hand over his jaw, his face grim. River didn't like what he was thinking, although these thoughts, he'd tried harder to keep to himself.

"You think my father was involved with this," she accused him, incredulous.

He didn't lie to her. "It's possible. You have no idea how bad this really is, River. Maybe he didn't either."

"Just because he took some photos doesn't mean a thing. My father would never have been involved with those experiments," River said with fierce conviction. "The soul that belonged to the body you saw in that cave was kind and gentle, but they weren't all like that." She shuddered, still nauseous from the images she'd seen in her head. "Some of them were more animal than human. But no matter what, they were all suffering and very desperate. My dad wouldn't have had any part of that."

She could tell he didn't believe her and it made her angry. She knew her father.

As Hawk examined the pictures, removing a few to stuff into his pockets, she tamped down her temper and tried again to explain. "My father was a good man, Hawk. Gentle and giving. A great parent. He wasn't responsible for any part of this. He wouldn't be."

Hawk nodded, humoring her, clearly not ruling out the possibility her father had been involved in the making of those monsters. River tried hard not to hate him for thinking it.

"We aren't waiting until nightfall to leave," he decided. "We should go now." He waved a hand toward the pile of clothes at the foot of her bed, then grabbed an old dusty rucksack off a shelf and tossed it to her. "Pack just what you think you'll need for the next day or two. We're going to summon this Wizard of yours," he said. "She was the one who sent us to that lab in the game in the first place. I bet she knows a lot more than she lets on."

River clutched the rucksack to her chest, wanting to defend Andy now as well, but not nearly as certain of her innocence as she was of her father's. She loved and trusted Andy. But did she think she was innocent?

"I'm coming with you."

Jake's determined voice sounded in the doorway and River whirled, Andy forgotten, wondering how much of their conversation he'd overheard.

She dropped the rucksack on the cot and crossed the room to put a hand on her brother's shoulder. "Sorry, Jake. The answer's no." She tried to smile and make light of it. "Your mother would shoot me before I reached the end of the driveway."

"River!" he protested, his adolescent voice cracking slightly as he patted the strap of his crossbow in a not-so-subtle reminder he'd saved their asses from a bear. "You need me."

While she appreciated his enthusiasm and courage, and his readiness to help, she also knew he was mostly interested in looking for adventure. He was a boy anxiously wanting to be a man.

He wouldn't thank her for pointing that out to him.

Hawk stepped up and did it for her, but in a far more tactful way. "You can't come. Your mom and brother depend on you."

Jake stared up at Hawk for a moment, hostility pinching his lips as duty warred with desire.

Duty won. He straightened his spine and squared his shoulders. "You're right. They do."

"Good man," Hawk said, and nodded toward the crossbow. "Now, what weapons do you have that you can spare?"

♦ ♦

They were coming.

Andy sighed as she wiped down a table, the half-empty bar noisy around her as people cheered, their attention on the hockey game on the wide-screen television over her head. The home team had scored its second goal of the first period.

She'd known River would be back, but she hadn't expected the Guardian to be with her. She should have realized he would find a way to keep them from being separated, and that he would never willingly leave her. It didn't matter. She couldn't have asked for anyone better to look out for River.

The Guardian, however, was never going to trust Andy and that created a problem. Guardians hated the immortals. Since immortals weren't all that fond of Guardians either, she didn't blame him for the prejudice. But she hadn't wanted another Guardian on this world, not yet. Not until she'd had a chance to fix the colossal mistake she'd made.

Andy took a few orders for food, her mind busy. Maybe she shouldn't have shown River that graveyard, but it was where the whole mess began. Andy tried to convince herself that by borrowing mortal souls, she hadn't meant any harm. Her mistake had been in showing others how those souls could be tied to bioengineered life. She'd thought she was helping to save this world. Instead Andy had unleashed a nightmare, and circumstances had aligned to keep her from correcting her mistake.

The virus she'd contracted would have killed her if not for River. What an ironic joke on the immortals that would have been—a microscopic organism, capable of mutation, therefore of living forever and killing an immortal. Because of River, Andy had survived.

Unfortunately, her magic had never fully recovered. She needed River's help, but not while River was under the protection of a Guardian. The Guardian would never allow River to do what needed to be done.

A cold shot of air touched the back of her neck as the heavy wooden doors of the bar pushed open. Andy looked around in a reflexive response, every hair on her head tingling to life.

Amos Kaye, the Monster Man, had sat in her bar only a few days before. Now George Johnson stood in her doorway, eyeing the crowd with distaste. Coincidence was unlikely since this wasn't the sort of establishment either man tended to frequent. Johnson, in fact, rarely left the capital city, so she could only assume he'd come here because of her. She'd really thought Kaye hadn't recognized her. She must have been wrong about that, but if so, he had to have some sort of sixth animal sense because she'd altered her appearance so drastically even she hadn't gotten used to it. Besides, what woman willingly added thirty years?

Of course, almost thirty years ago, the age difference had been marked. Now, not so much. She should have sold the bar to herself and changed her age and appearance again long before now, but she hadn't been able to summon enough magic to do so. She'd been saving it for emergencies, and tapping into River's game and the Dark Lord's prison had sapped what little energy she'd had in reserve.

Johnson was older now, too. His hair was solid white and the bags under his eyes more pronounced. He'd gotten a bit jowly as well. The charisma, however, remained unchanged. He commanded attention.

His eyes passed over her and she realized she'd been holding her breath. She let it out, then steadied it. She could be mistaken. Maybe he'd heard the food here was excellent.

Since patrons in the bar usually seated themselves, something he'd figure out in a minute or two, she went back to what she'd been doing. Once she took her orders to the kitchen she'd send out one of her staff to take her place waiting tables. Normally she liked the interaction with her customers, but this was one customer she had no intentions of willingly interacting with ever again. He might have come up in the world but he was still a sleazy opportunist more interested in profit than in people. Andy had been stupidly naïve to ever believe differently.

She understood human nature a whole lot better now.

Andy was turning to the kitchen, her pad in her hand, when cold, dry fingers fettered her wrist.

"It's been a long time," Johnson said to her, a smile that lacked any real sincerity fixed on his friendly politician's face.

Andy smiled politely in response, aware the regulars were watching them, likely wondering how she knew the province's premier. "I think you're mistaking me for someone else."

His fingers tightened for a brief second, then her wrist was released. "Sorry. You remind me of someone I once knew very well."

Too well, in fact. Andy hadn't understood the significance of his having a wife. When she did, her respect for him had dropped. And once she understood how little people mattered to him in general, she'd done her best to destroy all her research and make good her escape.

She tried not to let her emotions show on her face. If she did he would know for certain she was lying. She didn't think she could escape him as easily this time. She wasn't as strong now.

He was watching her closely. He'd always been an intuitive bastard. That was what made him so dangerous. It was too easy for people to believe in the image he wanted to present to the world.

"Can I get you something?" she asked. "Although we don't carry anything imported."

"You know who I am."

She should never have made that snide comment. Thirty years ago, he'd drunk imported. Now that she'd made the comment, she had to continue forward. He'd been lambasted in the press more than once for his extravagant tastes, and never once had he made any attempt to curtail them.

"Everyone in the bar knows who you are. What

they can't figure out is why you're here. Not that we aren't thrilled to have you," she added. "We don't get many famous people in here."

"Andy, isn't it?" She nodded reluctantly, and he got straight to the point. "Well, Andy, I'm here because of a business investment of mine. I'm looking for River Weston. I understand she's a friend of yours."

Andy wasn't afraid of the Johnsons of this world. She'd been around too long and seen too much for that.

She was deathly afraid for River, however.

"You mean the gamer?" Andy asked, allowing only moderate interest to show. "She's a customer. Or she was. Now that she's wanted for killing those other gamers, I doubt if she'll be back anytime soon. What happened to them was a real shame. Those were all nice kids." That much was the truth. They'd been smart, funny, innocent geeks who'd never done any harm to anyone.

Neither had River. River had simply been born to the wrong people at the wrong time and in the wrong place.

"So you don't have any idea where she might be?"

"None whatsoever." Andy had no trouble meeting his eyes because she was telling him the truth on that as well.

The regulars in the bar went back to watching the game, loud groans of disgust erupting as one of their favorite players got sent to the penalty box.

Johnson slipped a business card into her hand. "If she should happen to show, please have her call me.

Tell her I can get this whole mess straightened out."

Andy tucked the card into the pocket of her apron. Johnson thanked her for her time and left the bar, and Andy headed into the warmth and noise of the kitchen where staff was debating the merits of spitting in a customer's beer.

"Hey!" she said sharply and the debate ended, not that she believed they would have done it. She simply wasn't in the mood for their offbeat humor.

She pulled the business card from her pocket and examined it. Johnson may or may not know who she really was, but it didn't matter. She could take care of herself. He was closing in on River, though, and that was something she couldn't allow to happen.

She threw the card into the trash compactor. She hoped the Guardian was as good as he'd seemed in the game, because River was going to need him.

CHAPTER FIVE

♦

Jake led River and Hawk around the back of the house, then down the overgrown path leading to the old machinery shed at the far end of the property. He pulled a key from his pocket and removed the padlock. After lifting the metal bar that held the heavy wooden doors in place, Hawk grabbed one panel and slid it back on its track while Jake widened the other.

As anxious as River was to get moving, she couldn't

help but smile when she spotted her father's semire-
stored, 1945 four-wheel-drive Willys army Jeep next
to the aging John Deere tractor. The Jeep had been
her father's prized possession, something he'd built
from the ground up and worked on for years. In keeping with its original design the vehicle had no doors,
could carry a crew of three, had canvas seats, and
sported a fold-down windshield. She'd been far more
interested in video games than in ancient automo-
biles, but she'd listened to him talk about it because
he'd loved it so much. She wished she'd paid more attention to the things that had mattered to him.

Hawk was wrong about her father and she intended
to prove it. It gave her yet another reason for finding
that lab and the graveyard.

"I can't believe this is still here," she said, stepping
up to it and running her hands over the smooth primer
and the soft canvas roof. She wondered if he'd ever
gotten it running.

"It runs," Jake said, pride on his face as he answered her unspoken thought. "Dad and I had it out
on the road just before he d—died."

River noted the slight catch in his voice. Jake and
their dad had been close, and the loss still affected
him more than he wanted her to know. Guilt hit her
hard. She'd failed Jake over the past few years. She
couldn't replace their father, but she should be helping
Jake keep his memories of him alive.

Jake popped the hood and began fiddling with the
engine, his way of refocusing his concentration, and
she pushed her guilt aside for the time being. She

couldn't change the past, but she could work on the future.

"It has a three-speed, plus reverse T-84 transmission, full hydraulic brakes, leaf springs, shock absorbers, four-cylinder side valves . . ." As Jake continued to list off the specs, impressing even her with his knowledge, Hawk jumped into the driver's seat and tapped the speedometer. River scanned the dashboard while he examined the gauges.

"Bet you've never seen technology this old before," she said to Hawk.

He hardly seemed impressed by it, and she'd bet he trusted the restored Jeep about as much as he trusted her Wizard. "Let's hope I never do again." He looked around. "Where's the GPS?"

She nudged his arm. "Don't knock this baby. It might just be able to get us where we're going."

Hawk pushed in the clutch and turned the key. The engine choked and sputtered like an asthma patient before dying out. "Or not."

"You probably wouldn't know how to drive a stick shift anyway," she teased.

One eyebrow shot up. "It's basic technology."

Jake, who now had a streak of black grease on his cheek, peeked out from under the hood to state the obvious. "It needs gas."

River scanned the room, looking for a gas can. "I don't suppose you have any?"

He gestured toward a red plastic canister in a corner at the back of the shed. "Not enough to get you into the city. Dad just kept a bit for test runs because he didn't want the Jeep stolen. There might be enough to get you to the truck stop on Route 44, though." Jake stopped to rub his thumb and finger together. "But that'll cost you."

Hawk frowned, climbed from the seat, and joined Jake under the hood. "We don't have currency."

"You will soon enough," Jake said, amusement in his voice. He turned to River as she pulled the half-filled can from the shelf and adjusted the pour spout. "Won't you, River?"

River unscrewed the Jeep's gas cap. "Maybe."

Hawk leaned against the Jeep and folded his arms. "Is there something about your sister I should know?"

Jake laughed and the easy sound warmed River's insides. He was too serious most of the time. He'd been handed too much responsibility too early in life.

"Let's just say she has a natural talent for separating people from their money."

"Does she now?" Interest gleamed in Hawk's eyes as his gaze shot back and forth between them.

River made a face at Jake. "That was supposed to be our little secret. I haven't done that for a long time."

"I definitely want to hear this," Hawk said.

Jake's eyes lit up. "She used to play this magic card game, and—"

"And nothing," River interrupted. "It was just a silly game." Smiling at her brother and the pride light-ing his blue eyes, River shook the container to gauge the amount of gas inside. As she poured the fuel into the tank, she went on to explain. "Believe me, there was no magic involved." At least she hadn't thought so until now. She braced the canister on her hip and snapped her fingers. "The hand is quicker than the eye."

Jake snapped his fingers right back at her. "Not everyone's."

"I'm shocked," Hawk said.

River's face reddened until she could feel the burn. "I never kept the money."

"She gave it to me and Sam," Jake added.

Hawk cocked an eyebrow at her.

"What?" she demanded. "You always said I was an adrenaline junkie."

Hawk stiffened and she wished she could take those words back. He'd never called her an adrenaline junkie. Nick had.

That killed all the fun of the moment and she concentrated on the task at hand. After a quick calculation of gas and the amount of mileage they'd get out of it based on Jake's specs—these old Jeeps weren't known for their speed or fuel economy—she concluded that they might make it as far as the truck stop. If not, they'd have to walk the rest of the way. No big deal for her. She'd rested. Hawk, on the other hand, was dead on his feet and too stubborn to admit it.

She'd see to it that she drove and he slept.

After draining the canister into the Jeep's tank she screwed its plastic cap into place and tossed it into the backseat. Wiping her hands on her jeans she glanced up at Hawk and Jake, who'd been watching her.

Hawk turned to Jake. "Where did your father hide his gun?"

"Who says he had one?" River countered.

"He had one," Hawk said. "He had a family to protect."

Jake showed him a spot on the dust-covered wooden floor beneath the tractor where slats could be lifted up by two knotholes, just large enough for Hawk's fingers, to reveal a small recess beneath. In the recess sat a gun case, several boxes of shells, and the tools to load and clean the weapon. Hawk pulled a Glock 22 out of the case. River had used that gun for target practice more times than she could count.

"Nice," Hawk said approvingly, weighing the gun in the palm of his hand. "Light." He smiled at River. "This explains your choice of handguns in the final levels of your game."

"It's easy to use." River shrugged. "Except you need stronger thumbs than mine to load the final rounds. If you look under the gun case there should be a knife."

Hawk lifted the box but there was no knife underneath. River looked at Jake, then held out her hand. With a loud sigh, Jake hauled a six-inch-long switchblade from his back pocket and slapped it into her palm.

The sound of Melinda's voice calling for Jake rang out from the house.

"It's time for school," he said reluctantly.

River held up the knife. "And you were taking this with you?"

"Mom makes my sandwiches pretty thick."

"I'll bet."

River walked with her brothers to the end of the

driveway so she could say good-bye to them, tugging the neck of her sweater up against the bite of
the wind. The school bus rattled and groaned to a
stop just as it had hundreds of times when she was a
kid, only now dull red primer speckled its bright yellow finish.

River hugged the boys fiercely.

"I'll be back as soon as I can," she whispered in
Jake's ear. He nodded as if he didn't believe her, then
watched her from the grimy window of the bus as it
drove away. River waved until the bus rounded a corner and disappeared from sight.

"That thing's a death trap," Hawk observed as the
taillights vanished in a cloud of exhaust fumes.

"There are worse ways to travel."

They spent the next few hours showering and getting ready to leave. Hawk couldn't go out in public
with bloodstains and a bullet hole in his jacket, so
River raided the old bags of clothes in the attic and
found a red flannel padded coat of her father's to replace it.

After a heated debate Hawk finally conceded he
was too tired to drive, and while Melinda stood in
the kitchen doorway, River backed the Jeep from the
machine shed. River assumed her stepmother wanted
to ensure they actually left, not wish them a safe journey.

A lump lodged in her throat as she shifted gears
and watched the house shrink in the rearview mirror.
Then one wheel hit a pothole and she had to focus
more on her driving.

"We've got to do something about the way you're dressed," she said to Hawk. "You look like a bum."

He looked at the ill-fitting flannel coat he was wearing. "I take it that's bad. What do you suggest?"

"That we stop by Nick's apartment on the way to Andy's and pick up a few of his things."

"Someone shot Nick, and then Nick disappeared," he pointed out. "Don't you think whoever shot him might be keeping an eye on his place? Let's not forget about the police either. Or that our faces are all over the news."

"We could change our hair color," she suggested.

"We're not changing our hair color. The police on this world can't possibly be that stupid. We just need to keep out of sight." He yawned. "Maybe Nick's apartment is a good idea at that, if we can get in without being seen. Besides, I'd like to search it. He knew more than he was letting on."

"Nick's it is, then. But first, gas."

"If I find out he knew about that lab and the experiments, I'm getting a big fucking *Loser* tattooed on his ass," Hawk warned her, his voice hard. "In bright red, with about twenty pink hearts floating around it."

River didn't want to encourage him so she turned her attention back to the road.

After a few minutes, out of the corner of her eye, she noticed his head bobbling back and forth, and that he was fighting to keep his eyes open. Every once in a while his chin dipped. River chewed the inside of her lip. He was in a moving vehicle with no radio to distract him.

This was one battle he was about to lose and she had no intention of helping him out.

♦ ♦

Peters hadn't known for sure where he was headed when he got into his car, but after driving aimlessly for a half hour he realized he was en route to the small mountain town where River Weston had grown up.

The mountains were beautiful this time of year with the changing colors of the fall leaves and the startling blue of the clear, crisp sky, but Peters wasn't interested in the view.

He was going to take the job Johnson had dumped on him. He already knew that, but the part of his soul he hadn't sold wanted him to see what kind of bastard he'd become.

He hadn't wanted to know why River was so special to Johnson and the Monster Man, but now that he was about to sell her out to them he figured he should know his reason for it. He was already going to hell. He might as well make the trip worthwhile.

In terms of distance the trip to Hammonds wasn't very far. However, roads weren't maintained the way they'd been when he was a kid, and the potholes and broken asphalt made slow going for his poor old Buick. Chunks of rock from the cliffs had also broken free and occasionally blocked the way. The car didn't get much of a workout anymore either, and hadn't in years because of the price and availability of gas, and it wheezed and stuttered on the steep climb. Every so often Peters would have to pull over into one of the truck stops—flat stretches of pavement next to the rocky mountain face meant for long-haul trucks heading down the mountain that had lost the use of their brakes—and give his car a rest. The car rarely reached climbing speeds of more than twenty or twenty-five miles per hour even with the accelerator pressed to the floor on the good stretches. It also ate up gas at an alarming rate.

Luckily the mountain wasn't a straight uphill climb. Every so often he passed flat stretches of land that had once been settled but were now largely abandoned. Some towns had been hit harder by the virus than others, and some towns had simply been abandoned by residents who'd gone off to seek new beginnings elsewhere.

He remembered the days when the world had worried about overpopulation. Now the worry was how to keep the world's population connected. And, of course, there were always those who worried about making sure their area of population sat at the top of the food chain—with them crowned king.

He was about to help pass George Johnson the crown. There was always the possibility that elsewhere in the world some other country had a mad scientist working for it, but surely mad scientists were few and far between. The virus must have gotten rid of at least a few of them.

Peters watched the gas gauge on his dashboard dip slowly into the red zone. He might be able to find an abandoned gas station with a pump still on the power grid and a reservoir that hadn't been drained by looters, but he didn't want to take the chance. He also wasn't keen on getting his ass peppered with buckshot if the station's owner harbored a dislike for trespassers.

Trucks still ran service into the mountains and they couldn't travel forever without fuel. At the next plateau Peters saw what he'd been looking for—a truck stop that had seen better days, but appeared to be fully operational. A sign at the side of the road advertised gas at forty dollars per gallon, roughly the current rate. White paint peeled off the sides of the long, low building while a burned-out, not-so-operational ancient neon sign tilted crazily above the double glass doors. Most important, two glossy, almost-new pumps sat front and center. In a small parking lot next to the building sat a rickety, half-ton truck held together with what appeared to be baler twine, hockey sticks, and several sheets of riveted steel, and a rusted-out antique smart car. Two tractor trailers, visible from the road, were parked out back.

Peters' stomach growled when he spotted the paper menu posted on one of the glass-paneled doors, and he mentally counted the cash in his wallet and hoped they took Visa.

He parked the Buick next to the smart car and went inside. With gas at forty bucks a gallon, nobody these days let anyone pump it first. It was strictly pay up front, then load the receipt into the gas pump before filling the tank.

Peters looked around. To the right was a small dining area with a dance floor. To the left were a small convenience store, public washrooms, and showers for the truckers. The cash register faced the glass doors and the fuel pumps outside. He smelled coffee, and it smelled good.

He walked into the dining area and slid into a booth in a corner. The bench was covered in cracked black vinyl, and its memory foam padding had developed amnesia.

He pushed at the plastic salt shaker with his finger. The day wasn't getting any younger. He had to decide whether or not to travel the rest of the way to Hammonds or head for home.

The waitress, an older woman about his age with big, bleached hair, a tight pink uniform, and white, rubber-soled shoes approached him with her order pad in one heavily ringed hand.

"Coffee to start," he said to her before she could ask. "And can you tell me how much farther to Hammonds?"

She stuffed the pad into the pocket of her apron and fixed him with a look guaranteed to freeze his balls to his underwear. "You're the third person who's asked me that this week. Aren't you a little old for bounty hunting?"

It had to be a menopause thing. All women over fifty seemed to get bitchy.

"I guess I'll just take the coffee then," he said mildly.

She was back a few moments later. She set the coffee and a dish of creamers and sugar packets in front of him. Before she walked away she said, "Thirty miles."

Roughly another hour and a half, assuming she was telling him the truth. He could order some food and sit here and enjoy his last few hours of peace and self-respect before heading home, or he could continue on to Hammonds and make himself feel like a piece of crap. He wondered who the other two people were who'd asked about Hammonds. The police, Kaye, or someone he'd hired?

Peters took a sip of the black coffee, which was every bit as good as it smelled. He flagged down Mrs. Sunshine. "Can I get a burger and an order of fries?"

♦ ♦

The rich scent of strong black kaffa tickled Hawk's nose.

He slowed in front of the little shop where he and his late wife Cassie used to sit at a table in the sunlight and talk for hours in the prebaby days of their relationship. He inhaled the familiar, tempting aroma, smiling at the rush of memories it evoked, and would have stopped to grab a cup if he didn't have somewhere important to be.

But where exactly did he have to be?

He frowned and looked around him, momentarily confused about where he was and what he was supposed to be doing.

Across the street from the kaffa shop, in the wide courtyard fronting the Hall of the Great Lords, water spilled from an urn cradled in the delicate marble arms of the Fae Mother.

Hawk jogged across the street to the courtyard,

taking pleasure in the way the steady stream of water captured the morning rays of the planet's giant amber sun to reflect the colors of a rainbow. From the glittering pool at the Mother's feet, water funneled upward through the beautiful Fae's image in a continuous cycle. Meant to symbolize rebirth, the statue had been a gift to the Guardians from the Fae, and unlike everything else on Hawk's world, it ran on magic.

Hawk gazed into the statue's lovely face with its wide, expressive eyes, and with a tug at his soul suddenly realized how much River looked like the Mother. As he stepped up to the fountain to touch the tips of his fingers to the water and receive the Mother's blessing he caught his own reflection in the shallow pool. Dark eyes matched the color of his hair, which was cut short and combed to the side. His face was freshly shaven, smooth, and his dress clothes were neatly pressed, the fit perfect, comfortable.

He jerked back his hand in surprise. The Mother's blessing, which he'd received hundreds of times in his life, felt very much the same as River's touch, except with River, the feeling was magnified what seemed like a thousand times.

Where was River?

He turned around in a circle, scanning the growing crowd. Then, lengthening his stride, he hurried along the footpath skirting the courtyard, maneuvering through the masses of people all heading to work on the warm autumn morning. He cut across the patch of manicured lawn to the wide stone steps of the Hall of the Great Lords, taking them two at a time.

A sense of foreboding rippled through him and he clenched his jaw as he looked out over the courtyard, trying to gather his bearings and somehow figure out what was wrong other than that River was nowhere to be seen.

The mood of the crowd began to shift before his eyes, then one by one, their faces as well. The mass of people became a swarm of ugly red demons, the brilliant sun shocked into night as darkness blanketed the beauty of his world. A troll, long arms dangling down the sides of its twisted and hunched form, bounded through the double oak doors behind him, a goblin oozing green pus from its pores tight on its heels.

Hawk whirled around, afraid of what else might appear, groping for the gun he'd gotten from Jake. The gun was gone.

So was the Hall of the Great Lords.

Sweat broke out on his skin, his stomach clenched, and his mind screamed a protest. He blinked, locking his knees to help keep him upright. He threw out a hand to brace himself against one of the stone pillars, but instead of stone connected with hot, snarling flesh. Bloodstained lips parted, peeling back to expose jagged fangs too close to Hawk's face for comfort.

Demon.

The demon waved a dripping forked tongue at Hawk, then swiped at him with an enormous clawed paw. In a reaction more instinctive than conscious, Hawk sucked in his stomach and bowed his body backward to dodge an eviscerating blow. He'd had his guts spilled more than once by a demon, but then, it had been in the Dark Lord's virtual world. As long as he'd known it wasn't real, his body had healed.

Now he didn't know what was happening. He thought he was dreaming, but so much shit had happened to him he didn't dare take the chance of being wrong.

Crisos. If he was wrong, what would become of River?

Hawk was never one to flee a fight, but lessons learned had taught him that fighting the Dark Lord's demons was a waste of time, and his time was better spent in finding River. He had to know if she was okay. He bolted down the stairs to the courtyard below, empty now save for the monsters rallying in the street. Thunderous noise on the stairs behind him warned that the demon hadn't given up quite so easily.

Wind whipped his hair into his eyes as he ran down streets once lined with potted plants, cobblestone walkways, and lush, green patches of grass. Now shadows draped the crumbling ruins of the city, and the stench from the sewer drains made him retch. Imps—evil, monkeylike little creatures—scrabbled in the wreckage, tossing rocks and sticks at him and cackling wildly.

As he ran he caught brief flashes of his altered reflection in the blackened windows. His hair was still dark but longer now, more untidy, and his eyes . . . those were the blue eyes of a man he hated, the man who'd sold River out. He ran his hands over his face, except they really weren't his hands at all, and his jacket now sported a huge, gaping hole.

"Chase Hawkins."

The voice crowed with delight at the discovery of his name, stopping Hawk cold in his tracks. He recognized that voice from River's game. He was wearing the face that went with it.

"Calling yourself Hawk doesn't make you sound more like a guy," the voice added. "It makes you sound like you're gay and trying to hide it."

Hawk glanced at the blackened sky in an attempt to pinpoint the location of the speaker. "Shame you can't see what's tattooed on your ass," he shot back. "No one can accuse you of trying to hide what you are anymore."

Hawk could almost feel the love in the air during the few beats of time it took for his words to sink in. When they did, Nick didn't sound nearly as amused.

"I want my body back, you thieving bastard."

"So come and get it," Hawk invited. *And come get what you deserve, you miserable son of a bitch.* He wanted to keep Nick talking, to find out if he knew where River was.

"I do know where River is."

Too late, Hawk threw up the barriers he'd held in place for months and only ever relaxed when River was present. Nick had read his thoughts, and that scared the shit out of him.

"She's right beside you."

Nick was lying. But then Hawk felt her familiar presence, warm and steady, and he wasn't so sure. But she seemed safe, at least for the moment, and some of his worry for her eased.

But what in the name of the Great Lords was happening to him?

Pain erupted at the base of his skull, twisted down his spine, wrapped around his chest, and crushed his ribs so that Hawk couldn't breathe.

"Give it up, pal. You're fucked."

"I'm not your pal," Hawk said, his voice as calm as he could make it. He'd be damned before he let Nick know he'd gotten to him. But how in the world was Nick able to cause him so much pain?

Pushing past it, something he'd had months of practice in doing, he scanned the street, his eyes darting back and forth, looking for any escape as the Dark Lord's demons closed in around him. He might not know for sure what was happening, but he did know he wasn't going down without a fight. He had River to think about. He could feel her close by, but he had to find her and see for himself that she was okay—although seeing was not necessarily believing.

He had to find a way out of this nightmare.

Nick hammered hard at Hawk's consciousness, but Hawk fought him off. He tried to think, but thinking hurt. This couldn't possibly be real. He refused to believe in it.

Demons and imps surrounded him. He had to get away from them before Nick gave the order to attack, but there was nowhere to go but up.

Fine. He'd go up. He'd be okay as long as he didn't look down. He dug his fingers into the crumbling front of the building beside him and slowly began to climb, sliding the toes of his sneakers along the rough surface as he searched for cracks that could support his weight.

"Does she shout out my name when you're doing her?" Nick asked, making him stumble and lose a foothold.

Projected images flashed in his head. Hawk rested his forehead on the brick surface and tried to close his mind against them. River and Nick, kissing, touching, their sweaty bodies coming together over and over again. Hawk tore his thoughts away from the erotic slideshow, forcing himself to detach and focus instead on the room they were in. Other than a bed positioned in the center of the room and a blue comforter haphazardly thrown over their bodies, the only other piece of furniture was a single dresser.

Nick's room.

"You have about as much imagination when it comes to decorating as you do with sex," Hawk said. "Not much wonder she lost interest in you." River's soft, sexy moans reached his ears and it was all he could do not to throw Nick's body off the roof of the building he'd finally reached. That would fix the bastard.

That was it.

Nick wanted his body back. If this was real, he wasn't going to let anything happen to it. Hawk wished he'd figured that out before he'd climbed to the rooftop.

The rooftop did give him a better view, however.

Where once the glitter of the city's lights had blanketed its skyline at night, gleaming red eyes now sparkled as demons crawled through its crumbled remains. Hawk drew in a breath at the extent of the devastation.

A blow to the head had him careening backward, and Hawk tumbled from the rooftop and into a trash container with a thunderous clang.

He didn't bother to wait. He scrambled to his feet and launched himself at the first of the demons to turn on him.

There were too many of them, and although he landed a few good blows of his own, he heard and felt his bones crunching beneath their hammering fists. He stumbled, blood filling his mouth. He spit it out and swiped at his lips with the back of his hand. His heart thumped hard against his chest and it took too much effort to draw in air. They were playing with him. The real beating had yet to begin. They were going to pound him into the ground and leave him for dead. He was convinced of that.

No, wait. He couldn't be convinced of it. He had to remember that this wasn't real.

A darker, more deadly presence emerged from the gloom.

"Hey. Take it easy on him, Sandman."

Hawk heard Nick, his voice distant and alarmed, at the edge of his thoughts. The bastard was still there, touching his consciousness, and Hawk struck out again. His fist connected with a demon's solid chest plating. One of his knuckles popped.

"If you keep beating at him like that he'll have a heart attack, and we won't have a body."

That made no sense to Hawk. Who could Nick be talking to? Who besides Nick would want to beat him to death?

A demon knocked him to the ground, straddled his chest, and sliced open his collarbone with a taloned claw. Hawk rolled to his side, white-hot pain leaving him gasping for air.

He gave up. He was better off dead. He couldn't do this anymore. He started to shake.

"Hawk?"

Someone was calling him, but he was too tired and he hurt too much to open his eyes to find out whom. The shaking worsened.

"Hawk!"

It sounded like River. Hawk groaned through the pain. She needed him. For her, he'd open his eyes.

He blinked and her frightened face swam into focus. She had him by the shoulders, and now he knew why he was shaking so hard.

"Stop," he said to her, then put his hands to his head to keep it from falling off his neck. Everything hurt, even his hair, but the pain was fading. She let go of him and he sat up straight so he could see.

They were in the Jeep, pulled over to the side of the road next to the rocky face of a cliff. Day had long disappeared. It was cold and he tugged the flannel coat tighter around him. He had no idea where he was, or if it was real, or what he could believe.

But the voices were gone. So were the demons. All he saw now were cliffs, trees, and a panoramic, star-studded black velvet sky spread out like a blanket before them. He breathed in deeply, the sharp tang of pine thick in the air. His heartbeat slowed, became normal.

He had no idea where they were and he didn't like that. He turned to River. There was something more important he needed to know.

"Have you ever heard of the Sandman?"

CHAPTER SIX

♦

Spence sat by the monitor in front of the cryonic chamber where Hawk's body was entombed, a magazine open across his knees and a fringi fruit in his hand. He bit into its blush-colored flesh, the tangy juice tart on his tongue, and flipped the page of the magazine with a sticky finger.

Wrapped up in the latest study based on one of his research techniques, he almost missed the tiny blip on the screen.

The upended magazine fluttered to the floor and the fringi fruit clattered into the wastebasket as Spence tossed everything aside and jumped to his feet, nearly knocking over his chair in the process. His heart started to pound. The blip was gone so fast he wondered if he'd imagined it because he'd been so worried about it happening again.

Then he worried it had happened more than once and no one was paying close enough attention to pick it up.

He did the same thing he'd done the last time it happened. He programmed the data into the computer and had it process the results.

There it was. Spence rubbed his eyes, wishing he'd been wrong about that second blip. Hawk's brain had registered some sort of internal activity. Yet there was no activity at all on the screen monitoring his external consciousness.

Two days had passed. Spence didn't believe Hawk had twelve more days, yet he couldn't do anything about it because believing something to be true and proving it were two very different things. The blip was gone now. Everything looked normal.

"Spence?"

Spence looked up at the sound of a lab assistant's voice at the door. She was young, although he'd noticed that every year the assistants seemed to get younger. Her name was Shana and she was a promising student. She cared more about the work than any attention she received for it.

"Yes?"

"You wanted me to let you know when it was time to get ready for the reception."

He'd forgotten. A delegation of Fae had arrived and he was expected to speak. He stared at the computer screen, unwilling to leave.

Shana's long, straight, severe blond ponytail swayed in her wake as she entered the room. Her white lab coat was pressed and tidy, unlike his own. Spence felt like an unmade bed beside her. And very, very old.

"Someone else can deliver my speech," he said.

"Would you like to do it?" he asked hopefully. "I have all my notes ready."

"Dr. Jennings." She sounded like a disapproving teacher scolding a first-year novice. "They came to hear you. No one else is delivering your speech, especially not an intern."

He liked that about her. She'd known instantly he'd been serious. Anyone else would have found it incomprehensible he'd prefer to remain in his lab, and assumed he was joking.

Her clear blue eyes softened. "I'll watch the monitor for you, if you'd like. I promise I'll let you know immediately if anything changes."

She would, too, he knew. She would have him paged in the middle of his speech if she thought it important.

He watched the monitor, undecided. If the Fae knew the Guardians had endangered someone's life on their behalf, they would be appalled. Hawk was not expendable, regardless of what Jess and the Great Lords thought.

Neither was Spence entirely convinced they'd endangered Hawk solely on the Faes' behalf. Yes, Fae souls had gone missing, but not to the extent the Great Lords would have him believe. More and more, he suspected that was merely a convenient excuse. The Great Lords were searching for something, but what?

Spence stared at the monitor a few more moments. He trusted Shana more than he did most people. She would not let Hawk die if she could prevent it.

"Thank you," he said, accepting her offer.

"Comb your hair," she replied, and stepped up to the monitor.

The reception was to be held in the Hall of the Great Lords, but not in its council chambers. He went first to his office to put on his formal robe and to gather his notes, then crossed the courtyard. He paused at the statue of the Mother for a blessing, then hurried up the stone steps of the hall.

As usual he was late, but the Fae never minded such things, so the Great Lords did their best to hide their displeasure. Spence wasn't pleased to see that Jess had been invited, too. He figured that made them even.

The delegation of Fae consisted of about twenty people, most of them male. Even if he hadn't known the majority of them, they were easy to pick out in a crowd because they had a presence about them, an aura of calm that filtered through the room to touch everyone present.

They were also an extraordinarily attractive people. Spence lifted a drink from a serving tray, intending to sip it slowly, not especially caring about his own rumpled appearance but more conscious of it than usual.

He delivered his speech on the scientific process of separating the consciousness, the soul, and the mortal body, and the potential it offered for space exploration.

"The benefits are currently being balanced against the pitfalls," he concluded. "The possibility of exploring new worlds without the dangers the physical form currently faces is exciting. Transporter accidents alone have taken eight Guardian lives in the past thirty or more years. Feral and hostile planets also pose safety hazards. However, we aren't yet certain of the long-term effects on the three elements of mortal being. As well, exploration without physical presence means significant lag time in offering our combined assistance to worlds in need."

One of the Fae delegates approached him afterward. He was an older man with tightly curled gray hair and kind eyes. His name was Achala, and he was one of the spiritual leaders of the Fae, and therefore, also of the Guardians. Spence found himself totally at ease simply by being in his presence.

"Dr. Jennings, may I speak privately with you for a moment?"

"Certainly, Your Grace." Spence looked around and spotted a quiet corner of the room the wait staff had used for storing extra chairs.

He pulled out two of the chairs and offered one to Achala, who thanked him and sat down. Spence sat facing him.

"Dr. Jennings, your scientific research is fascinating, and well founded, I'm sure. However, when you speak of long-term effects on the three elements of mortal being, to what, exactly, are you referring?"

"I'm referring to the consciousness, the mortal body, and the soul," Spence replied.

Achala smiled. "I understand the three elements. I was curious about the dangers to them."

"At this point, the dangers are purely hypothetical other than the obvious dangers to the mortal body.

The dangers to the body by intracellular freezing are well documented and can be mitigated."

"What dangers do you see for the consciousness and the soul?" Achala pressed gently.

Spence sighed. "Your Grace, most mortal souls are not like those of the Fae. They aren't reborn. Therefore, there is no scientific evidence to back up my hypotheses. Until a consciousness returns to its body, there is no true method for determining damage to either the consciousness or the soul."

Achala frowned. "In theory, then, if recovered, there is no true method for determining if the missing Fae souls have been damaged until they are reborn, and given a consciousness and mortal form."

Spence really didn't care for the turn this conversation had taken. "There are always risks in experimentation. The real question is determining when the benefits outweigh the risks."

"Or vice versa." Achala looked at his hands, folded in his lap. "What risk do you suppose a damaged soul possessing magic might possibly present to the mortal world?"

"I'm a scientist," Spence replied. "I look at the facts. And statistically, the facts state that the benefits of Fae souls to mortal life far outweigh any possible risks."

"That's because you aren't aware of all the facts," Achala mused softly, and Spence didn't reply to that because no response had been expected. "Tell me, Dr. Jennings," he continued, visibly collecting himself. "You are widely regarded and respected as a man with high moral and ethical values. I want to know what you believe these hypothetical dangers to be to the consciousness and the soul of any Guardian undergoing such separation."

The skin beneath Spence's formal robe went clammy and cold despite the warmth of the crowded room. Nevertheless, he didn't hesitate to answer honestly.

"From early experimentation, it's been proven the soul connects the consciousness to the body. Beyond the obvious physical damage, including brain damage, I believe the consciousness is in a far more subtle danger because it's not so easy to measure," Spence admitted. "We're asking an individual to go for significant stretches of time without conscious rest. Unless the individual undergoing experimentation is strong-willed, the greatest danger he or she faces is dementia."

Achala was silent for a few moments. "Do you currently have anyone undergoing experimentation?"

Politically, Spence was now in well over his head. The Fae were spiritual leaders. They rarely became involved in Guardian matters other than on a moral level, and in actual fact, Spence was no longer convinced of the moral ethics of his cryonics experiment with Hawk. He had been at one time. He still believed the process was safe for short periods of time. But Hawk had been under too long, well past Spence's ethical comfort level.

His throat was dry and he took a long sip of his second drink. Who better to discuss this with than a spiritual leader?

"Yes," he said.

"Do you believe your Guardian's mental health is in danger? Is that concern the basis of your talk here today?"

Spence should have known the Fae would pick up on his dilemma. He wondered why the Great Lords had allowed him to speak today, since they, too, should have known.

"Colonel Hawkins is especially strong-willed. It would take a lot to test his mental strength," Spence said. "But yes, I believe he's in danger. He's been under far longer than any other subject to date. He should have been awake by now."

Achala placed his hands on his knees as if coming to some sort of decision.

"If you are worried about the safety of your Guardian's mind," he said to Spence, "then it's possible the Fae may be able to help him."

♦ ♦

"I couldn't wake you," River said. "You had me scared."

She still sounded scared.

"I'm fine." Hawk thought so, at least. "How long was I asleep?"

She hesitated before she answered, and Hawk knew she was going to tell him something he wouldn't like. "Ten hours."

"Ten *hours*?" He couldn't believe it. He turned his head, and beneath the faint light from the speedometer on the dashboard, noted the way she was looking at him. Her eyes were too big, too worried, and he felt like an ungrateful shit. She'd let him sleep because she knew he needed it.

Her soft mouth opened, but she didn't say she was sorry as he expected her to.

"Morpheus, Lord of Dreams," she said instead.

"What?" He ran his fingers through his hair, trying hard to convince himself he was back in reality. His head was so freaking messed up, he could no longer guarantee which way was up.

"You asked me if I'd ever heard of the Sandman."

Hawk could accept that he'd been dreaming of Nick. He could even accept that he'd been dreaming of beatings, because he'd been subjected to those for months. He couldn't figure out, however, why he would dream of a Sandman when he didn't have a clue what a Sandman was.

Unless he hadn't been dreaming. What if Nick's Sandman was Hawk's Dark Lord, and the two of them were screwing with his mind?

He shook his head in an attempt to clear it. If he went crazy now, River would be defenseless. Nick was dead. There had been a hole in his body to prove it. And the Dark Lord was contained by Fae magic, existing as nothing more than a thought.

Therefore, Hawk had been dreaming.

"Where are we?" he asked. The night was silent around them, lit only by the moon and the stars. River had pulled the Jeep against the rock face of a cliff where the steep mountain road had been widened enough to allow her to stop. It was obvious the road didn't get much traffic anymore, and hadn't in a long time. Grass grew between the cracks in the asphalt, and she'd parked behind a rockfall that partially blocked the Jeep from view.

"We ran out of gas about an hour from the farm," River replied.

Hawk rubbed his eyes. While he'd slept like a baby, she'd been exposed to the world for nine of those ten hours.

To top things off, he was starving. River must be as well. He could fix them up with some shelter for the night, but he doubted if he'd have much luck hunting with a handgun. "How far to the nearest town?"

She didn't answer. Instead she reached out and touched his fisted hand, her warm skin like a healing balm, and he didn't stop her from giving him a little of her natural energy. As the images of River and Nick came crawling back to the surface, Hawk stared straight ahead and tried to dispel them. He couldn't change what had happened in the past.

His heart began to slow and his fingers relaxed slightly, and as her soul brushed against his, need flashed in her eyes. He wished he could answer that need, but he couldn't. It was forbidden to them, and he wouldn't allow himself to get lost in her magic. Not again. He could accept whatever punishment the Great Lords might hand him, but the thought of River suffering for actions she didn't fully understand was intolerable to him.

Hawk drew away from her.

"What happened to you?" she finally asked, breaking the sudden quiet between them.

He sucked in a breath and took a moment to mull things over as he let it out slowly. "Bad dream."

"I tried to wake you." She handed him a bottle of water and he took a long drink before handing it back.

"Remind me never to go to sleep again." Forcing a smile, he tried to make light of it. "Ten hours should do me a couple of months."

"Why did you ask me about the Sandman?" she queried, refusing to let it go.

Hawk's smile soured. It wasn't as if he could lie about it, since he'd asked her the question in the first place. "I have no idea," he admitted. "It was something that happened in my dream. I don't know where I heard of it."

Absently, she had a hand to her cheek as if it hurt and Hawk reached over to pull her fingers away. Even in the dark he could see the swollen flesh over her cheekbone, and the skin changing color.

"I *hit* you." He couldn't believe it, although that explained why his knuckle still hurt.

"Not on purpose." She shrugged. "You took a swing at something and I got in the way. That was when I tried to wake you."

Crisos. He closed his eyes, feeling ill. He'd hit her hard. "I'm so sorry."

She laughed at his reaction, which made him feel worse. "It's already starting to heal," she assured him. "It was an accident. Stop being a baby."

How did he make her understand that, accident or not, causing her harm of any kind was unbearable?

"It's probably an hour's walk to the truck stop," River said. She tapped her fingers on the steering wheel. "Maybe we could try to jump?"

"Absolutely not," Hawk said. He stopped himself from taking her arm, afraid to touch her now. He curled his fingers into his palms. "You don't have enough control. We don't know what we might be jumping into."

"If Andy has magic, maybe she can teach me control."

River had far too much faith in this Wizard of hers and it made Hawk nervous for her. So far Jake was the only person in her life she could count on that he had seen, and Jake was a kid. "Maybe. For now, we walk. Let's get going."

She grabbed her rucksack from behind the front seat and Hawk handed her the gun. If she should need a weapon, he'd prefer she had something that didn't require her getting too close to her opponent. He didn't mind fighting with the knife. While he was confident she was faster, stronger, and smarter than most people on this world, the Fae reacted to threats and he didn't know what her reactions might be. Until her abilities fully emerged, she was a danger to herself and to others.

She wound her long hair into a knot and tucked it under a gray ball cap she must have gotten from Jake. With her heavy sweater and slight build, at first glance she could easily pass for a boy.

He cut down a few branches and draped them over the canvas-topped Jeep to keep it from discovery for as long as possible. If someone were looking for it they would find it. If they weren't, it might sit here for days.

"We should be able to hitch a ride with one of the truckers," River said.

"As long as they don't recognize us."

She bit her lip. "What if they do?"

"Then we kill them and steal their truck." He laughed at the expression on her face. "I'm kidding. This isn't a video game. We aren't killing anyone. Not unless they try to kill us first."

"No one's killing anyone, period," River muttered, and Hawk hoped she was right.

They walked along the deserted road by the light of the moon, both lost in their own thoughts. The road curved around the mountain, and before too long leveled off. The sound of music told Hawk they'd arrived long before the truck stop came into view.

The smell of greasy fries hung in the cold mountain air and Hawk's stomach squeezed in response.

Remembering that he looked like Nick and that Nick was a wanted man, he kept his head down as he opened the paned glass door and took a quick look around before gesturing for River to enter.

She stepped ahead of him and he let the door swing shut behind him. River led them to a booth in a corner of the small dining area. Beyond it was a dance floor. For some reason, that struck Hawk as funny.

The place was less than half full. Most were clearly locals. One middle-aged man, however, sat by himself at another booth with a single empty plate, a newspaper, and one cup of coffee on the table in front of him. He showed no interest in River and Hawk other than taking an initial look, and immediately Hawk tagged him as a cop.

"If we're going to eat," River said, "we're going to need some money."

Before Hawk could warn her, she slid from the booth and headed for the hall to the washrooms. As she did, she casually bumped into a heavily tattooed trucker deeply engaged in an intimate conversation with a large-breasted blonde girl wearing too much makeup. Hawk wondered if the girl's mother knew what she was up to.

"Pardon me," River said, keeping her eyes on the washroom doors, not looking at the man.

Hawk slid lower in his seat, incredulous.

River had picked the man's pocket.

◆ ◆

River followed the narrow hall to the washrooms, the stolen wallet in her pocket. As soon as she entered the ladies' room she hurried into one of the stalls, its pink-painted metal door sagging slightly on the frame, and quickly counted the cash in the billfold.

Truckers normally carried a lot of money and they kept a close eye on it. River figured she had about two minutes at the most before he noticed his wallet missing, and only then because he'd been distracted by a pretty girl.

Six thousand dollars. River took fifty, slid the rest back into the wallet, then left the ladies' room. She brushed past the trucker again, slipping the wallet back into his pocket, and rejoined Hawk.

Out of the corner of her eye she saw the trucker reach for his back pocket, absently pushing his wallet deeper.

"Tell me I didn't see you do that," Hawk said.

"You shouldn't have," River replied. "I'm out of practice." She eased into the booth, spread her fingers over the gingham tablecloth, and picked up a menu. "Did you want something to eat or not?"

Hawk rubbed at his collarbone, then grabbed a menu. As River signaled for the waitress she gave one more sweep around the room. This place was known for its grilled steaks and mouthwatering burgers, not for its high-class customers, and River hoped that boded well for her and Hawk. Most ordinary people wanted nothing to do with the law.

River lowered her head, a few strands of hair slipping free from Jake's old baseball cap and spilling across her cheek.

As Hawk studied his menu, the waitress, sporting a fifties-style, bubble-gum-pink uniform that hugged the swell of her curves a little too tightly, came up to them. She flipped open her order pad. "What can I get you?"

River took a quick glance at her nametag, then lowered her head and spoke into her menu. "Red Bull, please. And the burger platter with the works."

"Same for me," Hawk added, continuing to rub at his collarbone as if his clothes were chafing.

The woman paused, the wrinkles around her eyes

deepening as her piercing green eyes studied River. An uncomfortable silence settled as her glance darted back and forth between the two of them. Their faces had been splashed across the television screen every hour on the hour for several days now, and Ruth obviously recognized them. River and Hawk exchanged a look. What was she going to do about it?

Ruth flipped the pad closed. "What happened to your face?" she asked River.

River had forgotten about that. The swelling had already gone down and it didn't hurt quite as much, but she imagined the bruise was still spectacular. She should have taken two seconds to look at it while she was in the washroom. She hadn't thought about healing it beyond the pain.

She hadn't wanted Hawk to know just how hard he'd hit her.

"Loser husband," she replied. "So I'm running away with my boyfriend." She pointed to Hawk and gave him a loving smile.

Ruth twisted on the ball of her foot, spun around, and muttered, "Right. Red Bull."

River let loose a slow breath and Hawk eased back in his seat. He twisted to put his back to the wall.

"She thinks you hit me," River said, indignant on his behalf.

Hawk winced. "I did."

"Not on purpose!"

He contemplated her, his face expressionless. "That makes it okay?"

"That makes it an accident."

There had been something disturbing about the dream he'd had that had made him lash out, and River wanted to talk more about it, but it was a subject Hawk clearly wanted to avoid, and besides, this wasn't the place.

He'd asked her about the Sandman though, and that had gotten River thinking. Hawk had said he'd never heard of the Sandman, but Nick had.

What if Nick's soul was out there, trying to survive on a dead planet where the Guardians had programmed a virtual prison for the Dark Lord? She and Hawk had destroyed that prison, and when River had jumped from the compound with Nick in her arms, Hawk had stepped into his dying body.

What if Nick's soul was trying to make contact with Hawk, or to get back to his body? Shouldn't Hawk and River try to find a way to help him, to bring him home?

If they somehow did find a way to bring him back, what would that mean for Hawk? Would the two share one body, or would Nick, the rightful owner, drive Hawk out?

If he did, would Hawk be able to find his way home?

They hadn't eaten in hours, but River found she no longer had an appetite. She needed a Red Bull. Caffeine withdrawal probably explained her headache.

Hawk pitched his voice low and asked, "So what's next, River? How do we get into the city?"

She lowered her voice to match his. "I think our best bet is Lover Boy over there."

Hawk pinched the bridge of his nose. "You mean the guy you just robbed?"

"I only took a few dollars," she defended herself. "He'll never even notice it's gone. He'll think he spent it and forgot. Of course," she added, watching the trucker's hand slide up the blonde's bare arm, "we'll probably have to wait awhile for him. He doesn't look ready to leave anytime soon."

Hawk scanned the room again, nodding in agreement, but he didn't look happy about it.

River watched the waitress pull their drinks from the convenience store refrigerator.

"So this Red Bull," Hawk said, seeing what had caught her attention. "I'm finally going to see what the rage is all about?"

River rubbed her hands together in anticipation. "If you plan on sleeping, then I'd suggest—"

Hawk held his hand up and cut her off. "I don't plan on sleeping. Ever again."

River frowned. "You're forgetting you're back in the real world now. You'll need sleep again sooner or later."

A pause, and then, "In that case, maybe I'd better grab a couple for the road."

Hawk continued to rub at his chest and she was about to ask if she could take a look at it, but the waitress came back with their drinks.

Hawk cracked the tab on his, took a slug from the can, and a look of horror crossed his face. "I thought you said this tasted good."

River laughed. "Of course it does." She opened her

own can and took a huge drink, relishing the taste and more important, the aftereffects. "Pretend it's coffee," she suggested.

Hawk sighed. "I guess if you were able to pretend a snake was a big, fat juicy burger dripping with onions, maybe I can pretend this is coffee." He took another swig, then cringed. "Or not."

At his reference to their time trapped inside her video game and the Dark Lord's prison, her smile wobbled. Beneath Hawk's own shaky smile, she saw worry lines. He was a warrior, a fighter.

But he'd been through a lot.

The waitress returned a few moments later with their food.

As they were finishing, the glass doors swung open and cold air invaded the warmth of the diner. Two bikers clad in MX pants and jerseys filled the entrance.

The place fell silent. Hawk's empty can hit the table top with a clatter, the sound seeming to echo in the still room. River tensed. She knew trouble when she saw it, and from the expression on Hawk's face, he did, too.

The bikers' eyes swept the room as if they owned the place. They chose a table nearest the door. As they seated themselves, their leathers creaking loudly against the worn vinyl of the seats, the waitress immediately went to work on pouring them coffee.

"The regular?" she asked, turning over their mugs.

"Anyone here on foot?" the taller man with the shaved head and black handlebar mustache asked in a voice loud enough for everyone to hear.

The waitress shrugged. "Can't say for sure."

River watched Hawk as he looked them over, sizing them up, and her heart stopped. Both easily weighed in at around 250 pounds, and neared six-five in height. Hawk couldn't possibly believe he could tackle them both.

Hawk shifted restlessly across from her, and she tried to draw his attention. Undeterred, he continued to study them.

The shorter of the two pushed his long dark hair from his face, rested tree-trunk arms on the counter, and poured a generous amount of sugar into his coffee cup before saying, "We were out riding the trails and found an old Willys Jeep just a few miles from here. Seems I remember some old farmer had been restoring one. Isn't it his daughter who's wanted for murder?"

The waitress said nothing, but the way she tensed spoke for her. The tattooed trucker and his girl tossed a few bills onto the table and left, the doors swinging behind them.

"Get ready to move," Hawk said in a low voice.

He didn't have to tell her twice. Not with the way her senses were coming alive, warning of danger. River placed money on the table and a hand on her rucksack, ready to run whenever Hawk gave the word.

The waitress's hand clamped down on River's shoulder from behind.

"When I drop my tray, both of you head into the kitchen," the waitress said softly to Hawk. The kitchen's swinging doors were directly across from their table.

Hawk's eyes flew to River's face, silently asking her if the waitress could be trusted. River nodded because she didn't see that they had any choice.

The waitress piled their empty dishes high on her tray, then moved to the next table and added those to her already unsteady load. Instead of heading for the kitchen, she walked in the opposite direction. When she passed to the side of the bikers farthest away from River and Hawk, she dropped the overloaded tray.

"Now," Hawk ordered. "Don't look back."

River did as she was told, walking quickly for the kitchen doors, Hawk directly behind her. Once through the doors, and ignoring the startled face of the apron-clad cook standing over the deep fryer, Hawk put his hand on her back and steered her toward the back exit and out into the night.

The moonlight cast a long beam of light across the poorly lit parking lot. The trucker and his girl were climbing into the semi parked at the far end of the lot.

Before River and Hawk had a chance to catch up with them and try to hitch a ride, River heard hurried footsteps skidding in the gravel at the front of the building. The two bikers rounded the corner into the shadows.

The waitress had bought them a few extra seconds, but now they were on their own.

"Get out your gun," Hawk said to her, his jaw set and his voice grim. Like a modern-day gunslinger, his hand hovered near the knife tucked into his waist-band.

River's pulse hammered in her throat. She'd crammed

the Glock somewhere into her rucksack—not her smartest move—and she didn't dare take her eyes off the approaching men to find it. She fumbled with the catch of the rucksack and plunged her hand inside, her fingers scrabbling through her few possessions before closing around the barrel.

The gun wasn't loaded. She hadn't thought to put the bullets in before they'd left the Jeep behind, but the bikers didn't need to know that.

Hawk didn't need to know that either.

She briefly considered grabbing him and jumping, but that might put them right back at the river and they'd have to start over again. Jumping was a last resort.

River mentally tagged the men Fat Guy and Short Guy, although neither description was accurate. One was heavier set and slightly taller, but they were both enormous.

The semi's engine roared to life and the headlights came on, temporarily blinding River. Then the truck pulled out onto the highway and drove off, leaving River and Hawk without any transportation into the city. Or eyewitnesses.

Fat Guy ran a hand over his shaved head. "Going somewhere?" he asked Hawk. His eyes swept the parking lot, empty now except for an old Buick and two bikes. "Is that your car?"

"Yes," said Hawk.

Short Guy started to circle, his eyes on River, while Fat Guy kept his attention on Hawk. River's fingers tightened around the barrel of the Glock. She hadn't yet pulled it from the rucksack, although by the way Short Guy watched the bag, he knew she had some sort of weapon in her hand.

"Which one of you really killed those gamers?" Short Guy asked.

River pulled out the Glock and trained it on Short Guy, since it was obvious Fat Guy was more interested in Hawk. "I did."

Fat Guy laughed.

Hawk had been trying to keep both Fat Guy and Short Guy in his line of vision, but when he saw that River had drawn the gun on Short Guy, he edged away from her and closer to Fat Guy. River couldn't tell if Fat Guy had a weapon or not.

If Short Guy did, she hoped he took hers seriously.

"Stay where you are," Fat Guy said to Hawk. "She's wanted alive. You, they didn't seem to care about one way or the other."

Hawk stopped. "Who are 'they'?"

River couldn't figure that out either. She was a gamer. A software engineer. She'd been part of a team, and no more valuable than any of the other members. Investors stood to lose a great deal of money because the game didn't work, and without the team, it wasn't going to work anytime soon. Did they blame her for that?

"Who cares?" Fat Guy shrugged.

Hawk moved then, going for Fat Guy, startling River so that she almost dropped the gun. She brought it back up again and kept it on Short Guy, who didn't seem concerned for his friend.

Hawk drove his shoulder into Fat Guy's midsection, knocking the larger man back a few steps but not knocking him down. Fat Guy recovered his footing quickly and smiled down at Hawk, drawing a knife from the top of his boot. Hawk drew his own from his waistband, planting his feet shoulder width apart, and Fat Guy's grin grew wider.

Short Guy started for River and she quickly shifted her attention back to him. She had to trust that Hawk knew what he was doing, and that he did it before Short Guy figured out she had no bullets.

Short Guy continued to circle her, forcing her to turn her back to Hawk, and a weight dropped in her stomach. He was playing with her, and that made her mad.

The best defense was a good offense. Any second now, he was going to realize she was unarmed. River threw the gun as hard as she could, striking his forehead and catching him by surprise. His hands went to his face and she went for his stomach, ramming his gut with a flying roundhouse kick. He doubled over and she jabbed the heel of her hand into his nose, feeling the crunch of breaking bone. Blood sprayed.

"Son of a *bitch*." Short Guy went to his knees.

River heard a thud and a grunt from behind her, and her heart pounding wildly, she turned in instinctive response.

Hawk had driven his knife to the hilt in the soft inner flesh of Fat Guy's underarm. Hawk yanked the blade free, twisting quickly to the side to avoid Fat Guy's return thrust, then danced back out of range.

River grabbed up a handful of dirt, and darting forward, threw it in Fat Guy's startled face.

"Get back!" Hawk shouted to her, and she turned to flee.

She ran straight into Short Guy's bloodied shirt-front.

His arms went around her, lifting her off the ground, and she swung her foot wildly, trying to connect with his groin.

This time he didn't underestimate her. He tightened his arms, squeezing her until she couldn't breathe and her vision blurred. He wrapped one of his legs around both of hers, pinning her against him. Angry, and struggling hard to free herself, she tried to bite his arm but couldn't reach it.

"Drop the knife!" Short Guy shouted at Hawk.

Hawk stopped, breathing hard, but he kept his grip on his knife and one eye on Fat Guy. If he dropped the knife, River knew he was a dead man. Hawk knew it, too.

The motocross pants encasing Short Guy's legs were slippery, making it difficult for him to keep River pinned, especially when his attention was divided between her and Hawk. She worked a leg free, driving her knee up and into one of his elbows, then sank her teeth into his bicep.

Short Guy shouted in pain, finally releasing his hold, and she rolled to her hands and knees on the ground.

"Finish him off!" Short Guy panted at Fat Guy. "Otherwise, I'm going to kill her."

River's fist shot up and into his groin with as much force as she could manage. Short Guy went down and curled into a fetal position, moaning.

With his knife low and ready, Fat Guy barreled toward Hawk, who had moved instinctively to help River. Hawk whirled, throwing the knife he held in one fluid motion, striking Fat Guy in the throat. Fat Guy clawed at the knife, air and blood gurgling loudly from the gaping wound, and River clapped her hands over her ears.

A dark shape peeled away from the shadows of the building, and River screamed out a warning to Hawk.

"Behind you!"

CHAPTER SEVEN

♦

Hawk turned in response to River's shout, unarmed now but on an adrenaline high, ready to take on anyone or anything coming within an arm's reach of her.

Something hurtled past him to land on the biker River had managed to take down all on her own. For a moment Hawk thought it was human. Then it bent its head and ripped the biker's throat out with its teeth.

River screamed again, this time in horror, and Hawk threw himself at her and covered her head with his arms, pressing her face to his chest. She'd lost her gun. He would speak to her about that later, when—if—he got the chance.

The loud cocking of a double-barreled shotgun cracked the night air. Light streamed from the kitchen, the silhouette in the open doorway casting a long shadow across the cold ground. The shotgun bearer stepped into the parking lot, his weapon up and aimed steadily at the blood-drenched nonhuman crouched over the dead biker's body.

The waitress, Ruth, jerked the kitchen door shut behind the shotgun bearer and Hawk heard a lock slam into place.

"Christ almighty," the shotgun bearer said in disgust. "What is it with you Weres, anyway? Why do you always have to roll in the blood? Get on your feet, dog. Kaye's going to kill you for that."

It was the cop from the diner. Instead of being relieved at the rescue, Hawk instantly grew more alert. For a long, frightening moment he wondered if all this was real, then decided it didn't matter. He had to treat it as if it was.

A look of determination etched on his face, the Were turned on them all and ran his tongue over his red lips, a glint in his eye as he savored the taste. Then he inhaled deeply and grinned at Hawk. Hunger danced in his predator eyes.

"Hello, Nick," he said. "I always did love the smell of you."

Why did it not surprise him that Nick had known this thing?

When the Were's eyes locked on River, Hawk stiffened and he felt her shift beside him.

"We need to do something," she whispered, clenching her fists as if ready to fight.

Heart racing, Hawk angled his head and took in the two motorcycles. It was old technology, and he'd need a minute or two to figure it out. The chilling gleam in the Were's eyes, however, told him he wasn't going to get a second, let alone a minute.

"What we need to do is get out of here," Hawk murmured in a soft voice meant for River's ears only, but the Were heard it, too.

Hawk grabbed River's hand and pulled her against him, afraid more of what she might do than of the Were, but the old guy from the diner, the one Hawk had pegged as a cop, spoke again.

"He's not going to hurt you," the cop stated with certainty.

With the primitive hunger in the Were's eyes, and the way his bloodstained lips peeled back to expose sharp white teeth, Hawk had no idea why the cop would come to that conclusion.

The cop stared the Were straight in the eye.

"Why did you do that?" he demanded.

The Were smoothed his hair back as if grooming himself, all innocence, pretending not to understand the question, and Hawk recognized the animal response to a challenge. "Why did I do what?"

The cop waved a hand toward the slain biker. "Why did you rip his throat out? Did Kaye tell you to do that?"

The Were glanced at the dead biker like a smartass schoolboy caught stepping out of line, then ran his chin along his shoulder in a submissive, canine move. "Kaye told me to bring her in alive," the Were stated, not quite defiant but close. "He never said anything about anyone else."

"Who is this Kaye?" Hawk demanded, but the cop and the Were were locked in a battle of their own, and neither paid any attention to his question.

"Nobody likes cleaning up after you bastards," the cop said. He glanced with distaste at the dead biker, blood pooling darkly in the faint light of the parking lot. "I sure as hell don't. You've got thirty seconds to drag your ass out of here or I'm going to blow it off."

"You're bluffing," the Were said.

The cop lifted the shotgun and aimed it at him with steady hands. "If I've got to clean up one mess, I may as well clean up two. Fifteen seconds."

The Were started to back away, deciding the odds weren't in his favor. Hawk didn't think they were either. The cop was going to shoot him.

The Were turned to Hawk. "I'll see you later, Nick. That's a promise." He loped off into the woods behind the service station.

Hawk opened his mouth to speak, but the cop held up his hand for silence. He listened intently, then satisfied the Were was gone, he said, "You two get the hell out of here. You are in a shitload of trouble. That was just the beginning."

"What kind of trouble?" Hawk demanded. "Why don't you explain it to us?"

"Because I so fucking do not want to be mixed up in this shit," the cop snapped back, angry. "And because I'm willing to bet you know a lot more than I do. I don't know what your game is, Sutton, but I'm not falling for that bullshit girl act you pulled in my office again. That Were *knew* you. If you're mixed up with Kaye and his people, and you aren't playing straight with them either, then good luck to you. You're going to need it." He turned to River. "And I don't know who or what you really are, but right now I'm going to give you the benefit of the doubt because I do know you didn't kill those gamers. So if you really think you can trust this piece of crap, I'm going to give you a half-hour head start." The look he cast Hawk telegraphed pure contempt. "Personally, if I were you I wouldn't take my eyes off him."

Yet another person who hadn't liked Nick. Again, no real surprise. But Hawk's heart went out to River, who had to be hearing things that would only hurt her, because she was probably the only person on the planet who'd genuinely liked the asshole.

But she hadn't loved him. Hawk could be glad about that much, at least. And from the sound of it, Nick Sutton had fooled more than one person.

It was odd he'd fooled River, though. She had Fae instincts when it came to most people. What had made Nick special to her?

The cop lowered the shotgun, holding it in one hand and ignoring them as he surveyed the dead bikers. He walked over to the one Hawk had killed, yanked the knife from the body, and wiped the blade on the biker's shirt. He handed the knife to River. "Twenty-nine minutes."

He walked back to the diner's kitchen door where Ruth, the waitress, hastily unlocked it for him and let him inside.

Somehow Hawk doubted if he and River would be as welcome. They'd probably used up their quota of goodwill tonight.

He exhaled slowly, the adrenaline seeping away in the sudden quiet of the night. He searched the dark for the gun and found it not far from the biker the Were had killed.

Just as he'd thought. It wasn't loaded. He slipped it into his waistband, deciding to worry about that later. Time was running out.

River kept her eyes off the dead bikers, he noted. She liked danger and she could fight when she had to, but she didn't like causing death. She was such an odd mixture. As much as she was Fae, Hawk could no longer discount her Guardian heritage.

She frowned in the direction that the Were had disappeared into the forest. "How could whatever that thing was have known Nick?"

Hawk's insides tightened and he placed a comforting hand on her shoulder, hating Nick more than ever. He decided to spare River his opinion. "I don't know, but we can figure it out later. Right now we need to get moving. The cop wasn't bluffing. He'll turn us in."

She straightened, tearing her gaze away from the forest. "You're right." She secured her rucksack over her shoulder, pushed past Hawk, and threw her leg over one of the bikes. "Hop on."

Hawk studied her, noting how tiny her small frame looked sitting on top of that big bike, and not at all confident she could handle it. "It's my turn to drive."

River stuffed her ball cap into her bag, and holding the hilt of the knife tightly, she jammed the long blade into the ignition. She threw him a glance that would have killed a weaker man. "Get on."

This looked like the perfect machine to give her a killer thrill. Killer being the key word. She'd drive them off a cliff on this thing. They'd be safer jumping. Hawk folded his arms. "Do you know how to run it?"

River was busy checking out the controls. "Better than you do. It's a Suzuki DR-Z400 Supermoto."

She had him there, although he wasn't giving in. "I can figure it out."

"We don't have the time," she pointed out. "A half hour on this road in the dark isn't very much."

Once she broke the ignition lock with her blade, she twisted it to the on position, reached down and pulled the choke, then pressed the ignition. As the bike revved to life she grinned at Hawk, and in spite himself he smiled back. River never failed to impress him. When her magic caught up with her technical skills, the world should watch out.

After giving the ignition time to warm up, she flicked off the choke. "You coming or not?"

Hawk threw his long leg over the bike and straddled the vinyl seat behind her. "I hope you know what you're doing."

"Me, too," she said as she kicked it into gear and peeled out of the parking lot.

♦ ♦

Peters passed the shotgun back to Ruth, who propped it behind the kitchen's swinging diner entrance doors without a word.

He was pissed off and she could probably tell. He gave her credit though. When he'd flashed his badge and demanded the rifle he knew most store owners kept, she'd handed it over, no questions asked.

"Why did you help them?" he asked her.

She wiped her hands on the hips of her crisp pink cotton uniform. "Why did you let them go?"

Some of Peters' annoyance shifted to tired and weary confusion. "I have no idea."

"I bet I do." Ruth looked at him, an equal weariness in her eyes. "You and I both remember the days when that poor little thing would have been given a fair trial. Now she'll be lucky to last a week. Paying people rewards for doing what the law should be doing is vigilantism. It isn't right. At least we gave her a fighting chance."

Had they? Nick Sutton had connections to the Monster Man.

Peters hadn't known that the first time he'd met Sutton. Now that he did, he probably should have shot him when he'd had the chance. The reason he hadn't, and the real reason he'd let them go, was because of the way Sutton had tried to protect the girl.

That had definitely surprised Peters. At the police

station, Sutton had been all about protecting himself. He'd thrown up in a trash can when he'd seen the crime-scene photos of what had happened to the gamers.

But tonight, Sutton had shown none of that weakness. He'd fought and killed a man. Peters had watched him do it, ready to step in if he had to and hoping it wouldn't come to that. He'd watched the Weston girl fight off the other man, and that hadn't been quite normal either. She was too fast and too accurate.

Then the Were had shown up and Peters' stupid factor had manifested itself. That Were was going to report back to Kaye exactly what had happened tonight—minus the rolling-in-blood bit—and now Peters was in deep, deep trouble. He would have to explain why he'd been here tonight, and why he'd let Sutton and the Weston girl get away.

If he had any sense of self-preservation left at all, he had no choice but to accept Johnson's offer. Once he accepted it, decent people like Ruth—and thanks to Jesus there were still people like her left in the world—would never look at him as one of the good guys again.

His first leg of the descent into hell was the cleanup. If he could get that taken care of for Kaye and Johnson, they might let him live a little longer. The waitress was the only other person who'd seen the Were, and it had been dark. She most likely hadn't seen what it had done. One phone call to Johnson and within a few hours, he'd have the help he needed. He could drag the bodies around to the back of the building until they could be removed, well out of sight, and try to clean up the massive amounts of blood in the parking lot.

"Can I use your phone?" he asked Ruth. "And would you happen to have kitty litter, some garbage bags, and a shovel?"

♦ ♦

As River navigated the sharp mountain curves by the glare of a single headlight, the chill night wind whipping across their faces, Hawk wrapped his arms around her waist to help keep her warm.

He leaned into the turns with her as she effortlessly maneuvered them down the highway. He had to hand it to her: she really knew how to handle the machine. Her fast reflexes were a definite asset given the crumbled condition of the road.

The excessive speed he could do without. River, however, was enjoying the ride and he didn't have the heart to ask her to slow down, so he tried not to think about the sheer drop on one side of the road or the solid rock cliff face on the other. He hated heights. He wasn't too crazy about face plants into rock walls either.

With River nestled tight against his stomach, and his heart about two inches from his throat, he turned his thoughts to the Were. Someone had crossed wolf genes with human, with fairly sophisticated and scary results.

Who was Kaye? What was the connection between him, the Were, and the cop?

Why did he want River?

Hawk hugged her tighter, trying to gain comfort from the knowledge she was with him, and she was safe. The cop had let them go because he hadn't wanted to be mixed up in whatever was happening. He hadn't seemed like the nervous type. Therefore, this Kaye had to be one truly scary fuck.

A scary fuck and a Were. Hawk could connect those dots back to the monster in the cave, at least until proven wrong. Connecting them to the cop was harder, and then to River, almost impossible.

They met one car on their drive down the mountain. A large white cube van. River saw it coming before he did, switched off her headlight, and coasted them into one of the many little railed-off sections of road. The van sped past them without slowing.

A short while later River took an exit off the highway and they entered the outskirts of the city. Since River had modeled most of her video game after the things she loved, including the scarred and battered city where she worked and lived, Hawk recognized the general layout of the area—mountain on one side, a wide, lazy river on the other.

So far, this world was proving no different than her game—monsters and all. That bothered the shit out of him. The beauty of the Guardian world was going to take her breath away. He could hardly wait for her to see it.

River drove the bike into a deserted alley and cut the engine. She gestured with a nod up the steep mountain street. "Nick's apartment is that way. We can leave the bike here so it won't be seen."

Hawk pushed the bike to the other side of a trash container, facing it out in case they needed it in a hurry, and lowered the kickstand. He swung around to take in his surroundings and as he noted the empty streets, and the rows of townhouses, wondering what lurked in the darkness or behind the drawn curtains, he couldn't shake the feeling they were being watched.

"Are you okay?" River asked, pulling her ball cap from her bag and settling it on her head, tugging it low to hide her face.

He shrugged off his sudden unease, not wanting her to worry. "I'm fine. Let's get moving."

He pulled his hood up and kept pace beside her as they climbed the fifty or so feet to the front steps of Nick's apartment. Hawk, breathless from the short climb, tried not to wheeze too loudly. Nick, the lazy bastard, should have been in better shape considering where he'd lived.

River, on the other hand, showed no signs of fatigue.

There were two attached units although the front doors and stairs were separate. He didn't like feeling like a wimp so he took the stairs two at a time, then asked, "How do we get in?"

Instead of answering she lifted a planter, grabbed the key from beneath, and unlocked the front door. Hawk tried not to let the jealousy rising inside him show, or think about those disturbing images of River and Nick from his dream.

They stepped into Nick's kitchen and River automatically reached for the light.

"Don't," Hawk said, and captured her hand. "Not

yet." He moved through the kitchen and living room and drew the curtains for privacy. "We don't want anyone to know we're here."

Once the blinds were drawn Hawk turned on a lamp that gave off just enough light for them to find their way around, but not enough for anyone on the street to tell that someone was inside.

He followed River back into the kitchen, a little spooked by being in Nick's apartment. She was leaning against the counter, her back to the sink. She smiled at him with such undisguised relief in her eyes that at first he was surprised. Then he understood. This place, to her, was a safe house.

To him, it was creepy as hell.

As always, she picked up on his mood despite his best efforts to hide it from her. She moved into his arms, sliding her hands beneath his soiled jacket, the warmth of her fingers seeping into his flesh and playing havoc with his mind and body. He briefly shut his eyes, drew a deep breath, then opened them again. His gaze slid over her, taking in her beauty. She looked every inch a Fae in the soft light, and she made a small noise and moved her hand to his face. The heat of her palm brought on a shiver of need and his body responded to the growing heat in her eyes.

"River." He placed his hand over hers and squeezed, knowing he should end this before it went too far. Fae souls were sacred to the Guardians. It was understandable that he would be drawn to her, and most likely unavoidable. Not only was she Fae, she was a desirable woman, so the attraction was twofold. It was the reason Guardians and Fae of the opposite sex rarely traveled together. That made what he was doing twice as wrong.

He was desperate for the intimate contact all the same.

As she leaned into him, her breasts pressing against his chest, need unfurled inside him. He lowered his head, buried his face in her sweet-smelling hair, and filled his lungs. The whisper-soft velvet of her lips lightly brushing over his skin pulled him under, and he could feel himself drowning in her. Want burned through him, so strong his hands began to shake uncontrollably.

He fought an internal war, Guardian morality competing with natural male instincts, but when River went up on her toes, touching her lips to his skin, he let loose a low, tortured growl. She had no idea how much power she held over him. He was tired, mentally and physically, and every reason he had for staying away from her paled into insignificance. Her soul strengthened his. Physically, she strengthened him as well.

When it came to common sense, she destroyed him.

He circled his arms around her tiny waist, resting his palms on the small of her back, and anchored her body against him. He nudged her chin with his and when she tilted for him, his lips found hers. He kissed her without reserve and she responded by running urgent fingers over his body. He brought one hand around to her breast and stroked his thumb over her swollen nipple. She arched into his touch, her body needy, de-

manding, and his own urged him to answer those demands.

"Hawk," she rasped, her voice intimate, soft, and so
full of naked emotion it left him shaking.

Need pumped through his veins as she pressed
tighter against him. She didn't seem to know how to
control what she did to him, nor did she see any reason
to do so, but she hadn't been raised by the Fae. She
didn't understand why this was wrong, and he couldn't
begin to explain it to her.

But he was not going to take her on the kitchen
floor. He inched back, trying to salvage some small
bit of his control, and finally noticed the red rash on
her bruised face.

He ran his thumb over the rash, shame burning
through him. Neither did she understand what it did to
him to cause her pain, no matter how slight. At least
the bruise on her cheek was fading, although far too
slowly for his liking. She didn't mind sharing her
magic with him yet she spent very little on herself.

"Mellita," he whispered gently. "Sorry. I need to
shave."

River pressed her palm to his whisker-roughened
cheek, her eyes heavy with desire. "You worry too
much about unimportant things."

"And a shower," he added more firmly, sliding a
hand down her arm to capture her fingers with his.

She sighed and stepped back, but not before she
gave him one last, lingering kiss that very nearly made
him forget why the kitchen floor was a bad idea.

"The bathroom is right across from the bedroom."

Her voice trailed off and the sudden silence turned awkward.

Hawk stiffened as if he'd taken a knife to the gut. He hated that he was in her former lover's body, and that he couldn't seem to dispel from his head the images of the two of them in bed together.

"Thanks," he said, and turned to leave. When he reached the doorway, River's voice stopped him.

"Hawk?"

The pulse pounded in his neck and his muscles went rigid. He was being a bastard and he knew it, and he hated himself for it, but he couldn't seem to stop. Jealousy was an ugly emotion. "Yes?"

Expression troubled, she stared up at him with those too-big blue eyes of hers for a long moment, then seemed to change her mind about whatever she'd really intended to say. "What does *mellita* mean?"

The question lightened his heart, although having to explain it made him feel self-conscious and vulnerable, neither of which he liked. "It means *darling*."

She rolled that around in her head, then a smile backlit her eyes to replace a bit of the worry that continued to linger. "I'll make us some eggs."

He exhaled a long, slow breath of relief and said, "Okay."

Hawk began to make his way down the hall, pulling off his shirt as he went. He stepped into Nick's room in search of a set of clean clothes before he got into the shower. The heavy curtains to Nick's bedroom were drawn, so he carefully moved across the room and flicked on the small bedside lamp. As soon as he did, and the room came into view, his heart rose in his throat.

Crisos. Things had just gotten a hell of a lot more complicated.

♦ ♦

The last of the evening staff had long since departed and Andy was alone in the room.

She went around the bar, setting the straight-backed oak chairs upside down on the tables, getting ready for the staff to give the floor a cleaning before they opened again.

She hadn't used more than a whisper of magic in a long time. She no longer liked it the same way. Once, she hadn't thought she was doing any harm to anyone other than herself. Now that she understood the price her magic came with, she was less inclined to use it.

She also didn't have the strength for it. Not since the virus.

Andy ran her fingers through her long black hair, trying not to think about the gray streaks time had added to it. She should either color it or change her appearance. Maybe sell the bar and move on. It was beyond time for her to revisit her mistakes and try to rectify them, then start a new life.

She would have done so long ago if not for River.

Earlier that evening she'd swiped a tiny bit of soul from a homeless man who'd been desperate for a hot meal. She'd given him the meal, but only taken a very thin sliver of his soul in return. She would release it when she was done and he would never even know it had been missing. She'd be very careful not to damage it. She'd learned a lot during her time on earth.

She flicked off the overheads and let the glow from the streetlights outside the front window fill the room. Pouring herself a draft from on tap, she settled into one of the booths, closed her eyes, and let her mind wander.

She'd traveled so many places it took her awhile to find the right thread. Once she had it, she summoned the bit of soul she'd borrowed.

Then she jumped.

The lab hadn't changed much, which didn't really surprise her. Without magic to guide them, Johnson's research team could never have replicated the experiments she'd led.

They'd tried though. She could feel it. She walked the silent corridor by the soft gleam from the emergency lights, footsteps echoing, peering into the various lab departments. The smell of chemicals and antiseptic, more than anything, took her back.

She drew up short in the doorway of an open room. She'd spent a lot of time in this physio department, watching the Weres learn how to walk upright like normal humans. Many of them had been born too severely deformed to manage more than a hunchbacked, Quasimodo-style shuffle. Others could have passed for human on the street if not for their animal instincts.

Some things couldn't be changed. A mortal's nature was one of them.

Andy wasn't looking for anything inside the deserted lab, however. Everything of any scientific value had been moved to a more secure facility long ago. She was looking for the Fae in the graveyard.

She tested the door at the end of the long main corridor. It was locked. She pushed it with a precious bit of magic, careful not to expend too much, and the door opened. The frost in the night air scraped at her cheeks. Along with the cold she felt the sharp, bitter sting of despair.

Taking human DNA and growing it into a mass of living tissue until it could absorb a mechanical frame had been plausible. Making it a reality had required more than the limited scientific knowledge of the day.

Johnson had been too eager to meld man with machine and Andy had been too willing to help him. He'd meant it when he said that more than anything, he wanted to make the world a better, safer place. Johnson wanted it so badly, in fact, that Andy's magic had flared in response. She hadn't fully understood he wanted a better, safer world for him and to hell with the mere mortals in it.

She had loved him back then. One night she told Johnson what she was, and how her magic worked. He'd been intrigued by its possibilities, and to be honest with herself, so had she. She'd spent a number of years studying earth sciences, and mixing her magic with science had been a challenge she couldn't resist. She'd been more successful than she'd expected, but an immortal's magic, unlike the magic of the Fae, was limited. It ran out if it didn't have souls to regenerate it.

Kaye, apparently, had run out of magic.

Andy called softly to the Fae standing watch over the Guardian in the graveyard, asking permission to be allowed to approach.

The Fae's response was to blast Andy off her feet and back through the lab's outer doors, where she skidded on her back halfway up the tiled corridor floor.

Andy lay still for a few moments, panting past the pain. Then she rolled to her side and sat up, resting her head between her bent knees until the nausea passed. In the dead silence of the lab, her heart went out to the Fae.

She had done this to them. The Guardian had willingly sacrificed his soul for the Fae and their child to be safe, but it had been too late for the Fae. Her magical soul had returned to protect his. River was the key to helping release them. Once they knew she was safe, River could help convince the Fae to drop the magical containment she'd created around the graveyard. Andy and River could then set them both free.

First, however, she had to keep River safe.

Andy climbed to her feet, her hips stiff and her bruised back sore. She stretched, making certain nothing was broken, and hoped she had enough magic remaining to get her home. Under no circumstances would she draw on any of the souls still lingering around the remains of the failed experiments in this place.

She jumped again, unaware her visit had been caught on the security cameras she'd tripped when she arrived.

CHAPTER EIGHT

♦

River rooted through the cupboard drawers for a lighter, lit the pilot on the gas stove, then stuffed the lighter into the front pocket of her jeans.

She couldn't deny it was awkward to be in Nick's apartment with Hawk. She'd rather be in her own apartment, but she wouldn't feel safe there and Nick's was the next best thing.

Her whole life had been turned upside down and Hawk was all that kept her grounded. She got out the frying pan and set it on the burner with more force than necessary. She didn't like it that to him, she was Fae.

If being Fae meant she couldn't love whom she pleased, then she'd rather be human.

She'd just cracked an egg into the frying pan when a shiver slid down her spine. She stilled in the darkened kitchen and listened more closely to the early morning sounds of the building around her—the rumble of a water heater, doors opening and closing. None of those were cause for alarm.

She carefully leaned across the counter beside the small window overlooking the single stainless-steel sink and shifted the curtain slightly with her finger, glancing onto the street below.

Pale, predawn light whitewashed the waking city, its thousands of streetlights winking out one by one. As the wind picked up fallen leaves, dirt, debris, and what looked like an old paper ice cream wrapper, she searched the street for anything out of the ordinary.

She spotted the trash bin of a neighboring townhouse lying on its side, wet and soiled food remnants spilling across the concrete. That explained the paper ice cream wrapper. It didn't explain what had tipped over the garbage.

A slight movement in an alley across the street caught her eye, but before she could identify what it was, the shadow disappeared between two townhouses. River's unease dissolved and she let the curtain drop back in place, passing the incident off as a hungry animal in search of food, most likely a raccoon or possibly a bear. They grew more aggressive this time of year as they prepared for winter, and looting trash bins wasn't uncommon behavior.

She was about to go back to scrambling her eggs when she realized Hawk hadn't yet come out of the bedroom. Her gaze shifted from the window to the dimly lit hallway, unsettled and not wanting to be. Maybe he didn't like Nick's taste in clothes.

Or maybe something was wrong.

She pulled the frying pan off the hot burner and hurried down the unlit hall. Hawk stood shirtless in the middle of the bedroom, his back stiff and the muscles contracting as he stared at Nick's unmade bed.

At first she was angry with him. He had no reason to be jealous of Nick. She closed the small gap between them and placed her palm on his back, and he jerked away as if her touch burned his skin. He quickly spun around to face her and what she saw in his eyes changed her anger to alarm.

This wasn't about jealousy.

She glanced back at the bed, but all she saw were the rumpled comforter and mussed sheets. So Nick was a slob. She didn't think it would matter this much to Hawk.

"What is it?" she asked, and carefully placing her hand on his face she used a small flare of her magic to pull his concentration from the bed and back to her.

This time he didn't flinch away from her touch. Instead, as his hand closed over hers, emotions he couldn't seem to control flowed off him in waves. The fine lines around his eyes deepened and she gave another quick sweep of the room. Still unable to figure out what it was about Nick's room that disturbed him, she tugged at his hand. "Let's go into the other room."

Hawk followed her down the hall to the small living room off the kitchen and sat down on the worn, butter cream leather sofa. River never took her eyes off him as she moved to the other side of the room to give them both some space, sitting across from him on an ugly, faded orange recliner with worn fabric armrests. A small, rectangular glass coffee table separated them.

Hawk looked very much out of place in this room. He could pass for Nick's wilder, more exciting twin brother, but anyone who knew Nick would know this wasn't him.

Nick was a house cat. Hawk was a panther.

She leaned forward in her chair. "What's happening

to you?" she asked, spooked by the way he was acting.

He tapped his head. "It's what's happening in here that's the problem."

River knew one of his biggest fears was losing his mind and she couldn't blame him. He'd been through months of hell, and even a Guardian could only take so much. Worry for her only made matters worse for him.

Right now she was stronger than he was, and he needed both her and her energy more than he would admit.

"Talk to me," she said.

"I've seen that bedroom before," he stated with quiet certainty, tapping his head again. "In here. In my dream. When we were driving."

River wondered what that might possibly mean. Maybe it didn't mean anything. "Maybe you'd better tell me exactly what happened in your dream."

Outside, a car with a hole in its muffler roared past.

Hawk stared at the ceiling. "Nick, the little bastard, is in my head." He might have been talking about the weather, he sounded so calm, and it frightened her. "And he's not alone."

"That isn't possible," River said, because she didn't want it to be. The thought that she had failed Nick was something she didn't think she could bear. Thinking she might have done something to hurt Hawk was even worse.

Hawk scrubbed at his face with his hands. "He's in

there," he assured her. He let out a low, humorless laugh. "Either that or I'm going crazy."

"You're not going crazy," she said, despite the chill in her bones. "Maybe you'd better tell me everything that happened in the dream, and together we'll figure out what's going on and how we're going to fight it."

He told her everything, from finding himself back on his home planet to the projected images of River and Nick together.

Now she understood the source of his jealousy. She could understand why he thought Nick was in his head, because showing Hawk those thoughts of her was most definitely something Nick would do. He could be a lot of fun, but he could act like a spoiled child as well. That was how she'd known their relationship would never be serious.

"But I felt Nick's soul leave his body," she said. "I'm sure of it."

Hawk gave a shrug of his shoulders. "If the Dark Lord managed to shanghai my soul, who's to say he didn't do the same thing to Nick's?"

Hawk believed the body, the soul, and the consciousness were tied together. When the body died, the soul departed and the consciousness, the bond that connected them, ceased to exist. Hawk's body was alive on his world, therefore his consciousness maintained the connection.

Since Nick's body was also alive, then who was to say the same connection couldn't exist for Nick?

Tears clogged the back of River's throat and she fought to hold them in check. She thought of the tortured soul she'd touched in the attic and of her parents' souls when she had touched them in her game. Something kept them from finding peace. By healing Nick's body for Hawk to use, had she tortured Nick's soul?

Nick could be a jerk, but no one deserved that.

Immediately, Hawk's concern shifted to her. In two long steps he crossed to where she sat, kneeling beside her and placing a hand on her thigh. *"Mellita,"* he said softly. "What is it?"

She couldn't tell him because she didn't want to add to his stress. This wasn't about her worries or her guilt. This was about his concern for his sanity. "If Nick gets into your head, can the Dark Lord come with him?"

He tensed. "I don't know for certain. Which is why I can't let myself sleep."

"We aren't in a virtual world anymore," she pointed out. "Sooner or later, you're going to have to sleep."

Hawk's hand rubbed her thigh. "There are drugs to avoid that. I know what I need. I just need to know where to get them."

She knew where to get them, but she didn't like the idea of him resorting to drugs. Far better for her to use magic. "I could reason with Nick."

He didn't like that idea at all. "Stay out of my head," he ordered her. His mouth twitched at the corners. "I don't like being in there myself. There's no need for both of us to suffer. No sleep," he repeated. He shot a glance toward the kitchen. "I'm good for a while yet. Until I can get something stronger, does Nick have any coffee?"

"I'll check." River's stomach took that moment to grumble.

Hawk patted her leg, then stretched. "Why don't you finish cooking while I get cleaned up? We'll be able to think better once we're fed."

River watched Hawk's back disappear down the hall, then she returned to the kitchen. She listened as he ran water in the tub. He hadn't closed the bathroom door and he wasn't going to take a shower, because if he did, he wouldn't be able to hear what went on in the apartment. Sometimes his concern for her was nice. Sometimes it annoyed the hell out of her.

She searched Nick's near-empty cupboards. She grabbed a fresh pack of coffee from the freezer and went to work on making a pot. Even though she'd done it plenty of times before, going through Nick's cupboards now felt like an invasion of his privacy.

What if Hawk was right and Nick was inside his head?

Nick had been shot because of her. Her heart thudded as she revisited the terror of those last moments with him at the compound. She couldn't remember all the details, no matter how hard she tried.

She dropped two slices of bread into the toaster, sprinkled the now cold egg mixture with salt and pepper, and turned the burner back on.

Ten minutes later, after the coffee had finished brewing, she set their plates of food on the table and realized Hawk had been very quiet. She called out to him and waited a moment. When he didn't answer, she padded softly down the hallway and stopped outside the half-open bathroom door. "Hawk, your eggs are ready."

She listened but when she heard no noise she pushed the door open wide.

He was sprawled in the tub, his eyes shut and his head lolled to the side.

♦ ♦

Peters couldn't imagine anything worse than sitting in front of the Monster Man, barely able to keep his eyes open because he hadn't had any sleep, and scared shitless because he had to keep his story straight when his brain wasn't fully engaged. He had tripped up enough alibis in his time to know that depriving a suspect of sleep was a lot more reliable than a lie detector test.

It was too early in the freaking morning for this, especially after the crap he'd cleaned up in the night.

General Amos Kaye was every bit the creepy-eyed bastard he was reputed to be. Knowing who he was this time inched the creepy factor up several notches.

Peters tried not to let the shivers he felt enter his speech. "I had to let them go. A Were had just ripped the throat out of a guy, and cleanup always comes first." He inspected his fingernails. "At least that was the rule in the Westmount days."

Kaye leaned back in his chair, crossed his legs at the knee, and folded his hands neatly in his lap. They were sitting in the small conference room at the police station, and Peters wondered how much his soul was worth to Johnson and Kaye, and any of the others as-

sociated with this. So far he hadn't been offered any
real compensation other than his life, but that didn't
count because it was a shit life anyway.

"It's still the rule." Kaye fixed him with those bone-
chilling, colorless eyes. "Do you think you can control the Were?"

Peters couldn't say for certain. This Were was far
smarter than the ones he'd handled in Westmount, but
he didn't know if that was good or bad. Smart or not,
the Were didn't have any more control than the others
once he scented blood, and even being a smart Were
didn't make him brain surgeon material.

On the other hand, he'd responded immediately to
Peters' commands. "Can I kill him if I can't?"

Kaye studied him without blinking. "No."

That meant Peters was more dispensable than the
Were. Nice. "I can control him."

Kaye reached into the breast pocket of his overcoat
and pulled out a packet of photos. He placed them on
the table in front of Peters. "Take a look at these."

The photos were grainy and dark, and looked as if
they'd been snapped inside some sort of industrial
building. Taken at periodic intervals, they showed a
woman's figure walking down a hall, opening a door,
then being blown backward. Only two clearly showed
the woman's face. In the first, her eyes were squeezed
shut and she had her face turned to the side as she
tried to protect herself from the force of the blast. The
next showed her lying on the floor, her knees drawn
up to her chest as if she was in pain. She looked familiar but the photos weren't very good.

"Who is she?" he asked.

"She owns the pub on Argyle, not too far from here. She's also a close friend of the gamers. I want her watched, and if River Weston and Nick Sutton show up at her place, I want to know about it."

Now he recognized her. The younger guys sometimes went to that pub for lunch, although Peters only rarely joined them. She was a woman about his own age, well kept and very hot, but she'd been sick within the last few years, he recalled. That was enough to turn him off. Threats of the virus recurring tended to scare his generation away from public places. He couldn't imagine business was booming for her.

Peters decided it was time to show he wasn't a total pushover. He was already dispensable. If he took work from Kaye without any negotiation whatsoever, Kaye would assume he was easily intimidated and try to bully him every step of the way. "Why should I watch her for you? What's in this for me?"

"How about your life?"

"Not enough," Peters said. "Civil servants get paid shit. I'm pushing retirement and suffering arthritis. I'd like to live someplace warm." Not for a moment did he think he'd make it to retirement now, but he wasn't planning to go down without some pride. "And if you expect me to dog sit your Were too, there's more to this than I really want to know about. Don't tell me anything. I just want the danger pay."

"Fair enough."

Kaye named a figure that nearly knocked the chair

from under him. No way was Peters walking away from this alive. He would never see that money.

The knowledge was liberating. To hell with Kaye, Johnson, and all of the others involved in whatever this was. Peters was buying his soul back. First, he'd make sure the Weston girl wasn't a threat to anyone. Then, he'd help her escape. He would do as much as he could in the time he had left to try to right a few wrongs in the world.

Kaye was watching him, but he was very good at keeping his thoughts to himself.

"When do I start?" he asked once he judged enough time had passed to make it look like he was nervous about accepting, but unwilling to turn down the money. He wanted to look greedy, not stupid.

Or smart.

"Now." Kaye stood. "Come with me."

They went out to the street. Kaye's car was parked in a no-parking zone in front of the loading bay of a nearby office tower. In the backseat sat the battered and bruised Were, sullenly staring out the car window.

Kaye had known not to bloody him, so that was good, but he'd definitely beaten him into submission, and beating a Were into submission was no easy accomplishment. Peters didn't feel sorry for the homicidal little prick, but it didn't make the situation easier for him.

"Jesus," he said. "I can't take him out in public looking like this."

"That's not my problem." Kaye opened the door and yanked the Were out by the collar of his jacket.

"His name is Bane. He's going to do exactly what you tell him to. Aren't you, Bane?" Bane nodded, not meeting anyone's eyes. Kaye addressed Peters again. He handed him a cell phone and a battery charger. "Don't turn it off. I'll be calling you regularly for updates."

Kaye got into his car and pulled onto the street, leaving Peters and Bane standing alone in front of the loading bay doors.

"Not so tough without your shotgun, are you?" Bane said to him.

Peters cuffed the side of the Were's head, picking one of the most painful looking lumps for a target, reasonably secure in the knowledge it was too soon for Bane to forget the beating he'd received. "Shut up."

Bane subsided, although his sullenness deepened.

Peters considered the situation. He might have a use for the Were, whose instincts were more animal than human. That meant Bane would do whatever he was told, by whomever he respected. Beating an animal into submission was only one method of winning its loyalty. Feeding it was another.

Peters reached into his pocket for his car keys and decided it was worth the cost of the gas.

"We're going for breakfast," he said. "Keep your head down in the drive-through."

◆ ◆

"Hawk, wake up."

River seized him by the shoulders and shook him. His skin was wet and cold, and she had no bet-

ter luck waking him this time than she had in the
Jeep. She kept a close watch on his movements, ready
to dodge if he started swinging. Last time, he'd reacted badly when he discovered he'd accidentally hit
her.

His eyelids twitched rapidly and his legs flailed in
the tepid bathwater. As she watched, a bright red welt
formed on his cheekbone. Fresh blood flowed, trick-
ling slowly down his jaw before vanishing as if it had
never appeared.

He was healing himself in his dream. What was
happening to him?

"Hawk!" she called again, and still there was no
response. She knelt beside the tub, her legs and feet
wet from the bathwater that had slopped over the side
to pool on the cracked tile floor. Something had a grip
on his mind, and River wasn't going to let him battle it
alone. She knew how convincing an altered reality
could seem. She needed to do something and she
needed to do it now.

She kept one hand on his shoulder. She'd brushed
his soul before, and caught glimpses into his thoughts,
but she'd never tried to step into a dream. She didn't
even know if it was possible. But if whatever had entered his mind had done so through magic, then she
could do it, too.

She closed her eyes and forced herself to relax, a
difficult thing to do while Hawk was in trouble. As
she drew calming breaths she let her mind drift, searching for a thread the way Hawk had taught her when
explaining how to jump. The thread she searched for

now, however, connected Hawk's soul to River's. She found the fine filament and began to follow it, letting it lead her deeper and deeper into Hawk's subconscious.

Gunfire rang out.

River's eyes flew open and she spun quickly around, trying to find her bearings. Day had become night. Nothing looked right to her—not the buildings, the streets, or the red triple moons.

Where was she?

Since she'd stepped into Hawk's mind she thought it safe to assume she'd stepped into his world as well, but this was a dream so it was unlikely to be a true portrayal. She hoped not. It was awful and threatening, and she didn't like it at all. It reflected nothing of the little he'd told her of it.

The ground shifted beneath her feet as a deep, angry howl pierced the night. River stiffened, expecting the heaving pavement to crack open any second, then forced herself to move. Pressing against one of the many buildings edging the deserted street, she inched along its front. Across the street sat a small cafe. In a center square, a statue of a woman streamed water from an urn in her arms.

The peppery smell of sage, thick and familiar, stung her nostrils.

Magic.

Approaching footsteps pounded on the pavement behind her. She whirled in time to catch sight of a stranger slipping between two nearby buildings.

That had to be Hawk. He had a pack of oversized,

growling demons tight on his heels. She patted her body for weapons, but her hands came up empty.

This was a dream. She should be able to find weapons.

Unfortunately, it wasn't her dream. Her gaze swept the stores, looking for something, anything, she could use.

She tried the door to a dry cleaner's, hoping to find it unlocked. No such luck. She pulled off her sweater, wrapped it around her hand, and punched the glass. Then she stilled, listening to the night sounds and hoping she'd gone undetected. Tension coiled through her and goose bumps pebbled her bare arms when she caught the skittering sound of little feet scrabbling at the walls. Rats?

Imps.

Hawk hated imps more than anything, except maybe Nick.

Moving swiftly, she slipped her hand through the jagged glass and unbolted the door. Once inside she moved about the room in search of anything she could use. She found a broom, snapped it in two over her knee, and tucked the long end under her arm.

She lifted a portion of the counter and walked into a back room filled with dry-cleaning chemicals. She picked up a solvent, the label on its plastic bottle marked flammable. The liquid sloshed around inside the jug and she decided it might come in handy.

She thrust her hand into her front pocket and smiled with relief when she found Nick's lighter still there. Feeling much better equipped, she exited the dry cleaner's through the back door and listened for sounds of fighting. She had faith Hawk could look after a few demons alone, but she liked having her faith confirmed.

She cut through an alley, cursing silently at the sound of gravel crunching beneath her boots. The alley opened into a small, lush park with a flowering, vine-draped gazebo at its center. She hurried up the raised wooden walkway, slipped inside, and sank to the stone floor. Peering out over the top of a cedar ledge she could see into the deserted street, trying to decide where Hawk might have gone.

Footsteps in the alley warned her of someone's approach.

River crouched lower, listening intently, her heart ringing in her ears. She watched as a shape emerged from the darkness, uncertain at first whether it was man or demon.

It was a man, inching backward, coming closer and closer to her hiding place. She released a tiny finger of magic, wanting to be certain, and the familiar touch of his soul left her limp with relief.

"Hawk?" she whispered.

He spun around, feet wide and hands up, ready to defend himself. His hard gaze locked on hers, and then his legs ate up the distance between them. River backed up in awe. This man was all muscle and power, a stranger to her. Any traces of Nick were gone. From deep in his subconscious Hawk was projecting his own image.

He was clearly agitated, and River wanted to let

him know it was really her and not something he was dreaming. She held up the piece of the broken broom.

"Since this is your dream, can you give me a gun instead?" she asked.

He hesitated for a second, still uncertain. Then relief broke out on his face. "That depends. Are you going to put bullets in it this time or are you just going to throw it at things?"

River launched herself into his arms. She didn't care what he looked like. He was Hawk, and he was safe. At least for the moment.

His glance moved cautiously over her, his eyes still holding a hint of distrust. "How did you get here?"

"I followed the thread between us." She was proud of the fact that she'd used her magic on her own, and that she'd found him, and she didn't try to hide it. "You're dreaming and you need to wake up."

A wave of cool air brushed over their bodies and River shivered. Hawk scrubbed his chin. From the look of confusion on his face, River knew his mind was playing tricks on him. Careful not to startle him, she slowly reached out and gently placed a healing hand on his chest and tried to see through his eyes, to see what he saw.

As his body absorbed her heat and energy, he let loose a long, slow breath, then pinched the bridge of his nose. "Crisos."

"Hawk," River urged him. "Listen to me. You're in the bathtub, and you're asleep, and you have to wake up now."

He went quiet, his feet shifting restlessly. Tension

filled the air, frustration clouding his eyes. He winced, put his hands over his ears, and cursed under his breath. "Don't you see? I can't wake up. You need to get out of here. It's not safe."

The chill in the night air increased. River was as scared as she could ever remember being. Was Nick doing this to him?

No matter how hard she tried she couldn't see or hear everything. Hawk was shutting her out and she wasn't strong enough to break through.

"I'm not going anywhere," she insisted. "Not without you."

The muscle along his jaw tightened and he parted his lips as if about to speak, but then his head went up and he slammed his mouth shut. From somewhere close by, a scraping noise could be heard as if something heavy was being dragged through the dirt. He stepped into the gazebo with her, pushing her into the shadows and caging her between his broad back and the wooden boards.

"Do you have a weapon?" she asked quietly, trying to inch out from behind him, but he wouldn't allow her to move. When he shook his head, she handed him the broom handle and reached for her solvent and the lighter.

The scraping sound disappeared into the night. He shot her a look over his shoulder. "We need to move to a safer place."

In the game they'd had safe houses.

"Sorry," he said, reading her mind. "We don't have any safe houses here."

"How do you know?" she asked.

"I just know." He sounded amused and that in turn made River feel better. "But I may be able to think of something almost as good." He took her hand and tugged. "Let's go."

They bolted from their hiding place, cut through the alley, and headed back toward the main street, but before they could reach safety, a pack of wild dogs closed in on them from several directions.

As the animals advanced, River and Hawk stood back to back.

"This is your dream," River said. "Think of something."

"It might be my dream," Hawk replied, his voice grim, "but every time I think of something, someone throws up a roadblock."

"Whoever they are, they can't read my mind," River declared. "And I can think of something."

Intent on putting her solvent to good use she twisted the cap, but one dog attacked before she could douse it. From behind her Hawk fought off three dogs, using the broken broom handle as a weapon. She heard a yelp and a thud and would have smiled at the sound, but the sharp fangs slicing through her thigh and dragging her across the pavement had her moaning instead. She lost her grip on the solvent.

She heard Hawk's howl of frustrated fury as he tried to come to her aid, but the dogs were on him as well. She bit the inside of her cheek and dug her nails into the ground as she struggled to gain purchase. She freed one leg and kicked the dog in the muzzle, but the damn thing refused to let go. The scent of her blood filled the air, bringing more of the animals out of hiding. Fighting against the dog, and ignoring the pain, she inched closer to her solvent.

"Hawk!" she cried out.

He twisted, and reading her intent, he kicked the container closer to her. But in the split second he'd diverted his attention from them two dogs attacked, trapping him beneath their beefy paws and gnashing fangs.

River pulled the lid off the can and splashed the solvent over the dog digging its teeth into her leg. The animal yelped and released its grip. River kicked it in the side of the head for good measure and scrambled backward.

Grabbing her lighter from her pocket, she set the flame on high and tossed it at the dog.

Fire lit the sky and in the next instant, she was back on the bathroom floor, Hawk in the tub beside her, his eyes closed, his body lifeless.

In the far-off distance, River heard the echo of someone shouting her name.

CHAPTER NINE

♦

Nick threw himself onto a plush white leather sofa, propped his feet on a teakwood coffee table, and twisted the cap off an ice-cold beer. He only had his imagination to keep him comfortable, and this was as good as it got for him. If he thought too hard about it he'd be forced to admit his afterlife was the fiery armpit of hell.

To say Nick was pissed off was to understate the case. He wished he had something to kick, but all he had was a magical Dark Lord who couldn't use magic to find his own dick.

River had actually helped Chase Hawkins escape. The body-snatching bastard had taken over Nick's life, and now he had River on his side as well.

That River had gone over to the dark side and was helping the body snatcher didn't really make Nick feel warm and fuzzy.

He tried to think of what had gone wrong inside Hawkins' head, but Sandman was also pissed and that never helped. The seeing stones, too, were impossible to read, the images blackened and blurred. River had set off such a blast of magic at the very end that she'd scorched the inside of the stones.

That final blast of magic from River had scared the hell out of Sandman, and Nick wasn't entirely sure why. As far as he could tell she hadn't even known she'd done it. If Sandman hadn't let his uneasiness slip, Nick wouldn't have known where it came from either.

Nick didn't care about the magic. Not when he'd gladly knife his own mother in her sleep if it got him his body back.

The body snatcher was stronger than Sandman had expected, and not even the beatings he'd telegraphed through Nick had been enough to take him down. Chase Hawkins seemed able to take anything the Sandman dished out.

That was why Nick had left Hawkins a little calling card of his own. Sandman had been going about this all wrong.

Nick hadn't taken medical training for nothing. While Sandman had been beating the crap out of Hawkins, Nick had done a little brain exploration. He'd found his pineal gland, then danced around a little to stimulate melatonin production. Melatonin told the body it needed sleep, so increased production would make Hawkins tired. Once he was tired, Nick had left another slide show for him in the occipital lobes. A few good hallucinations should really weaken the bastard, and as long as Nick was careful, there would be no permanent damage done. He wanted his body back. He didn't want to end up scraping gum off the underside of restaurant tables for a living.

Neither did he want to spend eternity in make-believe land, drinking fake beer while sitting on fake furniture, since his imagination wasn't all that great and he wasn't very fond of the present company.

Nick drummed mental fingers. Sandman claimed

he'd tried to use River against Hawkins before and it hadn't worked, but Sandman didn't know River in quite the same way Nick did. Hawk hadn't liked those memories of his that he'd shared.

Nick was willing to bet that eventually, his knowledge of River would prove to be more than even Hawkins could take.

♦ ♦

Gasping for air, Hawk shot upright and gripped the sides of the claw-foot tub. Water sloshed onto the floor and his head snapped around as he searched frantically for River.

She sat in a pool of water beside him, her eyes wide, her lower lip between her teeth, and the fingers of her right hand biting into his shoulder. Magic crackled thousands of tiny whiplike pinpricks across his bare flesh.

He drew in a sharp breath and hastily scrambled to his feet, uncaring that he was naked and cold and dripping water everywhere. All he cared about was River.

Rooting his heels on the slippery porcelain tub, he gripped her under her arms and jerked her upright, dragging her slight frame to his. He ran his fingers through her hair, and his voice came out a bit too harsh as he dipped his head and breathed her name into her mouth over and over again. "River. Crisos, River."

Needing to feel every inch of her body pressed against his, and unable to hold her tight enough with the tub separating them, he stepped from the bath and onto the wet, tiled floor. "River," he repeated, his voice shaky from the riot of emotions careening through him as he gathered her into the circle of his arms. He pressed his mouth to her forehead and raced his hands over her curves, desperate to feel her heartbeat, to convince himself that he was awake, that this *was* real, and most important, that she was safe.

She had crawled into hell for him. He swallowed the lump in his throat. What if he had lost her? Panic rose inside him and he swiftly pushed it back, refusing to dwell on that dark thought because he'd be damned if he'd ever allow her to do such a thing again. He groaned deep in his throat. Her softness, pressed against his hardness, pulled a reaction from his body, and the slight sway of her hips told him she felt the pull every bit as much as he did.

In the blink of an eye the air charged with a different kind of energy, stunning him with how easily fear could morph into desire. They wanted each other, so much so that all it took was a simple touch to ignite the connection between their souls. Sexual energy swirled around the small room, and as need unfurled inside Hawk he buried his face in her neck, feeling the rapid beating of her heart beneath his palm.

As he worked to control his breathing, River delicately touched his face with the tips of her fingers, the soft caress pulling his thoughts back to what had happened and what it might mean.

She had unleashed her magic at the same time she had reached for his soul. She had no idea what she'd done to him by doing so. He closed his eyes. Before, there had been a connection between their souls. Now, she had bound him to her. She had broken one of the Fae's most sacred spiritual laws, and he didn't know what that meant for her.

He blamed himself. Each Fae was different. He'd assumed that because she was only half Fae her magic would be less. Instead it was more than he could possibly have imagined. She needed proper training, and he couldn't give that to her.

"Hawk, are you okay?" she whispered, her voice uncertain and filled with concern.

The distress in her tone had him inching away. He brushed her hair from her face to check for injuries. His gaze swept over her features and he ignored her question for one of his own.

"Are you hurt?" he demanded.

Her attention focused on his left cheek, which stung when he thought about it. Deep inside his dream he'd been cut, slashed by one of the Dark Lord's demons, and that injury had somehow carried over into his waking world.

"No, but you are," she responded. She ran her soft fingers along his cheek, sealing the wound with the healing energy of her touch. Her delicate eyebrows narrowed into a puzzled frown. "How on earth did you manage to fall asleep in the bathtub?"

"I didn't," he said grimly. "The water was warm and I closed my eyes for a few seconds." He hadn't fallen asleep, he had merely relaxed, and that was all it had taken. He wouldn't be making that same mistake again.

He tried not to think about how good it felt to be

touched by her because he wanted to be angry with her for disobeying him and entering his head. "You should never have put yourself in danger."

Her gentle, healing touch turned to a caress. "How could I possibly be in danger when I'm with you?"

Her question hurt him because he had already failed her on a level she didn't understand. He propped his hands on the wall on either side of her head, then dipped his chin to look in her eyes, her breath warm on his wet skin.

Her voice went soft, pulling him into a cocoon of need and desire. "Was I supposed to let you die, Hawk?" Her hand slipped from his face and with exquisite gentleness she ran the tip of her finger along his collarbone. "We're in this together, remember?"

How could he possibly forget? But Crisos, *he* was the Guardian, charged with protecting her. It was not supposed to be the other way around.

As she continued to stroke his damp flesh, a burst of warmth moved through his veins and for a split second he couldn't think, let alone breathe. River's warm, intimate touch derailed his ability to form a coherent sentence, or to think with any sort of logic.

Want, passion, and possession flared in her eyes, and his body tightened in response to the memories of the last time he'd made love to her. Her fingers burned his flesh as they raced over his bare skin. He gave a low, tortured groan full of want.

Crisos, he should put a stop to this, but here she was, brushing his soul and taking a part of him he had no right to give her. She destroyed all his emotional barriers and he no longer had the strength to fight her. Her magic had seen to that.

"Hawk."

When she said his name so softly and pressed her warm mouth to his, he didn't want to think about the trouble they were in. All he wanted to think about was touching her, kissing her, and blocking out the rest of the world as he buried himself inside her warm, welcoming body.

There would be time enough for regret later.

He exhaled a shallow breath and with a new urgency heating his blood, he splayed his hands over her slim hips, his eyes never leaving hers. His muscles bunched as he lifted her off the floor.

"Wrap your legs around me," he ordered softly, as the intense need to lose himself in her had him trembling from head to toe. She did as he said.

He couldn't bear the thought of touching her in the bedroom.

He carried her down the hall to the living room, his mouth taking possession and claiming hers, the soft blade of his tongue slashing urgently against hers and drinking in her unique sweetness. She kissed him back, her response so full of passion and need he tightened to the point of pain. Shifting restlessly in his arms, her eagerness and impatience let him know she wanted this as much as he did. Thin morning light filtered through the drawn blinds. Her arms tightened around his neck when he stilled and glanced around the room, desperately searching for the perfect spot to make love to her.

"The blanket," she murmured. Hawk caught sight of the cotton blanket strewn haphazardly over the sofa, and grabbing it with one hand, tossed it onto the floor. Two brown cushions followed.

Keeping her packaged in his arms, he dropped to his knees and gently lowered her onto the makeshift bed beneath them.

Enthralled in the moment, his hungry gaze brushed over her face, taking in the ruddy hue high on her cheeks, the way her dark, shining hair fell across the pillow and the warm desire swam in her eyes. A fine shiver skipped down his spine as he absorbed her beauty. His heart pounded so hard in his chest in response, breathing grew difficult.

"You cannot begin to imagine how much I want you," he whispered with effort. He tugged the hem of her T-shirt loose from the waistband of her jeans, sliding his hands over the slender curves of her hips.

River touched his cheek. Then she reached for his soul. "No more than I want you," she said. Her soft sigh of desire turned to demand. "Promise me that this time, you won't regret it."

His fingers stilled. If this connection between them was somehow discovered, they would be punished. He would lose his rank and any respect his people might have had for him. River, too, would be ostracized by the Fae.

Hawk's life had been destroyed once before, when he'd lost his family and everything he'd loved. He knew all about loss. River did as well. He wouldn't regret anything they did, or what was between them, because to him, River was all he had left that he valued.

He would, however, find some way to protect her. What she stood to gain from the Fae was far greater than anything he might lose.

He rolled to his back, pulling River with him so the hard floor was beneath him, not her. "The only thing I regret is the circumstances," he said. "I will make this up to you. That, I promise."

Instead of answering she pressed her lips to the base of his throat, then trailed kisses down his chest to his stomach. The brush of cotton and denim against his bare skin made him hunger to undress her, to feel her warmth pressed to his.

He ran his fingers through her hair and gave a slight tug. Her chin tipped up, their eyes locking. When she offered him a sensuous smile full of promises, he read her intent. Shaking, Hawk drew in a tight breath and braced himself.

"River," he said, but the rest of his words were lost on a moan as she wrapped her warm mouth around him. That first sweet touch of her lips made him react without thought. His hips lurched forward and he cupped the back of her head. River upped the intensity, using her tongue to drive him mad, the soft sounds she made turning his flesh to flame. Electricity coursed through his veins. She drew him in deeper, and as she made slow, skilled passes with her tongue, understanding hit. She was sharing her magic with him, offering her strength, and as he lost himself in her touch, his body drew from hers the same way she drew from him.

He hungered for so much more. Not nearly ready to give in to his needs, he forced himself to take in slow, steady breaths. He wanted to hold her, to kiss her, to pleasure her in return.

He wanted her naked beneath him.

"My turn," he said.

River fell back onto the pillows, an arm under her head as she looked up at him and took a deep, shuddering breath. "I need you inside me, Hawk."

The rasp in her voice aroused him even more. As lust prowled through him it was all he could do not to let animal urges rule his actions. A torrent of emotions washed over him, and he forced himself to slow things down, but when she looked at him with such pure desire, she destroyed any self-control he might have possessed.

With impatience written all over her face, she reached down and stroked him, driving him into a frenzy of want. Hawk threw his head back and let loose a low growl. "*Mellita*. I'll give you what you want, but first I need to taste you."

He went to his knees, toying with the button on her jeans. When she wiggled with impatience he reached up and gently, but firmly, brushed her mouth with the pad of his thumb. "First, I'm going to start here." With a light caress he dragged his finger over the soft swell of her breast. "Then I'm going to kiss you here." Her eyes lit when he continued his downward path. He touched her belly button, circling it slowly, then his fingers came to rest on her pubis. "And I'm going to finish right here."

As he spelled out exactly what it was he was going to do to her, she gave him a sexy smile of anticipation. Hawk had every intention of answering her needs, as well as his own, but first he ached to properly introduce himself to her body. They'd made love in her game, but this time it was for real.

He fingered the soft material on her jeans, then unhooked her button and snaked down the zipper. She wet her lips as he peeled the fabric from her shapely legs, removing the barrier between them. The slip of material she wore for panties quickly followed. He clenched down on his jaw and took a long moment to gaze at her nakedness as she lay there, opening her body and soul to him.

His gaze slid over her, taking his time to savor every inch of her beautiful body and the urgency coloring her cheeks. River surged upright, and ecstasy brimmed in her eyes when she pulled off her T-shirt, completely exposing herself to him. Hawk's mouth watered at the sight of her gorgeous breasts and the way her dark nipples hardened beneath his hungry inspection. She arched her back, eyes gleaming, and she brushed her thumb over one hard bud to tease him. Hawk's body throbbed in anticipation as her beautiful body beckoned his touch. He put his hands on her shoulders and pressed her back into the pillows.

She reached for him. When her fingers connected with his flesh a barrage of sensations overcame him, whispering through his blood and urging him to answer the demands of his body. With need pumping through his veins he positioned himself on top of her, using his elbows to keep his weight from crushing her. He dipped his head, taking full possession of her sweet mouth and claiming her as his.

A low moan rose up from the depths of River's throat with the tantalizing sweep of his tongue inside her mouth. Erotic heat pulsed through him as her hands trailed over his skin and explored his body.

His mouth left hers and he felt her shiver as he trailed kisses over her cheek and jaw, going lower and lower until he found the soft sensitive hollow of her neck.

His body rippled with want as he indulged in her softness. Moving with purpose he slid lower until his mouth was positioned over her breast. Her nipples tightened with arousal, coming to hard peaks before his eyes. He drew one pebbled nub between his lips to savor it. River arched her back and grabbed a fistful of blanket beneath her when he sucked her in deeper, running his tongue around the outer edge of her rosy bud. He stroked her left breast, teasing her taut flesh between his fingers while his mouth turned to her other mound, licking and sucking until she was wild with desire beneath him. He flicked his tongue over her flat stomach, his hands moving to her hips and his weight on his knees.

Her fingers raked through his hair and guided him downward to the spot that needed his tongue the most. Hunger for her clawed at him.

"Hawk, please." He glanced up at her, distracted by the urgency in her voice.

"Is this what you want?" He teased her, coming

perilously close but never touching the spot that needed it the most. Her body quivered in response and she gave a frustrated sigh of need that brought a smile to his face.

"Yes," she cried out, impatience lacing her voice and propelling him into action.

As he pressed a kiss to her warmth, her hips came off the floor. When she gasped he stroked deep, pushing in and out with his fingers until she grew slick.

Sensing her mounting desire, he picked up the pace, increasing the intensity. In no time at all he felt that first clench of her muscles. Pressure brewed between his own legs as her body tightened around his touch, gripping him hard.

Hawk held her while she rode out the powerful waves. When her body stopped trembling, she opened her eyes.

"I want you inside me. Now," she demanded.

Hawk's mouth covered hers as he pressed against her opening, and as her heat enveloped him tension coiled through his body and brought on a shudder.

Their tongues tangled as she lifted to meet him, forcing him deeper. Lust exploded inside him and he gripped her shoulders hard, sinking into her warm, wet heat. As their moans of pleasure merged, their bodies melted together.

His heart hammering, he brushed her hair from her face and moved urgently over her body. He angled his body to allow him to driver deeper, faster, but no matter how hard he tried he was still unable to get enough of her. She palmed his muscles and need streaked through him. His body shuddered at the onslaught of pleasure, so intense it was all he could do to hang on.

"More," she cried out, and thrust her pelvis against him.

Her words sent him over the edge. No longer able to fight off his release, he pushed deeper, driving himself all the way up inside her as her thighs hugged his hips. Pressure brewed in his core. His skin grew tight as she arched into him, meeting and welcoming each thrust.

Her legs tightened around his back, drawing him in deeper, his control slipping to the point of no return. She wrapped her arms around his neck. Loving the way she reacted to him, Hawk pounded into her with hot, hard strokes that had his body quaking and begging for release. She let loose a cry and he felt her muscles clenching, tightening, her hot liquid release spilling over him as she came for him a second time. Her sex clenched him so tightly he forgot how to breathe.

"Yes," she cried out. Bracing one trembling arm beside her head, Hawk drove deeper and brushed his thumb over her cheek. Blistering heat exploded inside him and hunger clawed at his insides as her body demanded a response from his. The blissful look spreading across her gorgeous face thrilled him, knowing he was the one who'd put it there. Need gripped him hard and River sensed it. She licked her lips, her heat reaching out to him.

"Come for me," she whispered, raising her hips in invitation and urging him on.

Hawk thrust forward, once, twice, then stilled his movements. He gripped her shoulders and held her tight as he lost himself to the pleasure. He threw his head back and let loose a growl of ecstasy as he released high inside her.

Gasping for breath, he feared for a moment he was going to black out. She wrapped her arms around him and he rolled to his back, taking her with him onto his stomach without withdrawing, her breasts pressed tight against his chest.

Neither one of them wanted to move.

Hawk felt River shiver and he shifted her to her side, reluctantly pulling out of her. "Hey," he murmured and brushed her hair from her face. "You cold?"

"A bit."

As he gripped the edge of the blanket and pulled it over her, he revelled in the feel of her soft flesh next to his. He drew in a deep, contented breath, and instead of feeling spent after an unbelievable round of sex with River, renewed energy sang in his limbs. He angled his head so he could see her face, and from the bright, heavy-lidded look she cast his way—not to mention the smile of satisfaction of his own—he knew their lovemaking had strengthened her, too.

They belonged to each other now. He wondered if they could possibly make it work. For himself, ostracism didn't matter. He had nothing of any value to him other than River. But she was Fae, and she possessed a level of magic, untutored though it might be, that left him in awe.

She would turn her back on the Fae without hesitation if you ask her to.

At that ugly thought, so selfish and utterly against everything he'd been taught to believe, the satisfied smile fell from his face and reality brought him crashing back to earth.

He was hers. But she would always, first and foremost, be Fae.

♦ ♦

Slipping Achala away from the delegation and into the cryonics lab hadn't been as easy or as dignified as Spence would have hoped.

The Fae spiritual leader, however, seemed unconcerned over climbing out a bathroom window and creeping like a criminal through the shadows between the school buildings.

Spence, on the other hand, felt as if he'd been transported in time back to his middle years at the academy, when sneaking out on the dons in the residence was the height of daring.

Young people were so innocent. Daring was exposing a spiritual leader to scandal.

Some young people weren't so innocent, however. When they walked into the lab and Shana realized whom he had with him, her shock and horror were so great he again felt like the student, not the instructor.

"Dr. *Jennings*," she breathed, disapproval heavy in her tone. "You were only supposed to deliver a speech."

Achala was far too polite to laugh out loud, although

Spence couldn't blame him if he did. The humor of the situation wasn't lost on him either.

"I delivered the speech," Spence assured her. "His Grace was interested in a tour of the facilities and I offered to escort him. I'm only taking a few moments of his time." He turned to Achala and introduced them. "Shana is one of my best and most trusted students. She's also responsible for my professional behavior."

Shana's face flushed as red as the third moon. "I meant no disrespect, Dr. Jennings."

Spence patted her arm. "I know that." He peered over her shoulder at the monitor. "Has anything happened?"

She bit her lip. "I tried to page you."

She had his pager in her hand and his stomach plunged. He'd forgotten it. How could he have forgotten it? "What's wrong?"

She scrolled through the streams of information on the monitor screen, Achala watching with interest, until she came to the pattern she was looking for. "There. Do you see it?"

Spence did.

"What does it mean?" Achala asked, coming to stand beside Spence to look at the monitor.

"I have no idea," Spence admitted. Although he'd bet it wasn't good.

"This belongs to your Colonel Hawkins?"

"This is what measures his internal brain activity, yes." Spence frowned. "But there should be no internal activity. Not without external activity first."

Achala examined the bank of cryonic chambers. Most were empty, intended for future research projects. Only Hawk's was currently in use.

"The colonel is in here?" he guessed, figuring it out through the process of elimination. It didn't take a scientist to see which one was occupied.

Spence nodded absently, paying little attention to the spiritual leader, too busy running through the trends in his head to see if there was some sort of pattern to Hawk's brain activity and finding none.

Achala placed his hand on the door of Hawk's cryonics chamber.

"Hey!" Spence said sharply, forgetting whom he was addressing for an instant in his concern over inappropriate behavior in his lab. "Please don't touch anything." Shana's small gasp brought him back to reality. "Your Grace," he added hastily.

The Fae dropped his hand to his side. "I understand your concern," Achala assured Spence. "But if I'm to try to follow the path to the colonel's soul, I need to be as close to him as I can get. Touching him would be best, although I understand that's not possible."

"You can do that?" Shana asked, her interest overcoming her awe of the Fae. "Follow his soul?"

"Up to a point." Achala smiled at her, his expression both gentle and apologetic. "I'm afraid it's not science."

Some of the worry Spence had been accumulating for the past few months began to abate, hope surging to take its place.

"Watch the monitor," he instructed Shana, unable

to contain his excitement. "I'll keep an eye on the chamber's controls. Your Grace," he said, straightening to address the Fae, "some of the greatest discoveries have been made using the most unscientific of methods. You are now in charge."

A faint smile crossed Achala's face. "I don't think we need to go so far as to put me in charge. Your permission to touch the colonel's chamber door will suffice."

Soft gray robes rustling around him, the spiritual leader of the Fae, and of the Guardians, too, ran his hands over the door of the chamber and Spence tried not to flinch. The controls to the chamber were so sensitive he immediately picked up on the readings caused by the Fae's light touch. Shana's sudden alertness behind him indicated she'd picked up some readings as well.

"I'm in the area outside the colonel's consciousness," Achala said. His fingertips stopped on the chamber door and the readings Spence had observed became static. His eyes were closed and his breathing had deepened so that his words came out without inflection, mere exhalations of sound. "The path is very faint, but it is there. Once I go into the area inside his brain, no matter what happens, please don't interfere. Don't touch me, and don't alter the controls to the chamber. I will protect him as best I can."

Unease unfurled within Spence. He didn't doubt for a moment that Achala would protect Hawk. Who, however, was going to protect Achala?

Shana must have had a similar thought. "Spence,"

she said, apprehension lifting her voice. "Stop him. This isn't a good idea."

Spence started forward, but another sharp command from Shana brought him to a halt before he could take more than a few steps. "It's too late," she said. "He's inside."

This was an even greater disaster than before, and threatened to worsen. Spence had assumed that Achala would never put himself in danger. He should have asked the Fae a few questions. Now all they could do was watch and wait, and hope for the best.

He ran over a list of all the things he'd done wrong that day. He had told a Fae spiritual leader about an experiment the Great Lords had wanted kept private. He had hustled the same Fae out a bathroom window and brought him to the cryonics lab without anyone's knowledge or permission. He had allowed the Fae to endanger himself on behalf of a Guardian military leader who wouldn't welcome the risk.

Worst of all—because really, Achala had to accept some of the blame for this by not being 100 percent honest—was the fact that Spence had jeopardized the career of a promising student. If they were discovered, she would be punished as well. Medical ethics dictated that a student was responsible for his or her own conduct. Students did not have to accept tasks they believed to be wrong. While she'd followed Spence's lead because she respected and trusted him, the Great Lords would not hold her blameless.

"Do you know what I forgot?" Spence said to Shana. "I forgot the reason Hawk accepted being cryonically frozen in the first place." He had been more interested in the science behind it than in the politics. He was getting too old for this type of research. "Now I've sent a Fae spiritual leader in search of a Guardian who is investigating the disappearance of Fae souls." The enormity of what he'd done yawned before him, a great, gaping black hole of stupidity. "You need to get out of here before someone figures out this is where Achala and I disappeared to and comes looking for us."

"I wish we'd asked His Grace to hook up to a monitor before we let him near that chamber," Shana said, keeping one eye on her screen and another on the Fae. "I don't dare put wires on him now. He said not to touch him."

"Did you hear me?" Spence asked.

Her fingers flew over the keyboards as she sifted through new information flashing on the screen. "Yes," she said absently. "And I'm ignoring you."

This was what it all came down to. Even his own students ignored him now. If Achala returned unharmed, Spence was handing in his resignation and retiring.

He tried not to pay attention to how slowly time was dragging. Achala stood motionless in front of Hawk's chamber as if he'd been frozen himself, his fingertips glued, unmoving, to the door.

Then the readings showed movement.

"He's back!" Shana cried, unable to hide her relief.

Achala's eyes flew open and he swayed, and Spence ran forward to help in case he should fall. Mindful of the Fae's warning, however, Spence was careful not to touch him without permission.

Achala held out his arm for assistance and Spence took it, guiding the Fae to a chair. He then grabbed a medical scanner and ran it over the Fae's head and chest, relieved to see that the readings were well within the normal range.

"Did you find him?" Spence asked once he decided it was safe for Achala to speak. The Fae was fine. Now he wanted to know about Hawk.

Truth be told, he had a hundred other questions to ask as well. His resignation could wait a little longer until his curiosity had been satisfied.

Achala opened his mouth to reply just as hurrying footsteps echoed in the hallway outside. The lab door swung open.

"What in the name of the Mother Fae is going on in here?" the First Lord demanded, his expression thunderous and his words like shards of ice.

Behind him stood Robert Jess with a false look of concern plastered on his traitorous face.

CHAPTER TEN

◆

The slant of the sun on the wall told her morning was passing them by.

A new wave of energy sang through River. She'd had the knack, from when she was a child, of drawing strength from some deep reservoir within herself and using it to stay up all night for several nights in a row. Her parents thought she was sleeping. Instead, she'd play video games.

She was able to pass some of that energy over to Hawk during lovemaking. To her, it was a win-win situation.

She smiled and lazily stretched her limbs, not the least bit bothered by the thin, industrial-gray carpet or the hardness of the floor pressing against her back. With contentment careening through her bloodstream, and a heavenly grin on her face, she tilted her head to the side to soak up the sight of the man stretched out beside her.

Her smile slowly faded. He looked to be about a million miles away as he stared at the stippled ceiling. He wasn't wearing the expression of a man who'd just had great sex.

Her bliss evaporated. Gathering the blanket tighter against her naked flesh, hyper aware of the turmoil emanating off Hawk and darkening the mood, she pushed up on her elbows to see him better and tried not to sound pissed.

"You promised me no regrets," she said.

"And I don't have any. But we didn't take precautions." His gaze slid over her body and settled on her stomach, and a light dawned. He'd told her that a female Fae could only have one child, and that the child had to be able to host a Fae's magical soul.

She wasn't sure how procreating was handled on his world, but River was an educated woman well acquainted with the use of birth control and disease prevention. "I'm clean and I've had my quarterly contraceptive shot."

"And Nick?" he asked. "Is he clean?"

"Good God, yes," River said, not wanting to think about Nick right at that moment. "He had total paranoia about STDs."

"He was probably worried about his equipment falling off," Hawk remarked sourly. He checked himself out under the blanket. "For the record, mine is better."

Interesting. It seemed it didn't matter what world a man came from, his penis was always his most prized possession.

The mood was definitely broken. River suspected that had been his intention. Hawk said he had no regrets, but despite the fragile bond between their souls, she knew he'd made her a promise he might never be able to keep. He was a Guardian, and to him, the Fae were sacred.

She didn't feel sacred. She felt ordinary. Despite never having known them, River resented the Fae with all her heart. She would, however, thank them for the use of magic if it had helped Hawk regain some of his strength.

"How do you feel?" she asked.

He held his hands out to examine them, turning them over for a closer inspection. "I feel good," he admitted. "Alive."

"Then what's the problem?"

He scrubbed his chin. "I didn't stop to think this through."

"Is that so bad?"

"Where you're concerned, yes."

River sat up, and assuming the lotus position, she took a deep breath and reached for his hand. "You weren't in a good place, Hawk. You needed my energy. That's a human body you're in. It's not going to hurt you to take whatever help I can offer."

One eyebrow shot up. "So that's what this is about then, giving me your energy?"

She stared at him, willing him to spontaneously combust. "Why are you being such an ass?"

He cupped her cheek with his free hand. His touch was warm but far from gentle. "Because I hate having to touch you with another man's body, in another man's home," he said fiercely. "I hate that you being Fae means I'm not meant for you. And I hate, more than anything, that someday, you'll most likely carry another man's child." The pain in his eyes made River's heart ache in response. The pain in his soul made hers want to weep. "I loved my daughter more than you can imagine. Losing her nearly destroyed me. When you have that child with someone else, I will know it because your soul is linked to mine. And it will be the same for me as losing my daughter all over again. Worse, because I'll have lost you, too."

River's palm slapped the carpet. "I am not one of your Fae. I don't follow your Fae laws. And only I will decide who is meant for me." Grass shot from between her fingers, thick and green and lush. She jerked her hand off the floor, startled. "What's happening?"

Hawk's expression was equally startled. Then his

lips tugged upward at the corners. "A temper tantrum, I'd say. Someone must have tracked in grass seed on the soles of his shoes."

River swore under her breath. This was the second time she'd grown plants when she was angry. She'd grown them in the game as well, and that made her wonder if Hawk was the catalyst. No one made her angrier, and to her knowledge, she'd never done anything like this before she met him. "How can I keep it from happening again?" she demanded in frustration.

"You'll have to find the answer to that from the Fae."

Hawk rolled to his feet, fast, sleek, and graceful. The strong, predatory way he carried himself, and the commanding way he moved across the room, made River catch her breath. Nick had never moved like that. They were nothing alike.

Naked, he turned to her and ran his fingers through his mussed hair as he lingered in the door. Silence stretched as they exchanged a long look, and she felt his anxiety as if it were her own. She didn't bother suggesting that it didn't matter what body Hawk wore, or what he needed to tell himself to make it through another day. There was chemistry between them, one that went well beyond the physical.

"Let's eat," he said, "and then we'll go find your Wizard." His hands fell to his sides and he twisted on the balls of his feet. "Let me get dressed."

River unfolded her legs and gathered her discarded clothes, deciding a bath was in order after she ate and before they hit the road again.

As Hawk disappeared down the hallway, River quickly climbed into her clothes, pulled back the curtain, and stole a glance out the living room window to see what was going on in the outside world.

She took in the empty sidewalks, the trim lawns, and the blue sky. Everything looked very ordinary.

It might look ordinary, but she felt like Dorothy from an old movie she used to watch with her mother. Except she couldn't click her heels three times and find herself back home, because home no longer existed for her. In the blink of an eye, all she knew and loved had changed.

She went back into the kitchen and put the plates of food into the microwave. She heard Hawk mopping up the water in the bathroom, then a closet door opening and closing in the bedroom. A drawer slammed. As the timer on the microwave chimed Hawk came around the corner, looking uncomfortable in Nick's jeans and a navy T-shirt that sported a slogan for the province's top-ranked brewery.

"Classy guy," Hawk said, frowning down at the slogan. "Very deep."

"Why not just pick another shirt?" River asked.

Hawk's frown turned to a grin. "If I could, I'd dress him in women's underwear, high heels, and a pink tutu."

That grin had her heart doing back flips. When she first met Hawk, he'd been through so much he'd forgotten how to smile. Overlooking the constant Nick bashing was a small thing if it made him happy.

River placed the plates on the table and sat across

from Hawk. As she bit into her now-soggy toast, she could tell by the way his expression grew serious that he wanted to talk about the situation they were in. They'd never really talked about what had happened at the truck stop. Too many other things had been going on since then.

"Who was the cop?" he asked, getting straight to the point.

River chewed, then swallowed. "He could be the one investigating the murders."

Hawk dug his fork into his eggs. "If so, why did he let us go? Why didn't he bring us in for questioning?" Frustration moved over his face, and his jaw tightened. "How did the Were know Nick?"

River didn't like to think that Nick had gotten himself involved in something dangerous, but the fact that he was dead indicated he had, and that he'd gotten in over his head. Neither did she like to think that maybe he'd gotten her involved in it as well. Those men at the compound had been coming at her with a syringe, and Nick had known them.

She jabbed at her eggs and took a bite, forcing herself to eat only because if she didn't, Hawk would worry about it.

As she sat and chewed she thought about those last moments with Nick before he'd been shot. Her memories remained blurred, hard to grasp onto. What had Nick said at the very end? She thought long and hard, refusing to let go of the thread she was diligently pursuing and then finally it hit her.

Kaye.

She swallowed the last of her eggs, lowered her fork, and placed her hands in her lap. "I can tell you what I do know."

"What?"

"The cop mentioned Kaye. And the Were said Kaye wanted me alive."

Hawk's eyes lit up, clearly hopeful for a lead. "You know who this Kaye is?"

River's heart started to race and the kitchen grew too warm. "He's the one who shot Nick."

Hawk let out a long, slow breath and planted his elbows on the table. "Then he probably knows what you are. Or at the very least, that you're different."

Her head was aching now. "How could he have known? I didn't even know."

"Nick must have known, too," Hawk added. "Or suspected. And he wouldn't have been the only one. How many people in your life know you very well? Or knew you?"

She studied Hawk's face, could almost hear what he was thinking, and she didn't like it. Denial rose, sure and swift. "My father had nothing to do with any of it. He would never tell anyone anything that might hurt me."

"He might if he thought he was helping you." Hawk frowned, deep in thought. "It's the little things you do that set you apart, and someone would have to know you fairly well to notice them. So we have Nick, your father, and let's not forget about your Wizard." He played with his fork, balancing it upright on his plate with his fingertip. "Don't forget we found a bioengineered monster on your father's property either."

"That means nothing." Thinking about its twisted soul bothered her. So did calling it a monster. River pushed her empty dish away, the food sitting like a lump of dough in her stomach. Her headache spread down her neck and into her shoulders. At least she'd been able to help the poor creature find peace.

Hawk relented and let the subject drop. "Only one of those three people can still answer our questions. We need to find out what your Wizard knows." He glanced at the clock. "We should show up at her pub around closing. How late is she open?"

He was right. They couldn't very well head out onto the streets before dark, and they had hours to go until nightfall. "I'm not sure. One in the morning? Two?"

"I don't want us to get there too early," Hawk said. "But we don't want to get there after she closes either."

River stood and gathered their plates. "Even if it's late, she'll open for me."

◆ ◆

Andy opened the door to her apartment at the back of the pub and immediately tried to close it again.

She'd hoped it was River. No one else used the back door. She didn't recognize this man.

He put a shoulder to the door and pushed his way in. Andy had to step back or be run over.

Heart pounding in her chest, she grabbed for the baseball bat she kept by the door. She didn't want to scream for help. Somehow she didn't think this was something the lunchtime crowd needed to find out about. If all else failed, she'd summon her magic.

"Relax," the man said, reaching for something in his coat pocket. "I'm a police officer."

He showed her his badge, which didn't make her heart rate slow but did make her relax her grip on the baseball bat. He looked to be midfifties, with graying red hair and tired eyes. She didn't think he was any immediate threat to her, although she was sensing danger.

She set the bat back against the door frame. "Since when do police officers force their way into people's homes?"

"Since your picture was taken in a place you shouldn't have been." He pulled some photos out of another pocket. "Recognize these?"

Andy hadn't known about the indoor security cameras. In her day the outside of the lab had been so well protected by Kaye's mechanical monsters, it hadn't occurred to her that he'd monitor the inside now as well.

"My God, I look old," she said.

His lips twitched but he didn't come right out and smile. "I have three bodies in the morgue, another two dumped off the side of a mountain, a Were in my squad car, and the creepiest bastard imaginable yanking my chain. That's not even taking into account General Kaye. So forgive me if I'm blunt. What the fuck is going on?"

"Let me guess," Andy said as she handed the

photographs back to him. "The creepy bastard is George Johnson."

He did smile this time, but it held no warmth. "At least with Kaye you can tell up front he's nuts. Johnson hides it a little better."

"George isn't crazy," Andy corrected him. "He has no conscience. That makes him a sociopath."

They looked at each other, sizing each other up.

"Well, well," the police officer said finally. He slid the photographs back into his jacket pocket and wiped his hand on his pants. "I didn't think there was much left in this world that could surprise me. The Were told me the truth. He said you knew more than you let on. He also said you shot at him the night he killed those gamers."

Andy wondered what her options were. They knew she'd been in the lab. They knew what she was, and they knew what it took to contain her. So why had they sent this very normal looking man to bring her in?

They hadn't. They'd sent him to watch her. They were looking for River, and once they had her, then they would come for Andy. That meant this man had approached her without their permission. It also meant she and River still had a chance.

"Too bad I missed him," Andy said. "Would you mind giving me your name, Officer?"

He hesitated for a split second, confirming her suspicions. "Jim Peters. Constable."

"Have a seat, Constable Peters." Andy gestured toward her small round maple kitchen table and its two matching chairs. "If you want to know what's going on, you're going to have to give me some information in return."

Again, he hesitated. Then he pulled out a chair and sat. And he waited.

Andy could respect that. He was very ordinary. No magic, no hint of craziness, and he didn't seem like a sociopath. But he had to be good at something or he wouldn't have an unattended Were in his car. He also wouldn't have been entrusted with watching her. Both Peters and Johnson knew what she could do.

"I'll go first," she said with a smile, resting her elbows on the table and leaning forward, her chin braced on the heels of her hands. "Why did you approach me? You must know that George will kill you for it. Since we're being blunt," she added.

Peters looked at her, weighing his words carefully. She liked that. Stupid people irritated her, probably because she'd once been so very stupid herself.

Peters shrugged. "He's going to kill me anyway. I'm a walking dead man. You're a friend of River Weston's. I want to help her."

She'd gotten a lot better at reading people over the years, but she couldn't read what was in their souls. They had to offer them to her in order for her to do that.

She wouldn't put River at risk. "Why would you want to help River? Do you know her?"

"No, I don't know her." He rubbed his eyes and suddenly, he looked even more tired than when he'd muscled his way in. "She's innocent. She didn't kill those gamers and we both know it. So then I have to ask myself why the Monster Man would be after her, and it can only be for one of two reasons. Either River is a monster herself, or she has something the Monster Man wants. If she has something he wants, then I want to make sure he doesn't get it."

"She's not a monster," Andy said. She met his eyes. "And I don't believe you."

It wasn't so much that she didn't believe him as that he wasn't telling her everything. He had another reason for wanting to help River. Something private. She wanted to know what it was, but he was very good at keeping his thoughts to himself.

Seconds ticked by. Andy could hear the doors opening and closing in the pub, and the muffled sounds of the customers.

"Ever hear of Westmount?" he said finally.

"Just what was in the papers." That wasn't quite the truth, but it wasn't a lie either. She'd had no direct involvement with the project. Hers had come after.

Peters stared off into space as if looking back in time. "Monster Man was a doctor back in the middle of the epidemic, right when things started to get ugly and wars were breaking out. A few rich people found out about his plans for a super army, and offered to fund it, then test it in their gated community. I led the first wave of Weres. When they started to get out of control I left. Right after that, the Weres turned on Westmount's residents." He sighed and faced her again. "I saw it coming and didn't do anything to stop it. I've lived with a lot of guilt over it."

That, Andy believed. She knew all about living

with guilt. It still didn't explain why he would suddenly choose to help River.

"What else?" she asked.

He looked at her in surprise. "That's not enough?"

"You must have a reason for wanting to help River in particular. I want to know what it is."

Somewhere in the pub, someone dropped a glass and it shattered. They both started at the noise.

"I'd like to buy back a small piece of my soul before I die," Peters said in a rush. His face flushed red with embarrassment, and then he looked angry over being embarrassed.

He was telling her the truth. Andy could have wept with relief and rekindled hope.

"Trust me when I say I understand exactly how you feel, because those Weres were just the beginning of it all." She rested one hand on the table, tipping her head to the side as she continued to regard him. "In my other life I built machines out of Weres. I worked directly for Amos, and that was how I met George. They didn't have very much success with their mechanical monsters after I left." She said the last with a great deal of grim satisfaction. She'd hidden right under their noses, too.

But now they knew who she was and where to find her. They were also after River. That took away some of the satisfaction.

"Now it's my turn not to believe you," Peters replied. "If you could do that, they would never have let you walk away. And why are they just now discovering where you are? It's not like you're very well hidden."

Since they were placing their cards on the table Andy decided to go for broke. She had nothing left to lose, and if it got her help for River, then everything to gain. "They didn't find me," she said, "because I used magic to hide from them."

She'd thought he would laugh.

He didn't. He didn't blindly accept it either. "I've seen some strange shit in my lifetime, but this one, you're going to have to prove to me."

"Wait right here."

Andy got up, went into the narrow hall that led to her bedroom, and was back a few moments later with a box in her hands. She'd hidden it in the back of her closet, under the floorboards beneath a rolled-back piece of carpet. It wasn't exactly a unique hiding place, but it did the job. If someone had wanted to tear her place apart looking for it he would have found it eventually.

She handed the box to him. He looked at her, looked at the box, then opened the lid. His eyes narrowed. "Holy shit."

The box contained over a hundred pictures she'd taken of some of the more pitiful experiments. She let him sift through them for a few minutes.

"The trouble with Weres," she said, "is that they have a low to moderate human intelligence level, but an animal's instincts. When I added bionics, I tried to give them a soul. I thought it might control those instincts. I didn't know I was doing any harm." That wasn't really true. She'd known. She simply hadn't fully understood the extent of the harm. She had River to thank for the fact she now did.

He placed the pictures carefully back into the box and closed the lid. He set the box on the table. "You expect me to believe you can give something a soul? What—you just pick them out of the air?"

"Something like that," she said. "Although attaching them to a mechanical Were was a bit more complicated. And they weren't random souls either. They had to be Fae."

"Naturally." He folded his arms and tipped back in his chair, preparing to hear her explain. "This has got to be good."

Where to begin?

Andy reached for one of the plants on the windowsill near the table. She didn't much care for plants, but they'd been gifts from River. The only reason they were still alive was because River stopped by on occasion and talked to them.

Andy placed her hand on the plant and concentrated. The plant, a leafy philodendron, began to spread, unfurling new shoots until they covered the table's smooth surface. A bead of sweat formed on her brow. The talent came naturally to River. For Andy it was hard work, and took more of her magic than she liked.

The legs of Peters' chair crashed to the floor. "Sweet mother of God," he breathed.

As much as she tried to keep the plants alive because River had given them to her, Andy needed to preserve her magic more. Reluctantly she withdrew it. As she did, the plant withered and slowly died. Where before a lush green plant had flourished, now curled, dried-out brown leaves littered the table.

"That," Andy said, "is how I managed to tie Fae souls to the monsters. I called them to me with magic. Fae souls have magic of their own. They would attach to the monsters, and their magic would then sustain life—just as I did with the plant."

Fae souls wanted life so badly they would attach themselves to anything mortal. That was the reason they didn't remain near their own world, but instead waited until summoned to return by Fae spiritual leaders for the birth of the baby they were meant to possess.

What Andy didn't tell him was that the Fae souls couldn't withdraw from the monsters if the monsters were killed. They needed to be released. Some of those Fae souls continued to linger near the remains of their bioengineered hosts.

Peters wore the shell-shocked look of someone who'd walked away from a near-fatal accident. To give him credit, he pulled himself together quickly. "So the gamer can do this as well?"

"She can do it far better than me," Andy replied. "And a great deal more. Amos Kaye will catch her, keep her drugged, and use her magic to summon souls to create monsters that make the Were look like lap dogs." Andy brushed the dead leaves off the table and into a small kitchen compost bin. "That's the future of the world we're looking at if they find her." She met Peters' eyes. "And they will find her. She has no idea how to protect herself."

"She's not exactly helpless," Peters said. He told her about what had happened in the parking lot of the truck stop. "And she's got Nick Sutton with her, so she's not completely alone."

"Nick?" Andy echoed, surprised and uneasy. That couldn't be right. She'd assumed the Guardian would be with her. What was River doing with Nick? "Are you sure?"

"No one was more surprised than me. But he's seriously looking out for her." Peters folded his arms. "Now tell me why I should believe that you're looking out for her, too, because from what I'm hearing, she'd be valuable to anyone who knows what she is and how to use her."

Andy ran her fingertips along the edge of the table, contemplating her cuticles. "I killed River's parents. Indirectly," she added hastily, seeing the change in his expression. "But the fault was mine. River's mother was Fae. Her soul attached itself to River's father's remains, and she won't leave him until she knows River is safe."

She closed her eyes, reliving that last night in the lab as she spoke.

She'd been alone, monitoring an experiment, when the Guardian had broken in. He'd thought the place was empty, and it might as well have been because she'd been so absorbed in her work he'd gotten a good look around before he stumbled on her. Andy didn't say it, she didn't even like thinking it, but the only reason she'd let him live was because of the pregnant Fae standing unprotected in the doorway behind him. Something inside Andy had rebelled at the thought of causing her harm. So she'd let them run—because she knew the monsters guarding the grounds would take care of them for her.

All she told Peters, however, was that she'd let them escape. He could believe what he wanted from that. She didn't want him to know about the darkness she'd once had in her. River had taken that darkness away, at least most of it, and now Andy needed to make certain that what had happened in the past sorted itself out in the present.

"I need to get River to that lab so she can free her parents," Andy explained.

But before she got River to the lab, there was one other thing she needed for River to do. It was selfish, but if River didn't do it, the world would become a much different place.

Peters carefully considered everything she said. Again, Andy liked him better for it.

"You can't take her to the lab," he finally said.

Maybe Andy didn't like him so much after all. "Try and stop me."

He held up a hand. "Hear me out. If Kaye and Johnson know who you are, or at least suspect that they do, then you can guarantee I'm not the only one watching you. You tipped them off already that you're interested in the lab and they'll be watching that as well. If you take River there, they're going to assume you're trying to use her for whatever reason it is they want to use her. You need to stay away from both her and that lab until we can figure out a way to get her there without them knowing. And once you do what you need to do," Peters added with grim determina-

tion, "you're both going to help make certain these
twisted experiments are over and done with. I'm
fucking sick to death of crazies and monsters. If you
were going to bioengineer something why couldn't it
be something with a warmer disposition? Why not
the Easter Bunny?"

"Rabbits have a very low level of intelligence,"
Andy explained. "Size is another factor against them.
Dolphins would have been interesting, but they're
aquatic."

It took him a few seconds to realize she was joking.

He scraped his chair back and rose. "I've been
gone long enough," he said, looking at his watch. "I'd
better feed the Were. In the meantime," he added, "if
River shows up, get rid of her as fast as you can. Stay
away from her for now. Give me some time to think
about it."

Andy wondered if she should genuflect. She murmured something noncommittal instead. Peters glared
at her, but she was no longer sensing danger from him
so he was wasting his time trying to intimidate her.
She would stay away from River, but there was still
something River needed to do and Andy thought she
knew how to get her to do it.

He reached for the door.

"If you could have any wish, what would you wish
for?" she asked him suddenly.

He froze, his hand still extended toward the doorknob. Then he dropped his hand to his side and turned
to look at her. "Self-respect."

Very interesting. She'd bet Constable Peters had a

past almost as misspent as hers. She captured his gaze and held it.

"You said you wanted to buy back a piece of your soul," she reminded him. "Self-respect is a part of that. So tell me: what are you willing to pay for it?"

♦ ♦

They played cards all afternoon and then, to River's amused disgust, she discovered Hawk was fascinated by the mixed martial arts on the fight channel.

She could appreciate the entertainment value. She had nothing against building fight sequences into her games, although she tried to keep it good guys against bad guys. She could also look after herself when necessary, and had proved it on several occasions.

But people bloodying each other for money wasn't high on her list of things to do or see.

"I'm taking a bath," she announced.

Happy to be alone with her own thoughts for a few moments, River grabbed a change of clothes from her bag and headed for the bathroom. She set the plug and grabbed a washcloth from the shelf behind her.

As she soaked in the warm water, she could hear Hawk rummaging around in Nick's room. Drawers creaked as he opened and closed them, then the hangers scraped across the metal rod as he dug through the closet. Since being in the bedroom unsettled him, she wondered what he could possibly be looking for.

She dried off and used Nick's blow dryer on her hair. Then she braced against the counter, glanced at her face in the mirror, and took in the strange woman staring back. She wasn't certain she cared for what she saw. Her skin was pale and her eyes seemed harder to her. She'd always been focused on her work, but now she didn't look like the type of person who laughed all that much either.

She looked like someone she'd see in the subway, only older.

She heard Hawk's footsteps trail down the hall, then fade as he entered the kitchen. Hinges groaned as he rummaged through the cupboards, and curiosity got the better of her.

She quickly dressed, then walked into the kitchen in time to see Hawk stuff a small black address book into his back pocket. He'd lit a stub of candle to keep the light in the apartment to a minimum and its tiny yellow flame danced, projecting distorted shadows across the walls.

He waved a hand to acknowledge her presence but he didn't say anything, and it was obvious he had something on his mind. She leaned her hip against the counter and watched him with interest.

He picked up the phone's receiver, turning it over in his hands as he figured out how it worked.

"What are you doing?" she asked.

He turned to face her. "I'm looking for clues but I won't know what they are until I find them." He pressed the redial button on the phone, then pressed the receiver to his ear. He crooked his finger and gestured for her to come close, holding the phone so they both could hear.

River pressed against him, her shoulder on his chest, and when a man's voice sounded on the other end, she caught her breath. Hawk glanced at her in silent warning and put a finger to his lips.

"Nick, is that you?" The man's voice on the other end of the line held equal measures of surprise and caution. River didn't know quite what to make of it.

Hawk held his hand over the mouthpiece and waited. "Nick. That is you, isn't it? Stay put. I'm coming for you." A pause and then, "Don't make me hunt you down."

When the line went dead, Hawk hung up the phone and snuffed out the candle's flame, plunging them into darkness.

"Who was that?" River whispered, although deep down, the chill in her bones told her she already knew.

He lowered his voice to match hers. "That's what we're going to find out." He gave a slight tug on her hand. "Come on."

When they reached the door, River grabbed one of Nick's old coats off the rack and tossed Hawk another one. After pulling it on, she threw her rucksack over her shoulder and kept tight on Hawk's heels. Through a small windowpane high on the door he peered into the night, and after he signaled that all was clear, she followed him out.

The cool night air whipped around them as they quietly descended the stairs, keeping close together as they ducked into the alley. River rocked back and forth on the balls of her feet, waiting and wondering if anyone would show up.

Less than ten minutes later, a black sedan crept up the hill and stopped in front of Nick's place. Two men exited the car, one from the driver's seat, one from the passenger side.

"Do you recognize them?" Hawk asked quietly.

Glass shattered, its glittering shards spilling onto the landing. The two men didn't appear concerned over getting caught for breaking and entering, which raised the fine hairs on the nape of River's neck.

She strained to get a better look as the men disappeared inside, then shook her head no.

Hawk put his mouth close to her ear, and she shivered when he said, "There's someone in the backseat of the car."

"Do you suppose it's Kaye?" She took a step closer, trying to get a better view so she could be certain, as anger, thick and hot, boiled inside her. He'd shot Nick. He'd most likely killed her other friends, too. He was one of the bad guys. She'd have no trouble at all kicking his ass and she'd do it for free.

Hawk grabbed her by the coat and drew her into the shadows. "If it is, I don't want you anywhere near him."

They waited in silence to see if the man in the car would show himself, but to River's disappointment he never moved.

A few minutes later the two men exited Nick's place, glancing up and down the street.

"Time for us to go," Hawk whispered. "They know someone placed that call and they're going to keep looking until they find out who it was."

They cut through the alley, crossed the backyards of a few townhouses, and kept off the streets as they made their way to Andy's in silence. Instead of fighting her anger River embraced it, using it to keep her senses on high alert. The distant sound of a garbage truck moving through the dark streets lent an illusion of normality to the night.

Then words Nick had spoken right before he was shot arose, unannounced, from the ragged remains of her memory. *There is a lot more going on than you know.*

But he had known, and he'd kept it from her. Hurt mingled with her anger. Nick was a lot of things, but she'd never taken him for someone who'd purposely endanger her.

"You okay?" Hawk asked, and when she glanced up at him it was only then that she realized she'd groaned low in her throat.

"Fine." Looking forward, she pointed into the shadows. "Andy's is just around the corner."

They negotiated the turn and River's pace picked up as they closed in on the pub. Her heart pounded harder as they approached. Andy would have answers.

River's gaze swept the streets, and finding them empty, free of danger, she practically ran the rest of the way to the pub.

Once there, she tried the door and frowned when she found it locked. Hawk moved to the window and pressed his face to the glass. "It's empty."

River glanced over her shoulder and shivered.

Hawk followed her gaze, instantly alert. "What's wrong?"

"Someone must be walking on my grave."

Hawk stiffened. "What's that supposed to mean?"

River shook her head, embarrassed at sounding so paranoid. "It's an old saying we have."

Hawk wasn't prepared to let it go at that. "But why did you say it?"

"Because I had an unexplained shiver."

"Yes," he persisted, "but don't you think it's an odd thing to say, especially since your life is on the line and we're looking for a grave?"

"I just said it, okay?" River pressed her fingertips to her temples and rubbed. "I didn't mean anything by it."

"What exactly does it mean?"

She glanced down at her feet, then at Hawk's, wishing she'd kept her mouth shut and her thoughts to herself. "It means that someone is walking on the spot where your grave is going to be."

Hawk stiffened, looking ready to pounce on anything that dared to move. "I don't like this."

"For the love of God, let it go." River turned from him in exasperation. "Andy has a back door to her apartment."

They made their way down a narrow side drive used for deliveries to the pub's kitchen, which was next to the apartment.

River tapped on the apartment door. When she got no response she tapped harder until eventually a light came on from inside. Relieved, she smiled up at Hawk who had worry written all over his face. His glance darted from her, to the door, to the street behind them and back to her.

He was freaking her out.

River heard Andy unlock the latch.

Andy inched the door open and stared at them with the same polite level of interest she'd show any of the random patrons in her pub. "Yes? What can I do for you?"

Taken aback, River straightened. This wasn't the reception she'd expected. "Can we come in?"

"It's late," Andy replied, tightening the belt at the waist of her lavender bathrobe, "and this bartender doesn't play psychiatrist after hours." She grabbed something off the window sill beside the door and pressed it into River's hand. River automatically closed her fingers around it, too startled to notice what it was. "Now, if you'll excuse me."

River's elbow shot out automatically to keep the other woman from closing the door. "Andy, wait a second."

Andy looked past their shoulders into the night and shivered from head to toe. The last thing she said before forcibly shutting the door in their faces was, "Imagine that. Someone must be walking on my grave."

CHAPTER **ELEVEN**

♦

As the heavy wooden door slammed in their faces and the warm peppery scent of magic curled around them, and River stared stupidly at the slip of plant Andy had thrust in her hand, Hawk's anger flared.

His first instinct was to knock down that door. River had been counting on Andy to point the way to the graveyard, or better yet, personally lead them to it.

Andy had some sort of connection to that lab and to what had happened to River's parents, and Hawk intended to find out what it was.

River's palm closed around his forearm, stopping him before he could ram into the door. He dipped his head and narrowed his eyes at her, and watched the confusion on her face shift into understanding.

"What?" he demanded.

River tugged on his arm, excitement in her tone. "Don't you see?"

"What I see is that your Wizard just turned her back on you." His intention wasn't to hurt River. It was to open her eyes to the truth about Andy.

Somewhere in the night a gunshot rang out, and they both stiffened. Hawk spun around to brace his back against the building, pulling River against him and shielding her with his body.

River recovered first.

She shook her head, lowered her voice, and slipped free of his embrace as if nothing had happened.

"You're wrong. She hasn't turned her back on me. Just think about the words she chose. *Someone must be walking on my grave.*"

Those words made Hawk distrust her Wizard more than ever and it was past time for River to accept it.

"You think that cryptic shit means something?" Hawk pushed away from the building and stood beside River. As they strode down the deserted street he scanned the darkness, half expecting an ambush.

River shot him a glance. "Those were *my* words. I said them moments before she did."

"And you just finished telling me they didn't mean anything. So now you're telling me they do?" Hawk was smart enough to know they weren't a coincidence, but he was damn tired of the Wizard's cryptic shit. His head ached fiercely and the energy he'd acquired from their lovemaking had begun to wear off, leaving him mentally unstable and physically shaky. What he hadn't told River, what he didn't want to worry her about, was that lack of sleep damaged the thalamus, a deep part of the brain, and that if he didn't sleep, eventually Nick's body would die. By helping keep Hawk awake with her magic, River was speeding the process.

He tightened his fingers into fists. They needed to hurry. Trying to figure out the Wizard was slowing them down.

"It's the graveyard, Hawk," River explained, speaking in whispered words as she hustled him past a boarded-up coffee shop, the sound of their booted footsteps on the cracked sidewalk cutting through the silence. "She sent us underground in the game, and I think she wants us to go underground now." River's breath turned to puffs of fog as she spoke.

As they rounded a corner Hawk noticed the broken strips of yellow and black crime-scene tape fluttering from a telephone pole and a nearby stair railing. He'd seen this in her game, but he didn't think it was something she'd coded. It looked too new.

River shivered at the sight of it. *Someone must be walking on my grave.* He recognized it now, even if she didn't. It had been all over the news. This was the spot where one of her friends was killed.

Hawk grabbed her by the arm and ushered her to the other side of the street. Not happy with the distance, he felt for his gun, somewhat reassured to find it in his coat pocket. "If the subway here in your world is anything like the one you created in your game, I think your Wizard is trying to get you killed."

"She's not trying to get me killed. But she's trying to tell me something. Do you remember the barrier in the game?" River turned to him, thoughtfulness in her eyes. "The graveyard was on the other side of it."

"Things in this world aren't exactly the same as they were in your game," he reminded her. "A real subway system isn't going to end in the middle of nowhere."

"No. But it has to end somewhere."

He wrapped his arm around her shoulder and kissed the top of her head, unable to argue with her logic even if he didn't like where it was taking them. She wouldn't be satisfied until she'd explored it for herself.

They walked in silence until they came to the

stairwell leading to the underground subway. It was pretty much the way Hawk remembered it from the game.

Not a good sign.

He peered into the black pit. In her virtual world they'd had flashlights, plenty of ammo, and a safe room to regroup in. Here in the real world, they were under-equipped and in over their heads. He didn't see any safe rooms either.

He sighed. "Are there demons down there?"

River's lips curved into a smile. "As a matter of fact—" Another gunshot rang out, closer this time, and she grabbed Hawk's hand. "We need to get off the streets."

Hawk wasn't about to argue. "Then let's move."

"Wait." River held him back, glancing around. "We need something red."

"What? Why?" he asked.

Nearby, a truck parked on the side of the street had an old red T-shirt tied to its trailer hitch. River unfastened it and started to lift the fabric to her mouth as if intending to tear at it with her teeth.

Hawk whisked it from her grasp and dangled it out of her reach. "Are you trying to make yourself sick?" he chided her. "If you want it torn into strips, let me do it. I don't mind if Nick gets a gum infection and all his teeth fall out."

River hooked her thumbs on her pockets and lifted an eyebrow. "How very selfless of you." She shot an anxious glance around that worried him. "We need to hurry. The streets aren't safe this late at night."

"The gunfire was a tip-off," Hawk agreed, his voice muffled by the fabric. She took the strips of cloth he handed her and tied one around her forearm, another around his. "What are these for?"

"To let the demons know we're friends." River started for the stairs, then paused to look at him, her eyes suddenly serious. "Remember they're just kids, okay?"

Hawk didn't like the sound of this. "River, wait just a sec—"

Too fast for him to stop her, she scooted around him and darted down the stairs. He had no choice but to follow.

The steep, crumbling stairs were in desperate need of repair. So was the water-stained subway platform below. Hawk tugged his jacket tighter against the chill dampness and watched River do the same. Rusted lights embedded in the walls flickered on and off, making their shadows elongate and dance.

The ancient transportation technology momentarily made Hawk forget why they were there. He leapt from the platform onto the tracks and crouched down for a closer look.

As near as he could tell without putting it to the test, steel-covered aluminum conducted electricity through a third-rail electrification system. A faint hum indicated the third rail was still live.

He shook his head, impressed by her eye for detail. "It's the same as in your game. We fried demons on these."

"We don't fry demons on these though," she said.

He looked up to where she stood on the platform above him. "But you said there were demons." Something scurried past his foot and Hawk, startled, sprang back. River, too, let out a small noise of revulsion. "This place is crawling with rats," he complained, not caring for them either. "Whatever possessed you to come down here in the first place?"

"Demons," she replied.

She was teasing him. She hadn't had much to joke about in the last few days, and it wouldn't hurt him to play along, but he had a feeling he was being stupid and missing an important clue in what she was saying.

He wasn't good at cryptic. A slight headache also made it difficult to concentrate.

Think. What kind of demons could entice her into a rat-infested tunnel and not make her want to fry them for it?

Crisos. He added a few other choice words as he puzzled it out. She'd said to remember they were just kids. He'd rather battle real demons.

He vaulted two-handed onto the platform beside her, landing catlike on his feet. "We're getting the hell out of here."

As he started to stand the world spun around him, and for a second, an image of River flashed in front of his eyes.

She lay sprawled across the tangled sheets of Nick's bed with her arms over her head, and her long, shining hair fanning the pillows. She wore a thin scrap of scarlet lace stretched across her hips and nothing else. A soft, sensual smile curved her lips.

That smile sent Hawk crashing to his knees, and the heels of his hands to his face as he tried to wipe away a memory that belonged to another man.

"Hawk?" He heard her calling to him and he shook his head against a ringing in his ears.

Except his ears weren't ringing. As the real world slid back into focus, the deep shadows down either side of the tracks began to shift and take form. The ringing turned into a chant.

Fight. Fight. Fight.

Hawk staggered to his feet, angry with himself for a moment of weakness that had allowed danger to come too close. He took two steps toward River before being stopped by a line of drawn knives.

Remember they're just kids, okay?

They were teenagers, to be exact. And they surrounded both him and River, swarming and separating them.

She hadn't seemed concerned before they'd entered the subway, and she didn't appear to be overly afraid now, but regardless of what she thought, these were not "just kids." These were gang members, sporting their colors, and he could not believe she hadn't thought it important to warn him of this.

She looked so small, crowded as she was by several of the larger boys, and then she disappeared from his view. Hawk's vision instantly shot through with red.

Again, he made a protective move toward her. A knife slashed across his arm, tearing his jacket and drawing a thin line of blood, letting him know that the kid who'd wielded it meant business.

"Make another move and you're a dead man," the kid said to him, eyes flat and cold and hard.

Hawk weighed the odds. Technically, Nick would be the dead man. Hawk would be free to find his way home. He wondered how many of the little bastards he could take out before that happened. Quite a few, most likely, but then where would River be?

He didn't like this, and really didn't like looking afraid of a young punk, but decided to trust River's judgment because he had only one other option.

The chanting hadn't stopped. Hawk craned his neck to see what was going on, and hoped like hell it wasn't what he thought. He stepped back, ready to sacrifice Nick at the first opportunity.

One of the older boys, no more than seventeen, tall and lean but with heavily muscled arms, pushed his way to the front of the crowd to stand before River. The black leather bomber jacket he wore had a gleaming red demon's head emblazoned on its back. The crotch of his worn denim jeans sagged almost to his knees. Steel chains dangled from his belt loops to his pockets. Hawk wondered what those chains held at the ends.

The chanting stopped.

"Who's it going to be?" the boy asked River, his voice overly loud in the sudden silence. "You or him?" He jerked his head in Hawk's direction.

A no-brainer. Hawk relaxed. Even in Nick's out-of-shape body he could kick that little snot's ass, and he intended to do so.

But River appeared to be thinking it over. "It had

better be me," she decided. "At least then you might stand a chance."

The kids surrounding Hawk were far from stupid. Before he could react to her words, his arms had been grabbed from behind and he found himself sprawled on his stomach, the air squeezed from his chest, and his cheek pressed hard to the cold concrete. Hot rage lent him strength and a few satisfying grunts of pain erupted from the boys as they tried to restrain him.

In the end, however, he had little choice but to watch and listen. Swearing released only a bit of his frustration.

Nothing overcame his fear for River's safety.

A roar of appreciation went up from the crowd. With his head pinned to the platform by a booted foot it was difficult for him to follow the action. The sound of a fist striking flesh made Hawk bite into his tongue, and he tasted warm blood.

The boys holding him down were placing bets on the outcome.

"My money's on River," one of them said. "She's won the last three fights."

Another disagreed. "The last was a year ago. Dan has grown two inches since then. And he's been practicing."

"But River fights dirty."

That observation was greeted by murmurs of appreciation. Hawk closed his eyes, gritting his teeth in frustration. What kind of a life had River been leading?

Most assuredly not the life of a Fae. He couldn't

help but lay blame at her Guardian father's door for that. Because of his weakness, River's mother was dead and River was exposed to violence and danger.

Hawk was proving no better than her father. Acknowledgment of that ate at him like acid.

From his prone position it was difficult for him to tell what was happening, but every once in a while he caught a glimpse of the action past people's legs. The boy called Dan spent a fair bit of time on his ass.

Another roar went up from the crowd.

"Told you," the one who'd bet on River said with satisfaction, and in an instant, Hawk was released and back on his feet, spitting fire. This time when he moved toward River, no one attempted to stop him but gave him a wide berth.

"Hey," River greeted him, wary concern in her eyes. "You okay?"

No, he was not. He was angry, frustrated, and emasculated. He wanted to punch the little shit beside her in the face, but from the looks of it, River had taken care of that for him. Blood trickled from one nostril and the boy dabbed at it with the back of his hand.

River, however, was unmarked except for the faded smudge of bruise on her cheek—the one that he had given her.

Hawk purposely stepped in front of her and faced the throng of teenage boys. A few girls littered the crowd as well he now saw, although not many. His chest tightened. Judging by their size, some of the gang members were no older than River's young brothers.

In fact, several were younger. The littlest children pressed closer to the biggest. They also wore strips of red on their sleeves, although no demon emblems.

His anger slowly ebbed away, replaced by an unsettling and uncomfortable realization. These were kids, just as River had said. Society's castaways. And they lived in the subway tunnels, fending for themselves and defending their territory.

Of course she would spend time down here among them. She was a Fae who had young brothers of her own, and therefore would be unable to resist trying to help them. Hawk had been a father. He swallowed a knot at the unbidden memory of his dead daughter. He wasn't immune to their circumstances either.

But their circumstances made them more dangerous, not less so. They would never completely trust River. Tonight was an example of that.

She began to introduce him to the boy she had fought. "Dan, this is—"

"I know who he is," Dan interrupted her. He took a bold step forward to stand eye to eye with Hawk. Hawk stood his ground as the boy studied him carefully, and with open hostility.

Hawk wasn't surprised by the boy's reaction. He had yet to meet anyone but River who had liked Nick.

River cleared her throat, more uncomfortable with this standoff than she'd been with the fight. Hawk caught the anxiety in her eyes and to ease her worries as well as to illustrate his protectiveness of her, he shifted casually until his arm brushed her shoulder. She stole a quick glance at him and the look on her face told him that while she appreciated both his touch and the gesture, they were unnecessary.

"How do you know Nick?" she asked the boy she'd called Dan.

"I've seen you walking with him before. I've also seen him walking with others." He stepped back and narrowed his eyes, his calculating gaze roaming over Hawk and the way he stood too close to River. "He seems different. He even carries himself different." A long pause and then, "But at least now he cares about you."

The last words were grudgingly spoken and suddenly, with male awareness, Hawk understood the underlying reason for his hostility. The boy had a crush on River and viewed Nick as competition.

Hawk suspected he had her presence to thank as the reason the gang hadn't cut his throat on sight, red arm badge or not.

River hadn't known of the boy's feelings for her until now. Her eyes met his, and she was the first to look away.

Feeling sorry for Dan, Hawk broke the awkwardness of the moment with a question.

"Is there a barrier at the end of this tunnel?" he asked. There had been one in the game.

Dan continued to ignore him and addressed River. "You don't want to go there. It's not safe."

"Why not?" River asked.

Dan lowered his voice and Hawk wondered if he didn't want the younger ones to overhear him. If so, it was a wasted effort on his part. All it did was bring them closer. "Strange things go on over there. It's no place for a girl."

"What kind of strange things?" she pressed.

He leaned in, his face inches from hers, his voice dropping to a whisper. "There are monsters."

River frowned. "Shame on you," she said, pushing him away. "Stop trying to scare the little ones with stupid stories."

Dan straightened, then shrugged. "It keeps them from wandering off by themselves." His voice returned to normal. "But seriously, we've heard noises. It's creepy. Nobody goes down there."

"We have to," River said. "We're looking for something."

"Something, or someone?" Dark lashes flashed over eyes too old for a face that couldn't yet grow a beard. He looked at Hawk, then back to River. "If you're looking for the animal that killed your friends, you won't find him down here." He pointed upward. "You'll find him up there."

The boy knew a hell of a lot more about those deaths than he was saying, and from the expression on his face when he looked over at Hawk, he thought Nick had some connection to them as well.

Not enough of a connection for him to say anything about it to River, however. That meant Nick hadn't been directly involved. Dan would have killed Hawk without hesitation if he had.

She turned back to Dan. "What do you know about my friends' deaths?"

But Dan wasn't saying anything more. Instead, he

lifted a small boy into his arms, then handed him over to River. "Matt's had a cold," he said. "Can you make him feel better?"

The child was thin and pale, and quite obviously ill. His nose had been running, and it had crusted onto his cheeks. River perched him on her hip even though he was far too big for it, then took the strip of red T-shirt off her arm and used it to wipe his face.

"He needs a doctor," Hawk said. Alarm bells were ringing in his head.

"Don't be so dramatic," River replied. "All he needs is a bottle of cold medicine and a good sleep." She pulled a few dollars from her pocket and passed them to Dan. "Wait another day to see if he gets better on his own before you spend the money on medicine," River said. She handed the boy back to Dan.

Dan wouldn't need to spend the money on medicine and all three of them knew it.

Hawk didn't like it.

Dan reached behind him and took a crowbar out of another boy's hand. He slapped it into Hawk's palm. "Take this." Then he called to a girl with dirty blond hair. Moving with quiet dignity, she passed River a flashlight.

"Thank you," River said to her, tucking the flashlight into her rucksack.

Hawk leapt to the tracks and lifted his hands to help River down.

"Let's get the hell out of here," he said. They rounded a bend, and then they were alone in the dim, sporadic light.

The side of his face stung. Hawk touched it, noting the wet stickiness on his fingers when he drew them away.

River made a small sound of sympathy. "Here. Let me take a look at that."

Hawk wiped his fingers on his jeans. "Save your energy, Dr. Weston. It's not that bad." He shifted the crowbar to his other hand and gave a grunt of disgust. "I should have heard them."

"Don't be so hard on yourself. They're used to these tunnels."

Hawk didn't want to admit to her the real reason he hadn't heard them because he didn't want her to worry.

He wanted to gouge out Nick's eyes every time he thought about it.

"You didn't hear them because you were paying too much attention to me." She tossed him a warning glance. "You keep that up and you'll get yourself killed."

"No. I'll get Nick killed."

He couldn't hide the satisfaction the thought gave him, and River stalked off in disgust.

Hawk went after her. He would happily give his own life to save hers, except right now he couldn't afford to get either himself or Nick killed. He needed to protect her, and keep her safe until he got her home. She couldn't act like some sort of faith healer and not draw attention to herself. It was a wonder she'd never been discovered before now.

As they moved past the next platform Hawk spotted

bright orange embers drifting upward, accompanied by plumes of black residue. The acrid scent of the smoke reached his nostrils and billowed through the tunnel. The heavy smoke carried the rancid scent of garbage and decomposing waste. He'd smelled some awful things in his line of work, but this had to be at least in the top ten. It was obvious the people living in the neighborhood above the entrance used the subway as a garbage dump. It spilled off the platform and onto the tracks. Someone must have decided to burn it, most likely to get rid of the rodents.

Hawk blinked the sting from his eyes and breathed into the crook of his elbow as they hurried past.

"Do you really think we're going to find the entrance to the graveyard down here?" he asked once he could breathe again. His words echoed eerily, bouncing off the walls of the tunnel.

"Andy sent us here for a reason. We should be looking for directions, some sort of clue." River frowned in thought. "Possibly even a door or exit of some kind."

"Why do you do it?" Hawk asked curiously. "Come here? Those kids don't need you. They can look after themselves. And to be honest, they would turn on you in a second if you gave them a reason to." They were children who'd had to learn their own moral code. Those codes tended to be harsh and without compassion. Hawk stepped closer, crowding her, wanting her to understand the danger she put herself in. "You don't know what you're dealing with."

"They're children."

Hawk exhaled slowly. "They're damaged. Dysfunctional. You can't save all of them. Maybe not even some."

She planted her hands on her hips and challenged him. "Isn't saving lives what the Fae do?"

Not exactly. Not in the way she meant. They created and preserved life. They didn't necessarily save lives. He bit back his frustration at her lack of understanding of the distinction.

"Not like this, they don't," he countered, but she had that look on her face, the one that said no amount of arguing on his part would change her mind. At times he admired her stubbornness. At other times, like this, it irritated the hell out of him. She refused to see reason.

"It might not be the way you're used to seeing things done, but it's the way I'm used to doing them. This is my world. This is my *home*."

Hawk absently slapped the crowbar against his palm as he glanced around them at the dank and dirty tunnel. The rank smell of burning garbage lingered in the air. He couldn't help but compare everything he'd seen so far to the wonder and brightness of his world, and to that of the Fae.

When he spoke, his contempt was impossible to contain. "*This* is what you call home?"

Immediately, he wished he could unsay his words. She withdrew as if he'd struck her.

"You've seen very little of my world," she said. "You don't have any right to judge it or its people."

That gave him pause. Her friends had been

murdered, she was wanted for questioning, and they were hiding in a subway that was home to a blood-thirsty street gang. Someone had been bioengineering animals with humans. Her birth parents were buried in an unmarked grave, their souls unable to find rest.

"I'm sorry," he said to her.

Dropping the crowbar, he blocked her path so she couldn't avoid him. He reached for her hands and drew her into his arms. She resisted at first, then buried her face in his jacket before melting against him. She didn't speak for a few moments and he ran one hand up and down her back, waiting.

"If my father and mother hadn't taken me in, I would have either died or ended up like Dan and the others," she finally said. "They weren't as lucky as me."

She had no idea how lucky she'd been. If she'd been found by the ones who'd killed her parents, she would most likely have ended up another lab experiment. Hawk didn't doubt that.

She was also correct. He had no right to judge her world. Judgment belonged to the Great Lords.

He cradled her face in his hands as he kissed her. "With you to love it, any world would shine brighter than the sun."

The flattery made her laugh, although he suspected he wasn't entirely forgiven.

Her hand still in his, they walked for several more hours until the light completely disappeared and they had to rely on the flashlight.

Just as Hawk began to worry about the life of the

batteries, they rounded a bend and reached the barricade.

River ran her fingers over the crumbling cement. "Do we go over?"

He regarded it thoughtfully. "Do we have any choice?"

Even though they were no longer in her game, a game that prohibited backtracking even if they ran into trouble, instinct warned him that once they went over that barricade, there'd be no coming back from whatever River's Wizard was trying to show them.

CHAPTER **TWELVE**

♦

Jess, the sniveling apostate, had at least had the decency to ensure Shana didn't lose her residency.

A large packing crate stood on one long, stainless-steel counter in one of the teaching labs and Spence tossed his personal effects into it with careless disregard for their safety. It didn't matter if something broke. It wasn't as if he'd need any of it again. He was retiring. Forced retirement, true, but he was sick of the politics regardless. He was a research scientist. He liked facts and probabilities. He rarely looked very far beyond the conclusions of his experiments once he'd proved they were viable and sustainable.

He heard something crack inside the packing crate

when he tossed one of his numerous plaques for scientific excellence onto the top of the pile. He wondered why he bothered to pack them. What was the point of recognition when in the end, it all boiled down to this? Shuffled aside for the latest rising star?

Yes, he was bitter. He'd gone from respected scientist to vilified lunatic in a matter of seconds. Worse, someone he had little personal respect for had moved in to take his place.

Achala had done his best to smooth over the situation, but the First Lord, while properly respectful, had bought none of it. Spence hadn't been allowed to sit in on the spiritual leader's debriefing with the Great Lords either. He'd merely been told to clear out his belongings, which was what he was doing. He saw no reason to prolong his departure.

What caused him guilt, however, was Chase Hawkins. Hawk, practically speaking, was a dead man. Not for a moment did Spence believe Jess could bring him out of stasis alive. Shana, too, would no longer be allowed to monitor what happened in the cryonics lab. She would have to earn back a level of trust from Jess, and that would be difficult. Jess was a suspicious little bastard who kept close watch over those he considered professional threats.

Spence should have followed his example.

He looked up as Shana entered the teaching lab. Her eyes were red and swollen from crying, which surprised him a little because she was normally more pragmatic than this.

"It won't take you long to get back into the lab,"

Spence said kindly. "For what it's worth, I'm deeply sorry to have put you in such a position."

Shana swiped at her nose with the back of her hand. "I don't care about that. I accepted this residency to work with *you*. You have a reputation for generosity with your knowledge and a talent for teaching that Dr. Jess could never hope to emulate. What's more, it's doubtful he will make any effort to try." She gave him a watery smile when she noted the expression on his face. "What?" she demanded. "You don't think students talk and compare notes about the instructors?"

Spence dropped onto one of the lab stools and allowed himself a moment of self-pity. This was what he was going to miss—the young people, eager to learn, who looked up to him and wanted to hear what he had to say.

Red light from the planet's three moons streamed through the windows. When the moons were full, as they were now, night was as bright as day, distinguished only by the color in which they washed the world.

"You and your fellow students are welcome to come by my home anytime to ask me questions," Spence said. "I'll be current for at least a year. After that, you should perhaps be a little skeptical of anything I tell you. Not only will I be out of touch with what's happening in my field, I'd imagine retirement won't be good for my short-term memory."

"If you're trying to cheer me up," Shana said, "you aren't going about it the right way."

Spence sighed. "You should be spending time with young people your own age, discussing fresh ideas and your future, not worrying about a stupid old man who didn't have the sense to keep quiet or quit. I should have done both a long time ago."

"If you had done either of those things," a voice in the doorway said quietly, "then I would never have discovered the trouble both of our races are in."

Spence and Shana both turned as Achala walked into the room. He did not wear his ceremonial robes. This evening he wore the black, fitted clothing and tall leather boots of the Fae when they traveled.

"You shouldn't be here," Spence said to him.

Amusement brightened the spiritual leader's eyes. "Why? Do you think the Great Lords will fire me, too?"

He had a point. "They won't be pleased," Spence cautioned him.

Achala waved a hand as if the opinion of the Great Lords mattered little to him, which it probably didn't. "I never got a chance to tell you what I discovered about your colonel before I was politely ushered off your world." Achala's eyes danced. "Purely for my own well-being, I assure you. They were most apologetic for your unprofessional behavior and deeply concerned for my health."

"The Great Lords saw no reason to debrief me on your discovery," Spence replied, dismissing the comment about his professionalism. The debriefing remained a sore point with him because Jess had been allowed to sit in whereas he had not.

Achala nodded in greeting to Shana, who could never seem to find her tongue with the Fae. Yet she had no trouble giving her opinion to him, Spence thought.

Achala pulled up a lab stool beside Spence and gestured for Shana to join them. She did so, looking both overwhelmed and uncomfortable, and Spence wanted to laugh. She was a brilliant scientist. Someday, he had no doubt others would stand in awe of her and she would come to appreciate what little value status really held.

"They had no reason to debrief you," Achala was saying, "because I told them nothing other than that Colonel Hawkins is safe, at least for the moment."

The relief Spence felt at the Fae's words was overwhelming. He was glad he'd been seated or his knees might well have given out on him.

Then, the addendum *for the moment* registered.

"That's excellent news, isn't it, Dr. Jennings?" Shana prompted him, more formal now because of the Fae's presence. Anxiousness replaced her enthusiasm when Spence didn't immediately respond.

Spence turned to Achala. "Is it?"

"Yes and no." Achala hooked one foot over a rung on the stool. The red glow from the windows highlighted the worry on his face that Spence hadn't picked up on when he'd first entered the room. "Your colonel is a complex man. To put it mildly."

Complexity could be good or bad. "Can you be more specific?" Spence asked warily.

"He's exceptionally good at protecting his thoughts," Achala admitted with a frown. "Some things I couldn't touch. However, he never knew I was there so I was able to pick up on more than I might normally have done without his permission."

"Isn't it unethical for the Fae to read someone's thoughts uninvited?" Shana asked.

Spence let out a mental sigh. She had to pick now to get over being impressed by status? "I'm not sure accusing a Fae spiritual leader of unethical behavior is the right way to get back into the cryonics lab."

Her look of horror made both men laugh. "It's completely unethical," Achala assured her cheerfully. "But under the circumstances I choose to grant myself absolution." He grew serious again and returned his attention to Spence. "That's because the circumstances are more than a little unusual. The colonel has found himself another body."

"He *what*?" Spence almost fell off his stool. Shana looked equally stunned.

Achala quickly explained what little he'd learned. From what he could gather, Hawk had taken on another man's body. The other man wanted it back and Hawk's consciousness was now under attack. Somehow, magic was involved.

"No *shit*," breathed Spence. Shana bit her lip but the look she sent him adequately expressed her disapproval.

"There's more." Concern etched Achala's face. "Colonel Hawkins' soul has become entangled with another's, and that soul, I can't read at all. It has magic, however, and I would guess that's how he's managed to claim this new body."

"Is that bad?" Shana asked, glancing uncertainly between them.

"Yes!" both men said in chorus.

"The use of magic is governed very closely," Achala explained to her. "If there's someone out there using it without the knowledge of the Fae, it can mean only one thing."

Spence's ulcer caught fire, a burning ember deep in the pit of his stomach.

"Dark Lord?" he guessed, hoping he was wrong.

"What else could it be?" Achala folded his hands in his lap. "I have to ask you something, Dr. Jennings, and I need an honest answer."

There was more bad news? Spence rubbed his eyes. "Go ahead. I'll be as honest as I can."

"That's not good enough." Without warning, Achala reached out with his soul's magic and caught hold of Spence's thoughts. Spence reared back in surprise.

"What are you doing to him?" Shana shouted at the Fae, all remnants of her former reverence disappearing. She rushed to Spence and wrapped her arms around him to keep him from toppling off the stool. "Stop it!"

"I can't. This is far too important," Spence could hear Achala saying past the spinning in his head. The Fae's soul searched his mind, sifting through his memories. The touch was gentle, as nonintrusive as possible and steeped in apology, but still, Spence felt violated. "I need you to answer this question."

Spence nodded, unable to do otherwise. The Fae

would have the answer from him as soon as the question was asked regardless of whether or not he cooperated.

The Fae leaned closer, and Shana tried to shield Spence from him with her body. She could not, however, stop the question from being asked.

"Did you know that Colonel Hawkins was a demolition man?" Achala demanded, and Spence heard Shana shouting for help as the world turned to gray around him.

♦ ♦

Standing on the platform of the subway, River eyed the cement barricade, her hands on her hips.

She hadn't yet forgiven Hawk for his undisguised contempt of her world. Another, smaller part of her worried he might be correct in his assessment.

"Your friends said they heard strange noises coming from the other side," Hawk said. "Judging by what we found in the game, we should be careful about going forward."

"I don't hear any strange noises now." River tried to see the barricade through his eyes, because from her perspective, going forward didn't appear to be an option. "Since this isn't a game, how are we supposed to get past this? Tear it down with our bare hands?"

"That's one possibility," he said thoughtfully. He tapped on the wall with the crowbar, then tapped progressively higher. "These are cinder blocks, but the bottom ones have been reinforced with rebar and filled with more concrete. See how the wall curves?" He pointed upward to show River how it narrowed where it met the ceiling. "Structurally, the probable place for a weakness is at the top. Those blocks are most likely still hollow. There seems to be a bit of water damage up there as well. I bet the roof leaks." He looked around. "Now I just need to find a way to get up there and check it out."

River shrugged her rucksack off her shoulder and played the beam of the flashlight from the subway tracks below them to the ceiling above. He was right. The concrete crumbled near the top. Knowing how much he hated heights she studied the structure, looking for some other way around it. She couldn't find one.

Neither could she see a way to climb. The barricade was smooth. In the game there had been a service ladder on the subway wall. Here, there was nothing. Because it was a tunnel with no natural lighting, she couldn't even find any plants to grow.

Except for the one Andy had given her.

She thrust her hand into her pocket, pulled out the slip of philodendron, and waved it triumphantly at Hawk. "Still think Andy's not on our side?"

Hawk's jaw worked. "Just plant it."

River had to lower herself off the platform and onto the ground beside the abandoned tracks in order to find enough dirt for the philodendron to take root. Hawk held onto the back of her jacket to steady her as she went over the side.

The dirt was dry and hard. "I need something to make a hole with," she said to Hawk. "Without a hole, the roots are going to spread out instead of down. I want it to have enough of a root system to hold our weight."

He handed her the crowbar.

River took it from him and managed to scrape enough soil away to satisfy her that the roots would take hold, then gently placed the slip into the dirt. She scooped soil around the plant, closed her eyes, and let magic flow from her palms. The plant shot upward, knocking her to her ass as it unfurled broad, giant leaves. Within seconds it reached the ceiling, then curled back on itself to spread away from the wall and down the tunnel into the darkness.

"That's enough!" Hawk said sharply, and River realized her magic was continuing to flow. She called it back and the philodendron's growth slowed, then stopped.

She tested the stem and the leaves. They were strong, although more slippery than she'd anticipated. The stem was as thick around as one of her legs, and although pliant, didn't seem inclined to bend more than a little.

She started to climb, using the base of the leaves like the rungs of a ladder. Hawk let her go first since she was lighter, and in a few minutes she reached the top of the wall.

River ran the light over the cinder blocks. As Hawk had thought, water dripped in a slow, steady rhythm from the roof and the concrete had rotted in places. She chipped at it carefully with the butt end of the flashlight. Chunks of crumbling concrete clattered down the wall.

Hawk pulled himself up beside her, his jaw clenching tight at the sound of concrete pebbles hitting the
platform below them. He never looked down.

"Shine the light over there," he said, and River
zeroed the light in on the spot he indicated. Hawk
studied it for a moment. "Move back and cover your
face."

He reached over their heads, took a firm hold on the
base of the leaf above them, then swung out with his
legs. Three good, hard kicks later, he'd knocked out a
hole large enough for them both to squeeze through.

"Hand me the flashlight," Hawk said.

River handed it to him and he poked his head and
shoulders into the opening. She heard him swear.

"Why can't anything ever be simple?" he growled,
pulling his head back and wiping cement dust off his
arms. "I'm going to have to make the hole bigger so
you can send your plant through. We'll need it to get
to the platform on the other side. It's too far to jump."

"The plant should be able to make the hole bigger
by itself," River replied. She reached up, grabbed hold
of a leaf, and concentrated. "Give me some room." A
shoot sprouted from the base of the leaf, lengthened,
thickened, and punched through the hole in the wall
like a giant green fist. Cement blocks and chunks of
mortar tumbled past them and Hawk threw his arms
around River to shield her with his upper body.

The dust slowly settled. Hawk, one protective arm
still tight around her, shone the light on a hole now big
enough for the plant, Hawk, River, and a few football
players to pass through.

"I don't know my own strength," River said into the sudden silence.

"No shit." Hawk gave her a quick squeeze, then released her.

They crawled through the hole and climbed down the plant to the platform below. Ahead of them, a few subway trains sat, rusting and dormant, where the tracks converged and the tunnel ended. A set of stairs to their left curved up toward daylight.

"We're at the central station," River said, surprised.

Hawk tensed. "What's wrong with that?"

"I don't know," she admitted. "The station's been boarded up forever, since at least the start of the war."

They'd walked a lot farther than she'd thought. The station was in the next town over, part of the greater city area that had been abandoned long before she'd been born because it was primarily a business center and the government had concentrated its restoration money in the more residential areas. She hadn't considered that this was where the tunnel would end. It was nowhere near forest and the mountains as the graveyard in her game had been.

"We've been walking for miles and have nothing to show for it. No graveyard. No lab." River was cold, damp, tired, and hungry, and she didn't bother trying to hide her frustration and disappointment. Yet despite everything, she refused to give up on her faith in Andy. "Maybe we need to find another tunnel."

Hawk took her hand and hooked her fingers through a belt loop on the back of his jeans. "Right now we have nowhere to go but up, and I want us to stay together."

Hawk hefted the crowbar.

River followed him up the stairs, the fingers of one hand curled through his belt loop, her other hand holding the stair railing.

Again, just as it had before they reached Andy's, cold brushed her soul, although this time it was magnified a thousand times. She drew up short, tugging Hawk to a standstill. He half turned on the stair above her so that her grip on his jeans pulled her against his hip. He narrowed his eyes and peered into the darkness behind them.

"What is it?" he demanded, and River knew he had felt the cold touch, too, through her.

Sweat collected on her brow as she tried to find the right words. "It feels dead," she said reluctantly. She frowned. "I don't know how else to explain. Where there used to be something, now there's nothing. It's like a black hole, only instead of an absence of light there's an absence of souls. They're gone. And they've taken the space they used to occupy with them."

"So you can feel the empty holes where souls used to be, and Andy has us looking for a graveyard," Hawk said. "Nice."

"The holes would have been left wherever the owners died," River pointed out. "By the time a person is buried, their soul is long gone."

Hawk frowned and looked toward the top of the stairs. "Maybe you should wait here."

"Not a chance." Her grip on his belt loop tightened.

They climbed the rest of the stairs, and at the top, Hawk and River exited through the gate into the main part of the station.

It was raining outside. Water streamed off the station's domed glass ceiling, bathing the large central concourse in a gray, midday light. Two other gates barred the entrances to other subway lines. A long ticket counter ran along one end of the building, and the main entrance was boarded over, just as she'd expected it to be.

What she hadn't expected, even though she should have, was the row upon row of rotted and desiccated bodies stacked several layers deep the entire length and width of the station.

There had to be thousands.

Hawk didn't seem as surprised. She let go of his belt loop as he walked toward the remains closest to them, pulling the collar of his T-shirt up over his mouth and nose. "Stay where you are," he said to her when she started to follow. "I want to see what they died from."

On shaky knees, River turned her back to the room and leaned against the metal subway gate. He was back in a few minutes, his arm sliding around her to offer up warmth and reassurance.

"What happened to them?" she asked, turning into his warmth and soaking up his strength.

"My best guess is that this place started out as a quarantine area for people sick with the virus. After that, it became a dumping ground for the dead."

River had heard the stories, but before, they were

just that. Stories. Now she felt the need to justify what had happened here.

"When the virus first appeared," she told him, "my parents said people were dying so fast the hospitals couldn't take care of them all. Tens of thousands died in the first few days alone, millions worldwide. My mother was a nurse at the time and she said when they knew a patient wasn't going to recover they had to remove him from the hospital to make room for someone who might. It was a global pandemic and everyone was scared. They didn't have the time or the resources to treat the dying with dignity."

"And afterward, the city boarded up the station to keep survivors from coming into contact with the virus through the remains of the dead," Hawk said with sympathy and understanding. "They did what needed to be done, River. That's not always pretty."

People who'd caught the virus after the first wave had lingered a lot longer, she knew. They'd suffered more, too. Her mother had been one of those. The virus had remained dormant in her system for several years before making itself known.

Hawk looked around. "Let's get the hell out of here."

River moved in close to him, suddenly beyond tired, as if all the energy had been sucked from her body. They hadn't slept in what felt like forever, and the air in the station was suffocating her.

"You didn't touch anything, did you?" she suddenly thought to ask, alarmed. She and her father hadn't caught the disease from her mother. Some people were naturally immune, and simple household vinegar had proven to be all that was needed to kill off the virus, but she didn't like the thought of Hawk being exposed to it. Once it infected a person, it was incurable.

And nobody knew for certain whether or not it would return in yet another mutated form.

"I used the crowbar." Hawk caught her hand and led her toward the next subway gate, carefully keeping between her and the dead so she didn't have to look. "I'm pretty confident all the other tunnels and exits are sealed, not just this one, but let's make sure. We've got to find a way out of here." The skylight soared several stories above them. Hawk looked up, then crooked an eyebrow at her. "That's a last resort. There's got to be an easier exit."

He was trying to distract her by making her laugh. She didn't feel like laughing, but she did allow herself to be distracted.

"Before we go anywhere," she said, "we have to figure out why Andy sent us here. If she wanted us to find this, what was her reason for it?"

Hawk sighed. He paused at the gate to the next set of stairs and looked at her. "Has it occurred to you that her reason for sending us here might be self-serving on her part?"

"Has it occurred to *you*," River shot back, "that maybe I can't believe that about her?"

"Yes," he replied. He drew River into his arms and kissed her forehead. "I hope you always have the same faith in me that you do in other people. Now let me have the flashlight."

The other tunnels were sealed the same as the first

and all of the exits were blocked, just as Hawk had said. They returned to the main concourse.

"I could try prying a door open with the crowbar," he suggested, rubbing the back of his neck.

"You could," River pointed out, "but where would we go after that?" She was still wanted by the police. "We need to find out the location of that lab, and I'm sure the answer's here somewhere."

Hunger had her reaching for her rucksack and the crackers and cheese she'd taken from Nick's apartment. She yawned, exhausted, and started to draw energy from deep in her abdomen, the way she'd done hundreds of times before when she was running on empty and pushing the limitations of her body.

Hawk touched her shoulder. "Don't do that."

She paused in midstretch. "Why not?"

"I don't want you to use up your energy."

"If I don't use it," River said, yawning again, "I'm going to fall on my face. You worry about me too much," she added. "I'm used to going without sleep." She'd told him before that her whole life she'd been able to keep herself awake for several days at a time. She'd done it as a kid so she could stay up and play video games after her parents thought she was in bed, and she'd used the trick to get top grades in university and become a software engineer.

Only before, she hadn't known the trick was really magic. She frowned. When she did crash, she could sleep for several days. If that happened, who would look out for Hawk? He had no magic but hers to keep him going.

Hawk looked around. "There has to be a lounge area somewhere. Some sort of break room. We need to sit down and decide what we're going to do next. We can't stay here forever." He looked at the cheese and crackers she held in her hands. "And I don't know about you, but that's not going to keep me going for long."

Fine lines creased the corners of Hawk's eyes and suddenly, River began to worry about his physical health as much as his mental state. She'd never truly worried about that before. Both he and Nick had been the ones to worry over her.

They found a break room behind the ticket counter. It contained an orange, cracked vinyl sofa, a Formica table, and a few rusted, gray metal chairs, all covered in a thick layer of dust.

The minute River stepped into the room she felt a sense of peace. She drew it around her like a warm blanket.

Hawk shook the dust off an old transit jacket left on a coat rack by the door and wiped down the sofa as best he could. He sneezed, his eyes watering. "For the love of the Mother," he complained, rubbing at his nose with the back of his hand. "Nick's allergic to dust?"

"Hmm?" River responded vaguely, too lost in a wash of dreamy contentment to pay much attention to what he was saying.

Hawk looked at her sharply. "What's wrong with you?"

"Nothing. Nothing at all."

He reached for her, drawing her close, and placed

his thumbs on her cheekbones, his hands warm and solid on her skin. He drew down her lower lids and peered into her eyes. The concern she saw in his made her smile. She slid her arms around his neck and melted against him, every bone in her body turning to jelly. She pressed her forehead to his chest, the room reeling around them.

"If I don't use my magic I'm going to fall asleep on my feet," she confessed. As it was, he was all that kept her upright.

"I want you to save your reserves." He swept one thumb over her cheek and smiled at her, making her throat tighten. "You should get your energy the old-fashioned way."

She looked up at him as if he'd grown a second head. "You expect me to sleep in this place?"

"That's exactly what I expect." He tugged the ruck-sack off her shoulder, lowered himself onto the sofa, and drew her down beside him. "Come, lay your head on my lap. I'll keep a lookout."

She couldn't deny that the idea appealed to her, especially as exhaustion was about to pull her under whether she liked it or not. Still, she resisted. "What about you?"

She felt a shiver move through him as if he'd tasted something sour, and noted the brief hesitation before he responded.

"I can't sleep. Not yet. I'm sorry, River. That's just how it is."

"You know you have to."

"You first."

He patted his leg and River gave it serious consideration. She had to be practical. Hawk was okay for now, but when he finally crashed, and he would because she could only do so much for him, she'd need all her strength to keep him safe from his dreams. She trusted him completely, and despite the precarious situation they'd found themselves in, Hawk would never let anything happen to her.

She wanted to be able to offer the same guarantee to him in return when the time came.

As she relaxed into him, he guided her head to his lap and placed his arm over her body like a heating pad.

"Just a couple of hours," she cautioned as her body absorbed his warmth.

"Okay."

"Promise?"

He gave a soft laugh at her undisguised skepticism. "I promise. Now stop talking and sleep." He brushed his hands through her hair and she snuggled in tighter.

Comforted by his touch, his mere presence, and the overwhelming sense of peace pervading the room, her lids slowly fell shut and she felt herself start to drift off. Instead of fighting it she allowed herself to give in to her body's needs, even if only for a few hours.

CHAPTER **THIRTEEN**

♦

Peters lost them at the subway.

He was tired, hungry, and more than a little afraid. Three of his least favorite things. And he had nothing to show for any of it.

He'd followed the gamer and her boyfriend after they left Andy's and he'd waited for them outside the subway entrance, but they never resurfaced. Waiting all that time with a whining Were in the car hadn't improved his usually sunny disposition.

He turned the car around and headed back in the direction of the police station. He had to decide if he believed the pub owner's story. He did believe parts of it. It was more her motivation for helping River Weston he called into question, because anyone who'd had a connection with George Johnson and the Monster Man couldn't possibly be good. Peters knew he wasn't, and his connection to them was loose at best. If her story was true, Andy's had been a lot tighter.

So why had he said yes to her when she'd asked for a piece of his soul? Because he wanted to find out if he even really had one? Because he'd wanted so much to believe she could mend it if he did? Because for the first time in years someone had offered him a slight glimmer of hope that just maybe his life had all been worthwhile?

Jesus, he was pathetic. Andy was probably another freaking crazy. Which made him one, too.

"Shut the hell up," he snapped at Bane, who was complaining for the hundredth time about how hungry he was. The Were ate his own weight in fast food.

Peters rubbed his eyes with the heel of one hand and tried to focus on his driving. He needed to get some sleep but he couldn't do that if he had a wide awake, hungry, restless Were to contend with. He'd feed the little bastard, then take him back to the station to work off some of that excess energy. There'd be more than enough testosterone in the department's gym to keep Bane in line.

He picked up some burgers and fries and they ate them in the police station parking lot. When they finished, he led Bane through the cubicles and corridors to the back of the station and the gym.

A few of the officers openly stared when they entered the sweat-steamy locker room.

Too late, Peters realized he'd forgotten about the cuts and bruises on the Were's face.

"What the hell did you do to him?" one of the men asked, looking up from removing his running shoes and doing a double take.

"It wasn't me, it was his mother," Peters replied. He opened his locker and tossed Bane a pair of clean shorts and a department T-shirt. "Put these on," he ordered the Were. "You can run in your bare feet. It won't kill you." He turned back to the cop who had spoken. "This is my sister's dumbass kid. She didn't like the birthday present he gave her and I had to take him into protective custody."

"Hardasses must run in the family," he heard someone mutter behind him.

"Looks like it might have skipped a generation," another one added, his voice equally low. "That guy took a beating."

Ignoring them all, Bane stripped off his clothes. As he did so, there was a collective intaking of breath. Peters tried hard to keep his own shock under control. The Monster Man had really worked the Were over.

This was the same Were who had torn three innocent people apart for the pleasure of tasting their blood. He needed to remember that. As Peters thought of those crime-scene photos, a lot of his pity dissolved but not all of it. Bane hadn't gone after those gamers on his own initiative. He'd been ordered to do so by someone who'd known full well what might possibly happen and hadn't really given a shit.

Bane's grin became feral as he jerked Peters' T-shirt over his head.

"She didn't like her Mother's Day gift either," he said, shaking his dark hair from his face, and the room went silent.

Peters wanted to kick his ass. "Shut up and get on the treadmill." He patted his sidearm. "And if you don't run the full twelve miles I'm going to shoot you."

The cop who'd been removing his running shoes tossed them into his locker with extra enthusiasm. "I bet your family Christmas is a blast."

Peters shrugged. "He loves holidays. There's a masochist in every family."

He sat on one of the weight benches so he could keep an eye on the Were while he ran, his long, muscular legs easily eating up the miles. Peters wasn't gay, in all honesty didn't even really like talking to men, so the thought of banging one held even less appeal, but he knew a seriously good-looking guy when he saw one. Compared to the creatures at Westmount, on a scale of one to ten Bane was a solid twenty-five. Whatever DNA sequence the Monster Man had used for him had paid off.

It made his blood run cold to think of how many more Weres like Bane might be roaming loose, undetectable to the average, unsuspecting person. If Kaye managed to up their intelligence quotient by even a few more points, the world was going to be in serious trouble. Thank God they couldn't reproduce.

Holy shit. They couldn't reproduce, could they?

Peters tried to remember his twelfth-grade biology, but that had been about a hundred years ago and the teacher had spent most of his time in class bumming weed and Visine off the students.

Then again, it was highly unlikely the Monster Man would let any of his Weres roam completely free. Peters relaxed. He needed to focus on one problem at a time.

The first problem was Andy. Did Peters really believe her?

Yes.

Peters had a good sense for reading people. That was why he didn't like very many of them. Most were full of bullshit. When Andy had asked him what he was willing to pay to earn back his soul, then asked for a piece of it in exchange for its return, he'd agreed willingly but not seriously. His soul was part conscience, part self-respect—a compilation of all the pieces that made him a decent human being. He could sell it but no one could give that back.

And yet deep down inside he wanted to believe that she could give it back to him, and there was no harm in that. He would get River and Sutton to the lab for her, but at the same time, he would make certain they stayed safe. If his soul could indeed be restored, then he was going to go out with it clean.

Because he could believe in Andy all he wanted, even owe her a favor, but that didn't change the fact that dealing with Johnson and Kaye meant he was a dead man.

But he'd be a dead man with a clean soul.

The Were finished his run in just over an hour.

Peters made him take a shower, then led him to lockup. He needed to sleep and he wasn't going to be able to do so with an unrestrained Were in the same room.

Once he'd gotten some sleep, he and the Were were going hunting. River and Sutton hadn't come out of that subway, and there were very few places underground for them to go. All of those places ended up at one central location.

Peters would find them. He slammed the door to the Were's jail cell and the automatic lock slid shut.

But when he found them, he needed to convince them to trust him. He thought about that for a moment.

River trusted Andy. She'd demonstrated that by showing up at her door.

If Andy gave him a message for River, River was more likely to trust him as well.

◆ ◆

Hawk played with a lock of River's hair, her head nestled in his lap, enjoying watching her sleep as much as the feel of the slow, steady warmth of her breath against the inside of his thigh. If not for an overwhelming worry, he could sit with her like this for hours.

Things in his head had gone seriously wrong. Along with the unexpected images of River, he was now having moments of memory loss—little flickers of blank screen, as if his mind's eye had suddenly blinked. He didn't think those had anything to do with Nick, yet he couldn't be certain of that.

But if they had nothing to do with Nick, then they had something to do with his real body. Spence had warned him cryonics had limitations, and that his research only guaranteed Hawk's safety up to a certain number of months. Hawk had no way of knowing how many months had gone by, but he suspected a lot. More than Spence had allocated.

Which meant Hawk might be pulled at any time, and if that happened he didn't know what his chances of survival might be. Only that Spence had given up hope of him ever returning on his own and decided there was nothing to lose by pulling the plug on the experiment.

While Hawk had been trapped in the Dark Lord's

prison, he'd done nothing but hope for the day Spence would try to revive him. He'd been afraid of it, too, for fear his body wouldn't make it and the Dark Lord would then have a claim on his soul as well as his consciousness.

Now he was afraid again, but this time, not for himself. If he should suddenly be pulled, he needed to convince River to jump with him. She possessed a link to his soul, and that was connected to his body. If she followed the thread of his consciousness on her own, she should still be able to find him.

But he hated the thought of her jumping blind, and really, by following the thread of his consciousness, that was what she'd be doing. Too many things could go wrong. No, he needed for her to be ready to jump with him, at the same time he was pulled. Even if Hawk didn't make it alive, River would at least be safe with the Guardians. They would see that she got home to the Fae.

He traced the curve of one delicate ear with the tip of his finger, careful not to disturb her, lost in his thoughts.

Hawk had loved his wife deeply, and as River had pointed out before they entered the concourse-turned-morgue, when souls departed this life they took the space they'd once occupied with them. He would have an empty place in his heart for both his wife and his daughter forever.

But Hawk belonged to River now. Not only had she captured his soul, she'd found her own place in his heart. He didn't know if he could survive the hole it would leave if anything happened to her, and it had nothing to do with her being Fae.

He also didn't know if he could stand by while she returned to her people without him. He could make an appeal to the Great Lords, then to the Council of the Fae. The worst that could happen was that they'd refuse him, and since that was the position he was already in, he had nothing to lose.

He heard a faint whisper of sound in the main concourse. His head went up and his hand stilled where he'd been lightly stroking the side of River's neck with the backs of his fingers. The building was old and not maintained. The noise could be anything.

He slid from beneath her, easing her gently onto the cracked vinyl seat. She rolled to her side with a soft sigh and a slight frown on her lips, then tucked her elbow beneath her cheek. Her breathing steadied, and just that quickly, she was again fast asleep. Hawk's mouth quirked at the corners. She might be able to go for a few days without sleep, but when she did sleep, nothing short of an earthquake was going to wake her.

He listened at the door of the break room but heard no further sounds. He stepped into the main concourse. It was empty except for the rows of the dead.

Hawk had seen far worse than this in his travels. He'd meant it when he'd said to River that the people who'd organized this had done what was necessary. Pandemics were ugly and difficult to contain. The only real surprise was that the place hadn't been burned to the ground when the worst of the pandemic had passed, or been turned into a memorial. Instead, it had simply been forgotten.

Odd. Why might that have been?

He turned from the main concourse and walked back through the ticket booth to the break room. He opened the door. It creaked loudly on dry hinges.

River's eyes flew open and she arched her back, throwing her arms to either side of her and stiffening as if in convulsion. Hawk crossed the room in several steps, reaching out to take her by the shoulders and steady her, but before he could do so she vanished.

His hands came in contact with nothing but empty space and warm vinyl.

♦ ♦

At first River thought she was dreaming. Yet the pounding of her heart and the fear her head might explode from the sudden influx of blood suggested her situation was real.

An emotional stimulus had triggered an immediate emotional response without any evaluation by her consciousness. That meant she had jumped. She was certain of it. She had felt a thread in the subway station, and she felt like an idiot because she hadn't recognized it as such.

Hawk must be frantic.

She turned around in a slow circle, attempting to find her bearings, needing to calm herself down and let the adrenaline abate so she could pick up the thread and make the jump back. If she didn't, she'd be jumping blind.

As her heart rate slowed, little things about her situation began to register.

The time of day was all wrong. It was now night. And she was outside, alone in the dark save for the faint light of the slivered moon overhead, facing an institutional structure that gave her the chills and rattled her right to the core. She hugged herself to ward off a shiver. She didn't have to use her magic to know that something very bad was taking place inside that building, and that she had found the lab from her game. She recognized its exterior. While trapped in her game the Wizard had sent her underground, and it was then that she'd stumbled across the graveyard.

Andy *had* purposely guided her into the subway. She must have known about the thread leading to the lab and the graveyard.

But River had assumed the lab she was searching for would be abandoned. This one was not. Neither was the graveyard at the back. It teemed with bright, shining souls crying out for release. One of those souls shone brighter than the rest.

Pity and horror fed off the adrenaline racing through River's bloodstream. She didn't care that the lab wasn't empty, and while she knew Hawk had to be worried, she wouldn't pass up this opportunity to find where her birth parents were buried.

Her night vision was good and as she scanned the surroundings, she spotted security cameras attached to towers at key points along the ten-foot-high fence surrounding the lab. River was a software engineer by trade and she knew technology, even old technology such as this. The cameras would have a 360-degree view but a five-hundred-foot range, for human motion-detection capability. A larger target, like a car or truck, could be detected at a greater distance.

Someone, however, would have to be monitoring those cameras in order to catch her breaking and entering. It wouldn't matter if she were caught on tape. She'd already be gone.

River bent her knees, rested her palms on her thighs, and worked to quiet her pounding heart. Silence hummed around her as she took in the woods fringing the lab.

A deep, low growl carried in the night, giving her no more time to think. In the game a Were had attacked from the woods, and armed, bioengineered monsters had burst from the ground in the graveyard in ambush, keeping her from reaching her parents.

Her parents.

She rose from her crouched position and sprinted for the fence. The barbed wire at the top was an issue. She quickly called on her magic and in seconds, she'd grown a flowering shrub big and thick enough to support her weight. She swung over the barbed wire and dropped lightly to the ground on the other side.

Boots pounded down a walkway, the sound reverberating and cracking the silence of the night. Angry voices prompted her into action. It seemed the cameras were monitored after all.

She raced for the cover of shadow against the exterior wall of the lab and listened as the guards went off in a different direction. Hands behind her back to feel her way, she slid along the building, scraping her palms on the cold concrete wall, and when she rounded the corner, she found another fence. She reached out a palm to test the air around it, and there it was—a familiar surge of electricity, just as she'd felt in the game. Her parents were here.

A shift in the shadows stilled her movements and she quickly pulled her hand back as if the surge of magic had burned her skin.

"What do you think you're doing?"

The soft challenge caught River off guard and she whirled in surprise. From the shadows a slight figure emerged into the pale wash of moonlight, confidently stepping into River's path and blocking her way.

She was a small woman, exquisitely lovely, no taller than River and as fair as River was dark. In the moonlight her blond, waist-length hair shimmered to white. Magic curled around her, its peppery sage scent thick and heavy from recent use. The magic in River reached out in response.

She wasn't Fae, at least not entirely. River sensed that instinctively. She frowned, unable to accept what else her instincts were telling her. The woman was far too young, and her outward appearance too different, but on the inside, River knew who she was. She had known her for a long time and would know her anywhere. "Andy?"

"Who are you?" the woman demanded, her tone sharper and no longer holding its original level of confidence.

Panic ramped up River's heart rate. Beyond a doubt

this was Andy, but something about her felt wrong. Something inside her was missing.

Again River reached out with her magic, this time in search of the other woman's soul, and she found it in seconds. It wasn't missing, it was dormant—a tiny, shriveled seed that had not yet begun to grow. Andy's soul should have been in full bloom and filled with life. The woman recoiled from River's light touch.

"What's happened to you?" River breathed in dismay.

Wariness and a slight touch of fear twisted the woman's features. "You're Fae."

A blast of magic hit River like a slap to the face, stinging but causing no real harm. River drew back, not wanting to believe that Andy had struck her. "Andy, it's me. River."

Andy stilled, regarding her with a great deal more caution now. "You aren't Fae."

"I don't know what I am," River replied. "I thought you knew. I thought you led me here." This could not be happening. This could not be Andy. Had she landed in an alternate reality?

"Why would I lead you to me?" Andy took a few light running steps forward and launched a roundhouse kick at River's head. She was fast.

So was River, who ducked and dodged to the side.

She scrabbled frantically for the thread that would take her back to Hawk. He had warned her about the dangers of jumping blind. She didn't care about that. She needed him near her. She didn't know how he had survived all those months of uncertainty in the Dark Lord's prison, unsure as to what reality he existed in, because right now, River was so scared she couldn't think.

The cold night wind bit deeply and she tried to draw warmth from the earth to surround her against it, but with only a little success. The use of her magic remained frustratingly erratic. What good was it to her if she couldn't use it at will?

Andy swung back to face her but didn't immediately attack again. Instead she opened her mouth as if to call out for help, and without conscious thought, River caught hold of the night wind with her magic and spun a thick wall of air around the other woman, effectively holding her prisoner within its weave.

Panting, River found the thread she had jumped with. Having it near at hand, and knowing Hawk was no more than a few seconds away, lessened her panic and cleared her head enough to think logically.

She listened for signs of the guards.

There were two of them, near the fence, examining the plant she had grown and discussing whether or not they earned enough money to pursue an intruder who could do such a thing. They didn't like working here, but neither would openly admit to being afraid.

River had no time to wait while they made up their minds about what to do next. She couldn't leave without freeing her parents. She had no idea if she'd get another opportunity.

She turned to the inner fence surrounding the small graveyard and the source of the magic she'd felt, hooking her fingers in the wire and intending to climb. She stopped, pressing her forehead to the cold metal links, then looked back.

She couldn't leave Andy either. She had never questioned their friendship. She'd never had reason to do so. This woman wasn't the Andy she knew and loved, but Andy was inside her. River simply needed to find some way to release her.

She let go of the weave of wind and Andy fell to her hands and knees, a swath of blond hair draping a curtain across her face. River reached out in search of that small seed of soul she had felt inside Andy. When she found it, she used the one part of her magic she found the easiest to control. She cracked open the seed and told it to grow.

Magic flowed from inside her, feeding the seed, and within seconds the woman was Andy—at least on the inside.

The woman lifted her head. "What have you done to me?" she whispered, her eyes wide.

River hadn't done anything, really, except awaken a soul that had been dormant. She kept her distance, allowing the woman a few moments to adjust to the change.

A distant drone became the hum of an engine. Headlights swept the front of the lab as a long car drove up the tree-lined lane leading to the gate. River ducked into the shadows, her back pressed to the concrete wall, hoping she hadn't been seen and trying to calculate how much more time she might have.

Andy tilted her head to watch the progress of the car, climbing stiffly to her feet.

"You should run," she advised River, her voice tense, her eyes continuing to track the approaching vehicle.

Not if it meant leaving Andy in danger. She wasn't abandoning her parents either.

River seized Andy's elbow to drag her toward the graveyard fence. She resisted at first, then allowed herself to be led. River grabbed the wire fencing, found toeholds for her feet, and started to climb.

Andy held back. "We can't go over the fence," she said to River. "There are sentinels."

River had almost forgotten about those. In the game, they had burst from the ground with weapons firing. She paused, trying to think. She had so little control of her magic. What could she use against them?

"Andy. Can you use your magic to stop them?" River asked. The hum of the car's engine died away. Doors slammed.

Andy hesitated. "I don't have enough."

Running footsteps made River desperate. Hawk had told her she needed to be taught to use her magic. Andy knew how to use it. "If I give mine to you, can you use it for me?"

"You would trust me to do that?" Surprise filled Andy's voice with wonder.

"Why wouldn't I?" River replied, equally surprised. Andy had helped her finish the game. She would get her through this as well.

Andy took hold of the fence and smiled over at River beside her. "My name isn't Andy. It's Baliani."

River didn't ask how Andy could be Baliani. If she wanted to help her parents she had to do it now, and she would accept whatever help she could get.

They reached the top of the fence and again, Andy—Baliani—paused as if uncertain.

River swung a leg over. "Come *on*."

Baliani leaned her upper body over the top of the fence. As soon as she did, a blast of electricity shot out and struck her, lifting and propelling her backward. With a soft cry she fell from the fence, landing hard on her hip and her shoulder and skidding a few feet in the gravel.

River froze. Then she quickly drew back, intending to climb down to see if Baliani was okay. Before she could do so, a slideshow of images began to race through her head. Balanced on the top of the fence, she pressed the flat of her hands to her temples, trying to make some sort of sense out of what she was seeing and the emotions attached to the images—fear, pain. Love.

Overriding them all, however, was a deep outpouring of anger, and it was directed at Baliani.

River hadn't considered what it meant to find Andy in this awful place. She didn't want to consider it now. These were her mother's images and emotions she was seeing and feeling, but somehow, her mother had gotten things wrong. Terrible things had happened here, true, and were happening still.

But Andy wasn't the cause of them.

River dropped to the ground and rushed to Baliani's side.

Baliani sat up, brushing dirt and gravel from her arm, wincing with pain. River felt the faint rush as Baliani focused her magic and mended the scrapes on her skin.

Both women turned their heads in the direction of approaching footsteps.

Baliani grabbed River's arm. "It's Kaye," she said. "Run. I'll try to stop him."

Rage unfurled inside River at the mention of his name, fueled in part by the overwhelming emotions fed to her by her mother, and also by the memory of what he had done to Nick.

Fire ripped a path through her veins.

Barely registering what Baliani was saying, she flung her hands forward. The hot wall of her anger sent the approaching man hurtling backward through the air to land in a heap twenty paces away.

She stalked him, her eyes narrowed. She would reach her parents, and she would destroy anything that stood in her way. This was no man. This was a monster.

"River, no!" Baliani cried out in alarm. She stepped between River and the man writhing in pain on the ground. "This isn't a path you want to start down."

A low, warning rumble rose in River's throat. "Get out of my way. He hurt my parents."

Pain and remorse mixed with the wonder glittering in Baliani's eyes. "*I* hurt your parents. I swear to you, I never meant any harm to them, or to anyone else. Please, let me find a way to fix this. Let me find a way to repay you." A single tear traced a track down her cheek and she brushed it away with her thumb. "Let me find a way to thank you for giving me my soul. Don't let this gift to me lead to your first steps down a dark path you weren't meant to travel."

River lifted her hand and gathered her magic, determination sharpening her tone as she warned her again. "I said get out of my way."

But Baliani, more experienced with magic although perhaps not as strong, struck first. The thread back to the subway station that River held close now wound around her, binding her much as she'd bound Baliani with wind mere moments before.

The world tilted.

Magic shot from River's fingertips, sending a fireball of electricity blasting through the wall of the break room in the subway station. The fireball tore through the ticket counter beyond to skip like a stone across the main concourse floor before striking the double-doored entrance.

Hawk, flat on his stomach on the break room floor where he'd dived to avoid the flame, lifted his head and looked up at her in wordless concern and open-mouthed surprise.

♦ ♦

When Spence came around it was to the sound of his research assistant delivering a blistering lecture to a Fae spiritual leader regarding the dangers of interfering with the mortal mind, particularly the mind of an elderly man, no matter that the man was a genius.

Being called elderly bothered him almost as much as being called a genius. Spence was no genius. He was a stupid old man who'd forgotten that power and politics ruled the world, and not science.

He was lying on the floor, covered by one of the

thermal blankets from the emergency kit, a pillow tucked under his neck and head to keep his airway open.

"I couldn't have known Hawk was a demolition man," Spence interrupted Shana midsentence, his words coming out in a croak, "because there's no such thing. It's a military joke."

Shana, sitting cross-legged on the floor beside him, paused in her lecture long enough to pick up his wrist and measure his pulse.

Spence shook her off. "I'm fine." He wasn't one hundred percent though. "Help me up." He knew he sounded cranky, which he was. The floor was hard and cold, neither thing good for an old man's bones, and he hadn't liked Achala's probing. He glared at the spiritual leader. "I would have willingly told you anything you wanted to know."

"Forgive me," Achala said. Genuine concern lingered in his eyes as he studied Spence. A twist of magic spun from him to Spence, and immediately, Spence's physical discomforts disappeared. "I couldn't be certain you would, and I needed to know." Achala frowned. "Demolition men are no joke, military or otherwise."

"What is a demolition man?" Shana asked, apparently deciding to forgo the rest of her lecture, at least for the moment. She helped Spence to his feet and into a chair, fussing over him and making him feel both foolish and flattered.

"It's a term used in reference to training given to a few select soldiers," Spence explained. "Centuries ago, a demolition man was someone sent to a world occupied by a Dark Lord with the intention of destroying it. The Dark Lords were immortals. Destroying the worlds they inhabited was the Guardian way of neutralizing them. Without a world and a physical form, they became harmless." He shot a sidelong glance at Achala. "The Fae never cared for the practice."

"You're speaking of fairy tales," Shana said. What she didn't say, although her tone implied it, was that she thought both Achala and Spence were talking foolishness. Spence was inclined to agree.

"The stories are not fairy tales," Achala replied, his tone deepening and trembling with barely restrained anger.

"And the training of demolition men was supposed to have ended."

CHAPTER **FOURTEEN**

♦

Dust and smoke billowed in a thick cloud as a section of the concourse wall caved in, scattering brick and mortar in a slow landslide across the marble floor.

Then there was silence, broken only by the raw, rasping sounds of her indrawn breaths.

Stunned surprise held Hawk pinned to the floor as he tried to reconcile the woman he knew with the one standing over him, her arms spread wide, anger and rage pouring off her in hot, searing waves.

She paid no attention to him. Her attention was elsewhere, turned inward, and with a sickening lurch of his gut he understood she was searching for a thread.

That brought him to his feet. "River."

He spoke her name softly, as if she were some wild creature that might bolt if startled. The comparison was apt. She looked tormented, dangerous, her pupils dilated and swallowing the whites of her eyes. A tainted, oily darkness swirled around her, frightening Hawk more than he cared to admit.

Something equally as terrifying was the knowledge that River had jumped again, and with no conscious effort on her part. One minute she was asleep, the next she was gone. Fae reacted to danger out of instinct. He knew that, and had seen it happen more than once. But never in his life had he seen or heard of one reacting with such fury. Wherever she'd gone, something terrible had happened.

He fisted his hands at his sides and took another cautious step toward her.

"River," he repeated, trying to calm her but needing to be careful in how he proceeded for fear she might disappear on him again if she found the thread she was seeking.

She blinked several times before finally focusing on him. As she did, her blue eyes lost a bit of that crazed, deadly gleam. The darkness surrounding her faded to an ugly gray. Hawk forced his fists to unclench, inching forward a few more steps.

Almost there.

"I have to go back," she said to him, the intensity of

her rekindling anger slamming against him and sending him reeling. Crackles of energy lifted the ends of
her hair as again, she gathered her magic.

He regained his footing and reached for her.

She darted away before he could touch her, panic
edging out some of the anger. "I left without releasing
my parents. I left Andy there, too. I have to go back
for them."

He kept his voice calm even though he felt anything
but. "You went to the graveyard and Andy was there?"

Sharp, impatient eyes, more aware now, raked his
face. "Yes. That's why she sent us down here, so I
could find the thread. But now the thread is gone."
She frowned and spoke to herself. "Why didn't she
know me?"

Hawk took advantage of her distraction. This time
when he reached for her, she moved willingly into his
arms and buried her face in the front of his shirt. He
ran a hand up and down her back, trying to soothe her.
She smelled of fresh air.

It chilled him.

"Tell me what happened," he said.

She told him everything, about Baliani, who was
really Andy, and the deep emotions she'd felt from her
mother. "Kaye was there," she added, and he felt the
fury in her again begin to rise. "He's responsible for
what happened to my parents." She started to tremble.
"I don't care what Andy said. It wasn't her fault."

As much as he'd like to, this wasn't the time to
voice his own opinions about Andy and what was or
wasn't her fault. But at some point, he and River's

Wizard were going to talk. He needed to find out who she was, and more important, what she was. Fae laws were being broken, and Fae laws governed all of creation.

Something else River had said snagged at his attention. "The thread is gone?"

"Yes." She curled her fingers in his shirt. "I can't feel it at all anymore."

"That isn't possible," Hawk said, trying to puzzle it out. "Threads don't disappear. They're paths to places the Fae have gone. At the very least, you should have left your own thread behind you when you jumped."

"Maybe it doesn't work that way when you travel to the past," River suggested.

"No one travels to the past." Hawk stopped to consider that. When the Guardians transported they crossed through open space, and open space was outside of time. Therefore, the Guardians weren't affected by time until they reached another world. He couldn't say for certain what happened when the Fae jumped because their magic wasn't based on science and technology. "What makes you think you traveled to the past?"

She was starting to relax, although he could sense she was no less determined.

"Because Andy was younger," she explained. "My age. The fence around the graveyard was new. The lab wasn't abandoned either. The security cameras were old technology. And Kaye." Her voice shook with dislike. "He was younger, too."

Hawk tried to imagine the level of magic it would take to create a thread to the past that only one person could follow, and linked two different times to one place, but couldn't quite wrap his head around it. That didn't mean it wasn't true.

He tightened his arms around her, afraid she would try to jump blind when she didn't find the thread she was looking for. A crackling in the main concourse caught his attention. He lifted his head and sniffed at the air, then stiffened.

The station was on fire.

♦ ♦

The police officer was back.

Andy peered through the small pane of glass in the heavy wooden door, her heart rate accelerating when she saw who it was. She shot back the dead bolt and threw open the door, grabbing his sleeve and hurrying him inside.

She'd overslept. Bright sunlight streamed through the windows. She'd dressed in jeans and a white wool sweater, although her feet were bare and her hair was still wet from her shower. She didn't have on any makeup, and in this lighting, every wrinkle she owned would show on her face.

They certainly showed on his.

"What are you doing here? What if somebody saw you?" She fought off the urge to check the street to see who Kaye had watching.

"Nobody saw me. I cut through the parking lot next door," he replied, taking off his coat and hanging it over the back of one of the kitchen chairs. "And the second shift is asleep in his car out front."

Andy thought she heard him add, "Lucky bastard," under his breath.

"Would you like a cup of coffee?" she asked, her heart shifting back into a lower gear. She didn't wait for him to answer before reaching for the pot and a ceramic mug. The way he looked was answer enough. She held up the pot. "What do you take in it?"

"Black is fine."

He sat at the table and she placed the mug of coffee in front of him. She poured another mug for herself and leaned against the counter while he stared off into space as if forgetting that he was the one who'd come to her.

A troublesome thought arose. "Constable Peters," she began.

"Jim." He lifted the mug to his lips, blew on the hot, inky surface, then sipped loudly.

She started again. "Jim. Where is the Were?"

The question caught him off guard. He paused with the mug halfway back to the table. "I left him locked in a holding cell at the station. Why?"

Andy sagged with relief. "Because he'll have a microchip embedded in his skull. It's in his skull so he can't remove it on his own," she answered in response to the question in his eyes. "Kaye will be tracking every move the both of you make."

Jim laughed softly to himself. "That also means I can't leave him alone in one place for too long. Jesus, I'm getting old. I should have thought of that."

Andy lost interest in the Were now that she knew where he was. "Did you find River?"

"They went into the subway and never came out, and I wasn't going into that cesspit after them. I'm a cop. Those little gang bastards scare the shit out of me, and if I shoot any of them I have to fill out a report."

Andy didn't believe for a minute that anything scared this man, at least not much. She had no difficulty picturing him at the head of one of Kaye's mutant armies. He didn't bluff, and a Were would respect that. So would children.

And if River had gone into the subway, she was right where she should be. She would find the thread Andy had left for her all those years ago, and when she did, she would learn the truth about Andy. Sadness crept into her heart. River had given Andy her soul and for that, Andy would love her forever.

She hoped River could still love her, too, at least a little.

"You didn't go into the subway because you had the Were with you," Andy guessed, and knew by the way his eyes shifted from her face that she'd guessed correctly.

"The little fuckers would have pissed him off and I was too tired to clean up the mess. I'd have had to shoot him, and while that paperwork might have been worth it, explaining it to Johnson and Kaye wasn't."

Well, well. Tough Constable Jim Peters had a soft spot for children and animals. Andy was a little charmed by that.

She could hear the kitchen staff in the pub preparing for the lunch crowd. Soon she was going to have to go set up the tables and open the cash.

She wondered why he was here.

"What are the chances of them finding this lab of yours on their own?" he finally asked.

"Very unlikely." Andy hoped he wasn't getting cold feet. "It's deep in the mountains, with one road in. The road is booby-trapped with buried explosives."

"How am I supposed to get them there?"

"The Were," Andy replied. "He knows the way. He can lead you through the forest. It's safe enough going in." Coming out was another matter.

The look he shot her said he understood what she hadn't said. "How are *you* going to get in?"

"The same way I got out the first time," Andy replied. She'd taken enough of his soul to help her get in, but no more. Once back at the lab, she could rely on River to help her release the Fae. How she got out again wasn't something she intended to worry about just yet, but she had hoped the Guardian would be there to guarantee River's safety.

Andy still found it difficult to believe that the Guardian hadn't made it out of the game. Not after surviving months with a Dark Lord. While she liked Nick well enough, self-preservation was his primary motivator. She didn't trust him with River.

"What was your impression of Nick Sutton?" she asked abruptly.

Jim paused to consider. Andy liked the way he thought through his responses.

"Truthfully? I don't know what to make of him. My

first impression was that he was weak. A bit of a sissy. He tossed his lunch in a garbage can when I showed him pictures of—" He hastily reconsidered what he'd been about to say, sliding her a quick sideways glance before continuing. "But he had no trouble killing a man who threatened the girl. And he faced down the Were as well. He either puts on a good show or is two different people."

Understanding dawned. So the Guardian had made it out of the game after all. On the heels of relief came a quick spurt of pity. She'd liked Nick. He'd had potential. She had not, however, liked seeing him with River. It was a motherly issue, and River was as close to a daughter as she was ever likely to come.

"If Amos is tracking the Were, you won't have much time to get to the lab," Andy warned. "Once he knows where you're headed, he'll follow."

"I'm counting on that," Jim replied. The way he said it gave Andy chills. "But before I can head there, I need to get Sutton and River to trust me enough to come with me. I don't see that happening. Especially not with the Were hanging off my ass."

He was right, of course. The Guardian would never trust anyone when it came to River's safety.

River, however, was another matter entirely. If she could forgive Andy for what had happened in the past, she would offer Andy her trust.

Andy ran her hands up and down her arms for warmth even though the room wasn't cold. She'd had nearly thirty years to accept what had happened. For River, it was fresh.

But if River couldn't forgive, there was little point

in continuing. She was the only person the Fae would allow close.

"I don't know about Nick," Andy said slowly, "but I do know what you can say to earn River's trust."

♦ ♦

It was an odd message, and one he found more than a little intriguing, but Peters had accepted it without question.

He was taking a chance on leaving the Were in the holding cell for a little while longer, but he and Andy had agreed it was a risk worth taking. Regardless of whether or not River understood the message, Sutton would never let her get into a car with a Were.

Not the Sutton who'd planted a knife in a guy's throat back at that truck stop, at any rate. Something about that boy just did not add up. Peters couldn't remember the last time he'd so badly misjudged a person.

He had a second reason for leaving the Were behind, one he hadn't mentioned to Andy. He was grateful to her for passing on the bit of information about the microchip, because before he helped to get River Weston and Nick Sutton to that mountain lab she was so anxious they find, he had another task to accomplish.

Premier George Johnson was going to die.

He flipped on his flashers, turned the patrol car onto Main Street, then headed west. Andy had been certain they'd be at the central subway station.

He almost hoped she was wrong. That place gave

him the creeps. Nobody went there. Nobody. Not even the homeless. Back in the early days of the virus, the local police had donned white anti-germ-warfare gear and helped stockpile the bodies. He hadn't been on the force at the time, but he'd seen the archived news footage. A hundred years from now when the horror of the virus was long forgotten, descendants of the abandoned dead would have video evidence for their court cases against the government.

He'd heard stories that even after decades had passed, the graves of its victims could contain the live virus. Although he hadn't found any research to confirm it, and since his own days were now numbered it shouldn't matter any longer to him, he'd grabbed two jugs of vinegar from the supply room at work to douse himself with, just in case. Old habits died hard. Old fears died even harder.

Maybe he could lure Sutton and River out into the open so he wouldn't have to go into the station after them.

Traffic was lighter than usual and it wasn't long before the boarded-up station came into view. Once the pride of the city it was now nothing more than a grimy eyesore, blackened by time and neglect. The buildings around it had long ago been razed. None of their previous tenants had wanted office space next to a mausoleum the entire country was trying to forget.

As Peters approached, he slowed the patrol car to a crawl. Solid columns of smoke spiraled from the station's roof to spread in a thick blanket of cloud that blocked out the blue of the sky.

He hit the brakes hard, and gripping the steering wheel tightly with white-knuckled fingers, he started to swear. Could nothing in this life ever be simple?

Pulling up to the curb in front of the main doors, he leapt from the car and popped open the trunk. The riot gear wasn't much help—hockey playoffs were still months away—but the tire jack he could probably use.

He seized it and raced for the boarded-up entrance.

♦ ♦

The screech of nails being pried from the wood barring the main double doors told Hawk they were no longer alone.

Someone was trying to get in.

Good enough. He and River were trying to get out. And the last thing he wanted right now was for her to make any attempt at a jump.

"Breathe into your elbow," he ordered her as smoke started to fill the room, and immediately she did as she was told. Hawk didn't know what, or who, was on the other side of that door. If they were unfriendly, he was perfectly willing to go through them to escape.

He was willing to do so no matter what. Deciding whether or not they were allies took time they couldn't afford. The building was tinder dry. Already, ribbons of fire licked at the walls of the main concourse.

Rusted hinges squealed as one of the front doors cracked open for the first time in decades. Hawk blinked in the sudden onslaught of daylight. A shadow appeared in the doorway.

"You two okay?" a gruff voice inquired.

It was the cop from the truck stop. Hawk didn't question the coincidence. Instead he pushed his way through the door, keeping his body between River and whatever else awaited them on the other side of it.

The street out in front was empty except for the lone police car. The wail of sirens in the distance suggested it wouldn't be empty for long. Fire trucks were on their way.

Hawk glanced quickly from left to right, trying to determine in which direction they should run.

"Hold on a second," the cop said, his hands spread wide to indicate he wasn't a threat to them. "I have a message for River from Andy."

"Is Andy okay?" River's tone indicated her concern. Hawk's teeth ground together. In spite of what she'd told him had happened with Andy at the lab, she continued to trust her.

Hawk didn't.

"Let's go," he said to River, one eye on the cop.

The cop, however, kept his attention on River. "Andy's fine. She said to tell you that Baliani thanks you for the gift of her soul." He looked at Hawk then, and he shrugged as if in apology. "I have no idea what that means."

Neither did Hawk, but it clearly held meaning for River. Her face lit up and a lot of the anger and darkness she hadn't yet managed to release disappeared in a flash.

The sirens were closer now, horns blaring and air brakes blasting as the fire trucks navigated the city streets. Heat from the burning building rolled over

Hawk and the others, quickly becoming uncomfortable.

"Get in the car," the cop said. "I can take you someplace where you'll be safe."

River started forward to do as he said, but Hawk drew her back. "Forget it," he said to her. "We don't know what Andy's game is and I'm tired of trying to figure it out."

"She knows where the graveyard is," River replied. Hawk recognized the stubborn light in her eyes and knew he was in for a fight.

The cop turned to his car. He tossed the jack into the trunk, slammed it shut, then opened the driver's door. He looked at them across the hood, his face lined and weary, and he ran a hand through his graying red hair. "You're tired of trying to figure something out. I'm tired of shit in general. Do what you want. You have ten seconds to change your mind and get in the car. After that, you're on your own."

"Hawk," River said urgently, tugging on his hand. "I want us to go with him."

Hawk deliberated for two of those ten seconds. The cop meant what he said. The fact that he intended to drive off without them made it easier for Hawk to decide.

That didn't mean he had to like the decision.

He reached for the passenger door and held it as River ducked into the backseat ahead of him. He climbed in beside her. The engine roared to life and the cop pulled away from the curb seconds before the first of the fire trucks roared into view.

From the rear window, Hawk watched as flames shot through the roof of the building. He turned back to River. When he did, he realized two things. A pane of bulletproof glass separated them from their driver.

And the doors in the back didn't open from the inside.

♦ ♦

Spence opened and closed his mouth several times without finding the words to allow him to speak.

Achala was wrong. The Guardians had progressed beyond such barbarism, and what he suggested was barbaric indeed. Spence looked around him at the laboratory classroom, alight in the red glow of the triple moons. This was the place he'd called home for more years than he cared to remember. His scientific research had promoted life, not death.

But he was not the only scientist in the world. How many students had he trained who he'd thought did not have the proper respect for the work they conducted?

How many of those students had surprised him with their quick career progression?

He thought of Robert Jess, and his stomach turned over.

"I'm sorry, Dr. Jennings," Achala said gently. "I've touched Colonel Hawkins' mind. I know what I saw."

"You've touched Dr. Jennings' as well," Shana pointed out sharply. "Therefore you know he would have no part of such a thing."

Spence was moved by her loyalty. He wished he could believe it was well founded. He pushed a microscope aside with his elbow as he leaned on the workbench, trying to breathe. He hoped the pain in his chest didn't mean he was having a heart attack.

"Perhaps you can tell me exactly what you saw in Colonel Hawkins' mind that makes you believe this is true," Spence said. The words echoed faintly, as if he'd spoken with his fingers stuck in his ears.

"There's a part of his mind that's closed off to him," Achala explained. "Because it's closed to him, he has no need to protect it. Under a normal examination, no Fae would have found it." He smiled thinly. "But I was inside the mind of a military man possessing more fortitude than most. I chose to use less orthodox methods for examining him."

"You opened the door and you looked at the memories," Spence said. Unspoken understanding passed between the two men.

"Are you familiar with the research?" Achala asked him.

"More or less." It hadn't been his project, although he'd mentored it. "It was intended to help with post-traumatic stress disorder in the military. A soldier who'd seen action off world would have the option of locking away memories he no longer wanted to access. But it would have been strictly voluntary," Spence added. "No one has the right to take away memories without permission, and I don't believe Colonel Hawkins would have volunteered for it." He knew for a fact that he wouldn't. Hawk had steadfastly refused to allow Spence or anyone else to ease his grief over the loss of his family.

Achala was shaking his head in disagreement. "If your colonel had volunteered for this, his subconscious would have known that a part of his mind has been closed. He has no knowledge of it."

"That's not possible," Shana interrupted. Pale spots had appeared on her cheeks, and Spence suddenly recalled she'd done her undergraduate thesis on the subject. "If he'd undergone any sort of procedure, even involuntarily, his subconscious would remember that much at the very least."

"She's correct," Spence confirmed. Relief made him feel faint.

His relief, however, was short lived.

"Unless," Achala said quietly, "the procedure was assisted by a Fae."

Spence looked at Shana. Her shock mirrored his own, so he said what he knew she was thinking. "What you're suggesting amounts to sacrilege."

Achala smiled, obviously not offended, although the smile was tinged with sadness. "It's a good thing, then, that the suggestion came from a spiritual leader, wouldn't you agree?" He rested his hands on his knees, absently rubbing them, becoming lost deep in thought. "The question is, why?"

Spence turned to Shana. "My retirement is timely. I should be thanking Dr. Jess, not feeling so bitter."

A blond eyebrow lifted in cool reproof. "Don't think you're getting off so easily."

"I have to agree with her." Achala's hands stilled as he rejoined the conversation. His gaze rested thoughtfully on Spence. "I need a favor from you. But before

I ask it, first, how important is your reputation to you?"

The answer to that one was easy. "My reputation for my past work is above reproach," Spence replied. He reached into a nearby crate he'd been using for packing and lifted out one of his numerous gold-plated awards as an example. He tossed it back into the crate. Glass shattered, and Shana leaned forward with a small sound of dismay. "While it pains me to admit it, my reputation now is that of an old man whose shelf life has expired. That's something I can gladly relinquish." He looked at Shana. "Hers, however, is another matter."

Achala nodded in agreement despite her protests to the contrary. "Between us we can probably salvage hers. Yours will be gone."

Whatever the favor Achala was going to ask, it must be good. Spence had to admit he was curious and more than a little willing to say yes.

"Colonel Hawkins is in trouble," Achala said bluntly. "He's also unwilling to be pulled out of stasis or he would never have assumed someone else's identity. That suggests a few things to me, and I need to know if I'm right. I'd like for you to revive him.

"And once you revive him, I'd like for you to bring him to me."

◆ ◆

Hawk thought about kicking the door out, then decided it was a waste of his time. The car had undoubtedly been built to withstand it. Plus, Nick's skinny legs would probably snap under the pressure.

He carefully kept his thoughts private, although inwardly he was seething. He didn't like it that he could no longer rely on himself and his judgment to keep River safe, but the reality was that he couldn't, and it was time to admit it. Right now the cop was their only ally, and even though Hawk wasn't happy about being locked in the back of a squad car, he had no one to blame but himself for that. He could have gotten into the front seat. If he'd been thinking straight, he would have.

He might as well enjoy the ride. As he watched the street signs go by so he would know how to find his way back if need be, it quickly became apparent that they were headed out of the city, not in. He didn't know what that might mean, or if it meant anything at all.

His head ached.

He turned to River and she smiled up at him, but it was such a warm, sexy smile that it threw him off guard. Not that he didn't like it, but this wasn't the time or the place. What the hell was she doing?

He pinched the bridge of his nose, wondering if his tired mind was hallucinating again.

River began to play with the zipper on her coat. She pulled it up and down in a slow, sensual movement, and licked her bottom lip.

Hawk started to sweat.

♦ ♦

Nick couldn't remember the last time he'd had this much fun. Not only was he messing with the body-snatcher's head, he was getting to replay some of his favorite moments. It was a lot like downloading the images off a camera. He plugged them in, then they popped up on a screen. It was amazing, some of the shit he had stored in his head.

Life couldn't possibly get any better.

Come on, lover boy, he encouraged. *We both like it when she does this.*

But he was more interested to see how Chase Hawkins liked it when he realized she'd also done this with Nick.

♦ ♦

"What are you doing?" Hawk asked her.

Something was wrong. Seriously, mind-fuckingly wrong. No longer were they sitting in the backseat of a police car. They were inside Nick's bedroom, and River had stripped down to her ivory-laced panties.

Time suspended as Hawk watched her lithe form relax on the bed. Desire darkened her eyes to a deep, ocean blue. Long, curly lashes swept onto her cheeks. She crooked her finger and beckoned him to her. "Come here, Nick. I know what you want."

"Nick?" Hawk demanded, his legs suddenly shaky beneath him and refusing to move.

She pouted her lips, hooking her thumbs in the lace of her panties, and in that instant Hawk was sure he was losing his mind. Either that or he was asleep. And he was pretty damn sure he was wide awake.

Panic fired his blood, singeing the air in his lungs. He struggled to breathe through the flames.

She reached for him and he lost his balance, collapsing on top of her. He struggled against her roaming hands, trying to push himself away.

"Come on, Nick. Stop teasing," she commanded. Her mouth pressed over his and she kissed him deeply.

Hawk struggled to his feet and staggered backward. River laughed and the room began spinning. Completely overwhelmed and not knowing what to do, he blinked his eyes and opened them again, hoping the image would go away. A throbbing began at the base of his neck and traveled onward and upward. The ringing in his ears and the pain in his temples crippled him to the point of blindness.

He dropped to his knees. River slid off the mattress and came close, sinking to the floor in front of him. The heat of her body caused a flaring response in his own and he could stand it no longer. "Stop," he said.

"Nick," she murmured, and placed her hands on his shoulders. "Please. I want you. I want what only you can give me."

He struggled out of her grasp but then he could feel her, feel her warmth moving against him, pushing back the chill in his bones. His eyes slipped shut, unable to fight her off any longer.

"Please," she said again, more urgently this time, her voice growing louder and louder.

Hawk forced his eyes open. With her mouth turned down in a frown, and her hands on his shoulders, she was shaking him hard. "Hawk, please."

The bulletproof divider slid open.

"Is everything okay back there?" the cop asked, his eyes on Hawk in the rearview mirror.

Hawk sucked in a tight breath. He disliked showing weakness. As air filled his lungs his vision cleared and the world around him ceased spinning, the chaotic images no longer in his head.

"Everything's fine," he replied. His voice sounded steady to him, but tired. "Just a bit of a headache."

The cop regarded him for a few more minutes, then reached behind his head and slid the divider shut.

River placed her fingers under Hawk's chin and angled his head until he was forced to look at her, which was difficult for him to do. He hadn't yet shaken those images entirely. "Tell me what happened."

The headache started to fade.

"Did I fall asleep?" he asked warily, keeping his voice low so as not to be overheard by the cop in the front seat.

"I don't think so."

The concern on her face made his chest ache. He rubbed the base of his skull where a dull pain continued to linger. The possibilities for what had gone wrong were endless.

He needed sleep. Without it, eventually he would die. The hallucinations might be a symptom of that.

Dying in Nick's body didn't worry him too much. But what if the hallucinations, along with those blank patches of memory, were a symptom that his real body was dying?

Immediately, Hawk dismissed that possibility. If his own body were dying, Nick's life wouldn't be the one flashing before his eyes. The Mother couldn't possibly be so cruel.

No. The one that made sense—the possibility that scared him the most—was that somehow Nick was trying to get back into the mental driver's seat.

And not only had the son of a bitch found another way to tamper with Hawk's reality, this time he'd come close—too close—to discovering a way to drive Hawk over the brink of insanity.

CHAPTER FIFTEEN

◆

River stared out the car window with the undivided attention of someone too overwhelmed to think.

They'd left the city limits behind and driven east along the river valley for over an hour until they hit cottage country at the base of the mountain range. She vaguely recognized the area from a childhood trip with her parents.

Something was wrong with Hawk.

Worse, he was shutting her out and River tried not to worry too much over what that might mean.

The message from Andy, however, had done wonders to ease her concerns over their driver. He'd introduced himself as Jim Peters and he was indeed a police officer—just as Hawk had thought.

River knew something else about him as well. Andy had touched him. That was good enough for River.

Peters turned up a dirt road leading deep into the

woodlands. They emerged at a small boat launch on the edge of a lake. A trim log cabin sat back off the main road, down a footpath carved through the tall trees and thick brush.

River and Hawk climbed from the backseat of the cruiser and followed Peters to the front door of the cabin. Peters jiggled a key in the padlock, then pushed open the heavy door and stepped back so they could enter ahead of him. He tossed Hawk the key. "Nobody knows about this place. I come here to get away."

River did a quick scan of the place. A stone fireplace was the focal point on the north wall, dry kindling piled high beside it. Facing the fireplace was an old worn sofa that looked as if it had been well loved. A large black bearskin rug covered the polished wood floor, completing the rustic mountain feel.

Two doors led off the main room. She assumed a bathroom was behind one and a bedroom behind the other. On the south side of the cabin there was a small kitchenette with a microwave, and she prayed she'd find coffee in those pine cupboards.

Hawk wasn't the only one who never wanted to sleep again.

Peters checked behind the closed doors, then returned to the main room. Hawk stood by the window, looking out at the lake. River knew the scenery wasn't what drew his attention. He was looking for escape routes.

"We need to talk," Peters said.

Hawk didn't turn from the window. "Damn straight we do. This is twice now that you've shown up just in time to save our asses. So tell me. What—or who—are you saving us for? And why should we trust you?"

Testosterone levels in the room soared as the two men squared off, sizing each other up. While Nick had never been what anyone could call buff, Hawk knew what he was doing. He also had the advantage of age. Peters, however, was no slouch either, despite his more advanced years. And he didn't bluff. They knew that much about him already.

"I don't know who the hell you are," Peters said to Hawk, "and I don't want to know. But I do know that you aren't Nick Sutton. So don't give me bullshit about trust when I don't have any reason to trust you either."

"Andy," River said. Both men looked at her. "She's the reason you can trust each other."

Hawk looked at her as if she'd gone crazy. "You want me to trust him because of the *Wizard*?"

"Constable Peters trusts her." River turned to him. "Don't you?" It wasn't a question as much as a prod for confirmation.

"The jury's still out."

A sound like a rifle shot cracked across the lake. River jumped and Hawk's head went up. Peters never moved.

"That was a beaver tail slapping the water," he said. "Something disturbed it, but whatever it was, it was on the other side of the lake."

They were all tired and on edge.

"So what does Andy want?" Hawk finally asked Peters.

"She says she wants to right a wrong. And she needs River's help to do it."

"What kind of a wrong?" Hawk asked, his eyes narrowing in suspicion, but River thought she already knew.

Peters' eyes slid to River, then quickly away. "I'd prefer it if Andy explained. Some of it didn't make a whole lot of sense to me. The rest, I don't want to know about."

"She's part of the reason my parents are caught in that graveyard," River said to Hawk. "But not the whole reason." That Andy was once Baliani, River could accept. She could not, however, blame Andy for things Baliani had done.

Hawk had gotten that look on his face that meant he was about to start dictating orders to her. River hated it. Some meek, inner Fae mechanism always tried to respond, and she had to fight it in order to do as she, River, wanted.

She prepared for a battle.

"When is Andy coming to explain?" Hawk asked Peters.

A muscle ticked at the corner of the police officer's mouth. Otherwise, he showed little emotion. "She's meeting us at some laboratory in the mountains."

Hawk's voice got quiet. "And how do we get to this laboratory in order to meet her? Do you know where it is?"

"I've arranged for a guide."

"A guide to a hidden laboratory in the mountains where a Fae soul is held captive, and bioengineered, armed mechanical animals guard the grounds," Hawk mused. "What kind of a guide might this be?"

"A Were," Peters admitted. The muscle continued to twitch. "The one from the parking lot at the truck stop. The one who killed those gamers."

River's knees started to shake. The temperature in the room seemed to drop ten degrees. For some reason, Johnny's face came to mind first. He'd been amazing with 3-D design, and very funny. He'd died because of her.

They all had.

"Grab your things," Hawk said to her. "We're leaving."

"Hang on just a second." Peters stepped in front of the door, and with a sense of impending disaster, River knew he'd made a mistake. Hawk's hands clenched into fists and she grabbed his arm to hold him back. He shook her off. Peters pretended not to notice the threat of violence. "The Were is almost all animal," he said. "He didn't randomly decide to kill those gamers. Someone commanded him to do it. Aren't you the least bit curious as to who that might be? And why?"

"I am," River said.

Hawk, however, was not. "No. Get away from the door."

Again, River took hold of his arm, but this time to plead her case. "I need to know what's going on," she said to him. "I need to understand. I need to get to that lab and free my parents. Nothing is more important to me than that."

"And nothing is more important to me than you." Hawk would not be budged. "I will not trade one Fae for another. First, I'll get you to safety. Then I will come back for your mother, because believe me, the Guardians will not leave a Fae soul trapped on this world. Not once they know."

River opened her mouth to protest, but before the words could come out, Hawk's eyes rolled back in his head and he started to fold at the knees. He recovered almost as quickly, but in less than two heartbeats, Peters had him facedown on the floor with a service revolver pressed to his temple.

"I'm trying to be honest with you," he said to Hawk. "That's more than I can say for you, whoever you are." He eased the pressure of his knee against Hawk's back. "I'm going to let you up. If you make one wrong move I'm going to shoot you. Got it?"

Hawk nodded, but River could tell he was furious. She suspected he was more angry with himself.

Something was wrong with him, and all the worry she'd tried to suppress rushed straight to the foreground. This time she couldn't push it aside. Neither, however, could she miss this opportunity to free her parents. She couldn't explain why it was so important. She hadn't known them. But twice now, she'd felt their love for her. She couldn't turn her back on that.

But Hawk wouldn't leave without her, and he needed to go.

"Please, Hawk." She tried to draw his attention from Peters to her. "The sooner we do this, the sooner we can leave."

She saw in his eyes the instant he realized what she was really trying to say. This was the first time she'd actually agreed to go with him when he left. Until now he'd arrogantly assumed she would, or that he could somehow override her reluctance when the time came. That she might not want to go hadn't been something he'd even considered.

He didn't say anything for a long time. Peters waited patiently.

"You trust him?" Hawk finally asked her.

"I do," River replied without hesitation.

"Then okay." His attention swiveled to Peters. "We'll do this. But if the Were becomes a problem, I'll kill him."

"If the Were becomes a problem, I'll kill him myself." Peters holstered his gun. "He's an asshole and I can't turn my back on him. But he'll do what I tell him because he knows that I'll kill him if he doesn't." He cast one last glance around. "You'll find cans of food in the cupboard and a few things in the freezer. There are clean towels and soap in the bathroom, although it may take a little while for the water heater to kick in. You should have everything you need until I get back, most likely in the morning. Don't open the door for anyone else."

River frowned, not wanting to wait any longer. "Where are you going?"

"To get our guide. And to do a little shopping." Peters paused with his hand on the door. "Once we set out, we won't have much time. So whatever you need to do, be prepared to do it fast."

He closed the door behind him, and a few moments later, they heard the car engine start. The sound soon faded away, leaving them alone in the silence.

Hawk dropped onto the worn floral sofa and kicked off his boots with a soft sigh of relief. He threw a shaky arm over the backrest and sagged into the cushions. He stared at the ceiling and exhaled a slow breath.

He was more tired than he'd wanted to let on.

River went to the stainless-steel kitchen sink and twisted the tap. Cold, clear water flowed. She let it run for a few minutes, then filled the kettle and plugged it in.

She then pulled off her jacket and went to work on building a fire. Crinkling up old newspapers she found by the firewood, she placed them inside the hearth. Hawk made no move to help her, which told her a lot. Crouched on the floor, she glanced over her shoulder at him to make sure he was still with her.

He was watching her, an unreadable expression in his eyes.

"What's happening to you?" she asked. "First in the car, then just now? Please be honest with me. Maybe I can help."

Hawk rubbed his temples. "I'm seeing things," he admitted.

"What kind of things?"

Hawk rose from the sofa and crossed to the kitchen in response to the whistling kettle. He dug through the cupboards until he found coffee. He held the jar up. "Want some?"

River nodded, pretending to concentrate on building the fire.

Hawk dropped a teaspoon of the freeze-dried crystals into two mugs, then filled them with the steaming water. The aromatic scent drifted to River and her mouth watered.

She stood, brushing debris from the knees of her jeans. She glanced around for the matches. "It's Nick again, isn't it? How is it possible that he's in there when you're awake?" Not that she didn't *believe* it was possible. She did. She just didn't know how Nick was doing it. Reaching up, she grabbed the matches from the mantel, lit one, and held it to the newspaper. Once it flared, she straightened.

He was behind her now. She spun to face him.

"I'm done, River." She could hear the exhaustion in his voice, see it creased in the corners of his red-rimmed eyes. He cupped her elbows, pulling her against his chest. "It could be Nick, it could be my body deteriorating, or it could be my mind shorting out from exhaustion. If I don't get some sleep, this body will die. Not even magic can keep it running forever. If I do get some sleep, I might lose my mind. I can't protect you like this." He rested his chin on the top of her head. "Once this is over, no matter what the outcome with your parents, do you really promise to come with me? Because if you aren't going to be safe, none of this is worth it to me."

River disliked the assumption that she couldn't look after herself. She had done so for most of her life. But she was half Guardian as well and she understood his concern for her, because right now, she was so worried about him she would promise him anything.

"You could go now, without me, and once you've recovered your body, you can come back."

He shook his head. "What if my body is dying? What if I don't get the chance to tell anyone about you and your parents? I think I know now what's been happening to the Fae souls. The Great Lords need to be told, if not by me, then by you."

River drew her bottom lip between her teeth. He was asking her to walk away from her brothers and all that she loved. This was her world, and it always would be. But she'd made him a promise.

She wanted one in return.

"This is my home." She waved her hand around and held her ground. "If the Fae save worlds, then I want them to help save mine. I don't want my world defused. I don't want it stripped of technology. We've only now begun to recover, and without technology we'll die.

Still holding onto one of her elbows, he scrubbed his hand over his chin. "I can't guarantee that."

She stepped back, carefully extracting herself from his fingers. Hot anger flared. He thought her home wasn't worth saving. "Why not?"

He drew a breath and let it escape. "Your parents were sent here already to help save this world, and they never came back. When the Great Lords find out what's happened to them, more important, to your mother's soul, there will be no help for it."

She studied his face. "Do you think we can't be saved?"

"There is no *we*, River. This isn't your world. And it doesn't matter what I think." He reached for her but she stepped away. His hands dropped to his sides and shutters fell over his eyes. "My job is to report the facts. My opinion on them won't count."

River felt as if her world was on a collision course with the sun and she could do nothing but stand by and watch. "I see." She sank to her knees in front of the fire and poked at the kindling with one of the tongs. "The Guardians and the Fae are going to stand back and allow my world to slowly die."

"Stripping a world of technology isn't necessarily a death sentence. Most do recover," he said. "Given time."

But without technology, what would River have to offer it?

As he spoke, River threw a heavy piece of hard-wood onto the burning fire, and it flared so hot and high the heat sent her scurrying backward in surprise. The faint scent of sage lingered in the air.

Hawk's lips turned up at the corners. "You might want to learn to control your temper," he advised. "Growing plants isn't so bad. Playing with fire is a lot more dangerous."

"Both have their uses." She stood and brushed off her hands. Sidestepping Hawk, she walked to the kitchen and picked up her coffee. She would go back with him because she wanted to see that he was safe, too. She also wanted the chance to plead her case for her world.

She was about to tell him so. But when she turned to do so, he was on the floor, holding his head between his palms.

Their argument was immediately forgotten.

Her coffee cup crashed to the floor and within seconds she was kneeling before him. She took in his pained expression and the odd way he was looking at her, but she knew he was seeing something else.

What was going on inside his head?

She placed her hands over his. "Hawk, can you hear me?"

His eyes glazed over and his face paled. That was the extent of his response.

River didn't hesitate. She kept her hands over his to help create the connection. Closing her eyes, she let loose a little magic and exhaled slowly.

When she opened her eyes she was no longer inside the cabin, she was inside Hawk's head. She could see what he saw—her on her knees before Nick, her head bobbing back and forth.

Very nice, Nick. You bastard.

She didn't know why Hawk was upset. She was the one with the right to be angry. And she was pissed.

Hawk's voice was calm. "I'm going to kill him."

Take a number.

But as River got over the first heat of anger, she tried to remember that in reality, this was Nick's head they were in and that they were the trespassers.

"This isn't real. You're sitting with me on the floor of a cabin." She took Hawk's hand and ran it over the bearskin. "Feel that?"

His hand left the bearskin rug and settled on her leg. "I also feel you. You're sitting beside me."

As Hawk struggled to ground himself back in reality, River tried hard to think of a way to put a stop to this. Somehow, Nick had managed to tap into his brain. That meant he had some sort of connection to his body.

If River followed the connection . . .

It was far easier than she'd expected. There he was.

Nick lounged on a sofa, his legs stretched out in front of him. He had a crooked grin on his face as he, too, stared at the slow, sensual movements of River on her knees before him.

"We all know your dick isn't that big," she said to him.

His head swiveled around in surprise. "River?" He quickly recovered. "Do you like the show?" he asked her, sounding quite pleased. "All that medical research on the parts of the brain really paid off. This is almost as good as the video game. But not quite." His feet hit the floor and he leaned forward. "At least in the game, some jerkwad wasn't wearing my skin."

She could understand why he'd be angry. That didn't make her any less so.

"Nice trick," she congratulated him. *Bastard*. "But to be fair, we thought you were dead."

"I suppose I am," he admitted. "Believe me, it's overrated."

She wondered what it would take to get him to leave Hawk alone.

The answer was simple. Nick had one true love, and that was himself. "You should be dead. You were shot in the chest at close range," she pointed out. "You're a medic. You know what that means. No one took anything from you. You were already gone from your body before Hawk ever stepped in."

"So how come my body survived?" he demanded. "You'd save it for him but you wouldn't for me?"

That hurt her as much as he'd intended it to. It also surprised her. He cared more than she'd thought. "I didn't know how," she replied. He made a soft sound of disbelief. She tried to think what to offer him that wouldn't harm Hawk. "This is only temporary. What if I can give your body back to you?"

"Okay, do it. Give it to me."

Although she was angry, the hope in his eyes hurt her heart. "I can't do it just yet," she said. "I need Hawk's help for a little while longer. As soon as we're through though, I promise, I'll make everything right for you." She hoped she could do so. She thought she could.

He leaned back on the sofa, resting one foot on the opposite knee. He jiggled his knee up and down. "Here's the thing. I don't want to wait. That body is mine. And I don't trust him with it."

"You don't have to trust him. You have to trust me," River pointed out.

"While I appreciate the offer, I've made a new friend who's as anxious to get back into the real world as I am. Maybe more so. He keeps ranting on about virtual prisons and being a mighty Dark Lord." Nick ran one hand up and down the arm of the sofa, idly watching the track of his fingers and avoiding her eyes. "He hates your Guardian far more than I do."

A cold shiver tickled its way up and down River's spine. "You don't want to mess with a Dark Lord," she warned him. She wondered if the Dark Lord could possibly touch her, too, then decided he couldn't. She no longer owed him anything. But the last thing the world needed was a Dark Lord set loose on it again. It was damaged enough. "If you owe him a favor, he owns your soul."

"I have no problem with that. I can live without a soul. A body seems to be the deal maker. Besides." He hooked his eyes onto hers. "I'm well past believing you. I took a bullet for you and you've been fucking that guy."

The hurt on his face that he tried to disguise caught her off guard because she hadn't thought she was all that important to him.

Then a few more pieces of the puzzle began falling in place, and memories of their last few moments together began to crystallize into something she hadn't wanted to consider because she genuinely liked him.

"Wasn't it you who set me up for that bullet?" she shot back, putting it out there to gauge his response.

Again, she saw a flash of hurt on his face. "I looked out for you the best that I could."

He was a sorry excuse for a human being. He'd cheated on her, and he was chipping away at Hawk's sanity with intimate images of her that anyone with an ounce of decency would want to keep private.

But he cared about her in his own selfish way, and she believed him when he said he'd done his best.

He also knew a lot more about what was happening than she'd thought. "Who is Kaye?" she asked, trying to find out what she could. "And how do you know him?"

But Hawk, still physically next to her, chose that

moment to go into convulsions and alarmed, she severed the connection with Nick.

The abrupt disconnection left her disoriented.

She was no longer in Hawk's head, although she still touched his soul. She wrapped her arms around him, letting energy flow from her soul to his, and as she let loose her healing magic Hawk groaned, his soul grasping greedily onto it.

River continued to offer herself to him and Hawk continued to take. Light-headed now, she tried to ease back, not wanting to sever the connection but needing to slow down the drain on her magic.

"Hawk, please," she said, her tongue growing thick, her body turning to ice. Her lids fluttered and she no longer had the energy to keep them open.

He continued to draw from her, taking what he needed to refuel his body, until she could no longer think clearly.

Then Hawk's hands were on her shoulders, his fingers biting into her skin as he gave her a gentle shake. She felt as if she was watching a movie at half speed. Everything was happening in slow motion.

"Crisos. *River.* What have I done?" His voice echoed as if from the far end of a long tunnel. He tapped her cheek. "River, wake up."

The command in his tone brought out the Fae in her soul. She tried to speak, to tell him it was okay, that she was only going to sleep for a little while, but the words wouldn't come. They were clogged somewhere in the back of her throat.

At first, she thought she was floating. Then she realized Hawk was lifting her from his lap, his fingertips at her throat as if checking for a pulse. He carried her closer to the fire and placed her gently on the rug, warm palms creating friction and heat as he loosened her clothes and rubbed her bare skin. Then he covered her body with his.

He pressed his lips to hers. With the soft blade of his tongue he parted her lips and slipped inside. When she opened for him, he kissed her deeply, almost frantically. "Stay with me."

His tongue slashed against the sides of her mouth with hunger and possession as his hands traced the pattern of her body with intimate recognition.

She shifted beneath him, absorbing the energy his seduction created, and tangled her tongue with his. His heat scorched her body and she moved restlessly beneath him. As her internal temperature rose she drew a deep breath and inflated her lungs, then let it out slowly.

"That's it," he whispered into her mouth, relief lingering beneath his words. He grabbed her arm and placed it on the side of his face. "I want you to touch me, *mellita*. Show me you're okay. Show me you know who I am."

He kissed her again as she traced her fingers over his face, reveling in the feel of the rough growth on his cheek. It tickled her fingers, arousing the woman in her. Warmth began brewing in her stomach, her blood moving quicker through her veins and igniting a fire. As her lower region heated, her hunger for Hawk grew to new levels.

She slipped her hand around his head, and as her nipples responded to his touch, she held his mouth to hers. His breathing became heavy, his hands gripping her shirt with urgent need. Without bothering to undo the buttons he tore the material from her body. The plastic buttons popped free and fell to the floor, clattering across the wood as Hawk bared her breasts.

"So beautiful." The heat of his mouth washed over her skin, sending her body into quivers of delight.

He eased his mouth from hers and brought his lips to the soft hollow of her throat. As he kissed a sensitive spot, her lids slowly inched open.

He lifted his head, his eyes moving over her face with tender concern, his tension palpable. Genuine concern clouded his eyes.

She raked her fingers though his hair. "Are you okay?"

He closed his eyes for a second, his body slightly relaxing on top of hers as he pinned her to the floor. "I'm fine." Brushing her hair from her face, he shifted his body weight and whispered, "No, I'm not. I didn't know it would be so hard to stop." He held up one hand and examined it, frowning. "I don't know how that happened. I'd never do anything to harm you," he added. "You know that, don't you?"

"Of course I do," she replied, hurt that he needed to ask. His eyes locked on hers, an uncertainty in them that immediately dispelled the sting of his words.

They had a connection between them. Most of the time he tried to ignore its existence. He kept her shut out. But if she truly wanted in, there was little he could do to stop her. After all, she had not been able to stop him. She hadn't wanted to try.

"Let me show you an easier way to take magic from me that we both can share," she said.

He gasped as he, too, felt the warmth of their souls when they merged into one. River grabbed his hand and placed it over her breast, the desire for a physical connection now equally as strong.

His eyes darkened. He ran his thumb over her nipple and gave it a light pinch. She could feel the tension drain from him as he smiled at her.

"I think you should," he agreed, his voice loaded with promise. With that he lowered his head and made a slow, skilled pass with his tongue. Her body flushed hotter and her breasts grew heavy as he took possession of one and greedily drew her nipple into his warm mouth. He stroked her pink bud with his wet tongue, circling around her peak until it hardened beneath his careful attention.

Embraced in his arms he continued to seduce her senses, scorching her body with the skilled blade of his tongue. River whimpered and arched her back, making no qualms about what she wanted, or what she needed.

As desire singed her blood and her sex fluttered, she gripped the tail of Hawk's shirt and tugged. His lips twitched as he pushed back from her, resting on his heels, and tore it from his body. A moment later he climbed to his feet and River's body grew needy as he loomed over her. Using hurried movements, he quickly removed the rest of his clothes.

Once naked, he turned his attention to her and she quivered all over. As sexual energy rippled in the air, he dropped back to the carpet and positioned himself between her legs. Deft hands swiftly released the button on her jeans, the hiss of her zipper cutting through the silence as he released it.

River wiggled restlessly, encouraging him to hurry. Instead he grinned, and slowly lowered her tight jeans down her legs and tossed them onto his. Her panties came next. He twirled the scrap of lace between his fingers before sliding them over her legs. As he added them to the pile of discarded clothing she lay before him, completely naked, and completely his.

He paused to look at her, his breath coming in a slow, labored rush. Dark scalding eyes locked on hers and she could feel his raw hunger reach out to her. As she watched his every movement in the firelight, her heart pounded harder and harder against her chest with the knowledge he was a part of her, and she a part of him.

As his primal essence completely overwhelmed her, she crooked her index finger and beckoned him close. He groaned out loud as he flattened himself along the length of her body. His hand brushed over her curves intimately, and River widened her legs to accommodate him.

His mouth found hers and he kissed her hard and deep as he settled between her legs. His lips left her mouth and moved to her ear. "You scared me, River," he murmured into her ear as he breached her opening.

She breathed in his earthy scent and said, "Nothing is going to happen to me, Hawk. Not as long as we're together."

The trouble was, neither of them could say for certain how much longer that might be. When he tensed, she leaned up and kissed him. She wrapped her arms around his shoulders and held him tight, wanting to make every moment together count in case they were suddenly parted.

As he entered her body, offering her an inch at a time, she bit back a breathy moan and closed her eyes against the flood of heat and sensations rocketing through her. It felt so good to be touched by him.

Hawk pounded into her, faster and faster, until it was impossible to tell where her body ended and his began.

Soon her body began trembling, her sex convulsing, and her moans of ecstasy echoed through the cabin.

Attuned to her needs, Hawk pushed deep, long strokes that finally pushed her over the edge. She gripped his back and let herself tumble into orgasm. Hawk drove into her one last time, arching his spine on a moan as release overcame him.

Perspiration melded their bodies together. The fire crackled and flared, removing the last lingering bits of chill from the room. River ran her hands through his hair and he inched back to admire the satisfaction on her face, his gaze stilling when he met her eyes.

She smiled at him and even though his touch filled her soul with warmth, a shiver moved through her.

One way or another, whether on this world or his, they were going to be separated. And River already knew, deep in her heart, that the life he wanted for her was not the one she would have chosen for herself.

CHAPTER **SIXTEEN**

♦

Nick really knew how to choose his friends.

Hawk, wearing nothing but boxers and not bothered by the cold, puttered around in the kitchenette. It wasn't so much that the cold didn't bother him. It was more that he enjoyed causing discomfort to Nick's body.

He'd hoped he'd been dreaming the first time Nick and the Dark Lord had attacked him, back on the mountain, but after talking to River last night, now he knew differently.

Nick wanted his body back badly enough for the Dark Lord to snag onto him. This presented yet another complication.

Hawk would not be responsible for the return of a Dark Lord, not even indirectly. Therefore, once River's parents were freed and Hawk could relinquish this body, Nick was going to take a flying leap off a steep cliff. The trick would be in making certain that River never found out what he'd done.

She stood by the window looking out at the lake. Earlier that morning she'd found an old sweater in the bedroom. Now she tightened the woolen wrap around her waist as she smiled over at him, the dying embers of the fire crackling in the hearth and making her skin glow.

They'd spent the night making love. A knot lodged in his throat and he tried to swallow it as he worked to convince himself everything would be okay, that they'd both needed the energy.

That was his justification for their actions. He dropped two pieces of bread into the toaster. It had certainly worked for him. He felt better this morning than he had in a long time.

Which meant the crash and burn was going to be spectacular.

Hawk carried coffee and toast into the main room. He lowered himself onto the floor and patted the space on the rug next to him. After she joined him, sinking gracefully onto her knees, he carefully pulled the coffee table closer with his foot.

He slid a mug across the wooden top until it was in front of her. "Sorry. The sugar is gone."

"That's okay." She took a sip, made a face, then her mug clunked as she set it back on the table.

Hawk's gaze moved over her. "Are you warm enough?"

"You're the one who doesn't have a shirt on."

He wanted to make another smartass comment about Nick and his body, but considering what he had planned for him, it was probably best to avoid the subject altogether. He handed her a piece of toast instead and she bit into it. When it crumbled in her mouth, she made a face. "No sugar in the coffee is one thing, but really. Dry toast?"

He smiled at her. "No butter either."

"Yum."

"It's better for you this way."

"That's a matter of opinion."

Hawk rested his elbow on the sofa and twined a finger through her hair. When she turned to face him, he grinned at her and stated, "It's not an opinion, it's a fact."

She didn't smile at him in return as he'd hoped she would. She wasn't her normal self this morning, and he finally had to accept a truth he'd tried hard to avoid. She didn't want to leave this world. She'd only said yes because of him.

She also thought the Guardians would sit back and allow her world to destroy itself.

Guilt weighed heavily on his conscience.

"Maybe someday I can show you my world," he said, tugging on the lock of silky dark hair wrapped around his finger.

She did smile then, briefly, although he could see her heart wasn't in it. "I'm sure it's amazing."

Compared to this world, which had barely begun to rebuild from disaster, his was a paradise. Only the world of the Fae could surpass it.

This might not be the best time to mention that.

He told her a bit about his world. He spoke of the cities, and of the university where he'd studied. He told her of the rivers and valleys, and of swimming at night by the light of the triple red moons. She listened attentively, but a part of her was somewhere else.

If he'd learned anything from married life, it was that the question he was about to ask her was always the opener to a conversation no one really wanted to have.

He asked it anyway. "What are you thinking?"

"I'm thinking about my brothers."

Of course she would be. She'd most likely never see them again. They might not be her biological brothers, but that didn't mean she loved them any less.

"Jake will look after Sam," Hawk said. He didn't know what else to say other than that. River was his primary concern. He wanted to say he would check on them for her, or that maybe she would be able to do so at some point in the future, but he didn't want to lie.

A knock on the front door made them both turn their heads. Peters' voice rang out from the other side. "It's me. Open up."

Hawk had begun to wonder if the cop would ever return. He hadn't been bothered by the prospect of him not doing so other than that time was running out, at least for Hawk.

Hawk ran his fingers through River's hair, cupping the back of her head and drawing her mouth to his for a quick kiss of reassurance. She tasted like coffee and unsweetened cinnamon. He wished he could tell her everything would be fine.

"You two okay in there?" Peters called.

River never took her eyes off of Hawk as he pulled back to answer. "Fine. Just give us a second."

Hawk went to the door while River gathered the mugs and the plates and took everything back to the sink in the kitchenette. Hawk could hear the tap running as she rinsed them.

Peters stepped inside, followed by a cold blast of air that foreshadowed rain.

"You were gone a long time," Hawk said.

Peters held up a large travel bag. "I told you. I had some shopping to do."

The bag contained winter gear for River. "I swung by her apartment," he said. "Where we're headed, she's going to need heavier shoes and a thicker coat."

The cop's thoughtfulness went a long way toward dispelling Hawk's lingering suspicions. If he planned to harm her, would he be so considerate of her comfort?

A gentler side didn't appear to be something Peters enjoyed displaying. "We need to do some planning, and we can't do it with that fucking Were around. I left him outside in the car with the radio on."

River came back from the kitchenette and sat on the sofa. Hawk stood by the window while Peters remained at the door to keep an eye on his car.

"The Were has a tracking device embedded in his skull," Peters began.

And Peters had brought him straight to them.

"That will make it easier for his handlers to retrieve his body from the bottom of the lake," Hawk replied. River let out a small gasp of dismay.

"Not so fast." Peters regarded him coldly. "You need to think this through. It won't take long for his *handlers* to know exactly where he's headed, but they won't know who's with him. Ten to one says they'll show up asap to find out who it is and what they're after, so once we get to the lab, I'll take the Were and head straight in. You two can circle around and approach from a different direction. They'll be tracking the Were. You'll be off the radar."

"The place is surrounded by cameras," River said.

Suspicion darkened Peters' expression. "How do you know that?"

Hawk interceded before she could try to explain. "Because it only makes sense they would have surveillance. They've gone to a lot of trouble to keep its location a secret."

Peters wasn't 100 percent satisfied, but he let it go. Hawk got the distinct impression he really didn't want an answer anyway.

"Andy is supposed to meet River inside the grounds near an inner fence. She said River would be able to find the place she means." River nodded when Peters looked at her for confirmation, then he continued. "Once you and Andy do whatever it is you need to do, you should run like hell." His eyes glittered with grim determination. "I'm blowing the shit out of the place and I'm not likely to get a second chance at it, so it's going to be good."

More than anything, Hawk loved a good explosion. "What are you using?" he asked.

"Two M32 grenade launchers and about fifty pounds of C4. I've also got a couple of MK16s. Hope you're feeling energetic," Peters added, "because you're carrying half of it. The Were is strong, but I wouldn't trust that bastard with a flare gun." He looked at River. "The MK16s are light. You can carry those."

Peters had been shopping for a great deal more than clothes. "The police in your town seem to have quite the range of weapons experience," Hawk said.

Peters shrugged, although the movement was far

from casual. "You seem to forget the times that we're living in. If you can't beat 'em, join 'em. Gun laws are a thing of the past. So are a lot of other things."

"You both seem to forget there's a Were waiting outside," River interrupted. They turned to look at her. Worry lines etched the corners of her full mouth. "I think we all know what happens when he's left unattended for too long."

Traveling with the animal that had killed her friends wasn't going to be easy for River. Hawk had to be careful not to forget that.

"You're going to blow up the lab with C4 and grenades," Hawk prompted, bringing the conversation back on track so they could be on their way and get this over with. He didn't give a damn what happened afterward. He and River would be gone. "I'm not sure fifty pounds will be enough."

"If it's planted properly I can make it enough," Peters replied. "The only problem with the C4 is that I don't have a detonator. I need extreme heat and a shock wave. I was hoping to find something inside the lab that might work."

"I can detonate it," River said.

Hawk read the disbelief on Peters' face. River, sitting cross-legged on the sofa with her slim build and large, almond-shaped blue eyes, gave off the appearance of delicate, childlike innocence, not a weapon of mass destruction. Hawk, however, had seen her in action and had the scorch marks to prove it. Fifty pounds of C4 should be plenty.

"She can, indeed," Hawk assured Peters, allowing

himself a small grin of anticipation at the prospect. "You're the one who should be prepared to run like hell."

Their plan was seriously lacking in detail, but without knowing what was waiting for them, there wasn't much they could do about it. Hawk rubbed his forehead, then stopped when he realized River was watching him.

"That's it, then," Peters said finally, his hand on the door. It groaned on dry hinges as he opened it. "Get dressed. We're leaving in five minutes."

As Hawk pulled on his clothes and laced up his boots, he tried not to think about the fact that their plan was lacking one major detail in particular.

Escape.

They left the cabin with half a minute to spare.

They were traveling in style, apparently. Hawk recognized the piece-of-shit Buick from the truck stop parking lot. He was glad not to be stuck in the back of the police cruiser again.

The Were was waiting with Peters in the front seat of the car.

"This is Bane," Peters said through the rolled-down window.

"Hey Nick," Bane greeted him. "We already know each other," he added to Peters. "We go way back."

Hawk decided he might volunteer to set some of that C4 himself. Throwing Nick's body off a cliff was too kind. Blowing the bastard into a million little pieces would guarantee he stayed dead.

He was conscious of River beside him, her tension

so thick he could taste it. He didn't offer her any comfort, or do anything to draw added attention to her, because the Were could sense it as well. Hawk could see the awareness of it in his eyes. He could also see that the Were enjoyed River's distress, and that it brought out the predator in him.

Hawk took the seat behind Bane. If he so much as twitched the wrong way, Hawk was going to ram the blade of his knife into the fucker's throat.

River edged closer and slid her hand into his. Warmth spread through him from his palms to his toes. He squeezed her fingers.

The Were flipped on the radio. They caught the tail end of something loud by a metal band from the turn of the century. Then the news came on.

Coming just days after the deaths of three young video game designers, there has been yet another murder in the city. Premier George Johnson, in town on undisclosed business, was found shot to death early this morning in a downtown hotel room. Police are releasing few details at this time. The investigation con—

Peters reached over and turned the radio off.

Hawk stared out the window and realized they had left the river valley and were heading into the mountains. They hadn't met another car for miles, although he'd already noticed that traffic was seriously light at the best of times.

He also realized he'd blanked out again. Peters had

said something to him that he hadn't caught, and River was looking at him. He hated the fact that she was worried about him.

"Are you okay?" she whispered.

He scanned the road ahead. "I'm fine. Just thinking."

Peters' eyes met his in the rearview mirror. Hawk went back to staring at the scenery. They turned onto a road with a wooden construction sawhorse blocking the way. The orange sign nailed to it said Road Closed. Hawk got out and moved the sawhorse, then dragged it back into place once Peters drove past it.

The rain in the valley turned to snow in the mountains. It dusted the landscape in a cleansing layer of white, and Bane rolled his window down.

River spotted a herd of deer on the side of the road. "Hawk, look."

She'd called him Hawk, not Nick. Hawk turned to take in the animals as River, too, realized her slip. She glanced at Peters, who was studying them both in the mirror. Something flashed in the cop's eyes before he looked away, confirming for Hawk that there were, indeed, things he'd rather not know.

Fair enough. Hawk didn't need to know why Peters had turned off the radio at the news some politician was dead either.

The deer flashed their white tails before darting off into the woods. "Nature's beauty," River murmured. "Like the mountains."

Already, she sounded homesick. But it wouldn't be long before the Fae world became home to her.

That thought didn't exactly cheer Hawk.

Bane inhaled deep, then growled low. "More like nature's dinner," he said and turned his head to face Peters. He licked his lips and offered Peters a look of pure, feral hunger. "Why don't you stop the car for a minute and let me out for a run?"

Peters struck him on the side of the head with the heel of his hand. "Roll your window up."

Sullen, Bane did as he was told.

Hawk didn't miss the way River kept shooting curious glances at the Were when she thought no one was paying attention. He thought he knew what she was thinking. She was wondering how this seemingly normal-looking person had done what he had to her friends.

"I'm a handsome guy," Bane said without turning around.

That startled her. "Sorry?"

"That's why you keep staring at me. Because I'm such a great-looking guy."

Hawk's fingers itched toward the knife in his pocket, but before he could make up his mind, Bane tapped a finger on the windshield. "Pull over," he said to Peters. "Right there. That's where we get out. The buried explosives start around the next bend in the road. You have to know where to get in."

They got out of the car. Hawk, curious, walked around the bend to see what was ahead.

A huge crater filled the space where pavement used to be. Blackened boulders, scattered rocks, and chunks of twisted steel littered the highway and shoulders of the road. Most of the dirt and loose debris had long ago been swept away by the wind and the weather. Nearby, the burned-out shell of a car teetered upside down on its roof, creaking in the wind.

"Huh," Hawk said, at a loss for words. At least this would slow down any pursuit.

"There were three people in that car," River said from behind him. Too late, he remembered her ability to feel the empty spaces left by souls.

He turned her around, and placing his hand on her back, gave her a gentle push. "Let's go."

Peters was unloading the trunk of the Buick, steadfastly ignoring the Were's complaints that he wasn't allowed to carry a weapon. Hawk handed the MK16s to River, along with some of the rounds of ammunition. Those were considerably heavier, but there was little he could do about that. Much as he'd like to, he couldn't carry it all. He shouldered the pack with half of the C4. He knew she was stronger than she looked.

There was no actual path. They had to rely on the Were to lead them, something that did not make Hawk feel at all good.

After an hour of steady climbing he was breathing hard. After two, he was ready to lie down and die. He wished he could blame it entirely on Nick's lack of physical fitness, but knew that wasn't true.

Peters was faring no better. Hawk hated that. It meant that neither one of them was capable of defending River if the Were decided to turn on her.

When they crested yet another ridge, Bane stopped abruptly and sniffed at the air.

What is it?" River asked him.

Dark eyes turned to her. "We're here."

Hawk stepped up beside him and looked at the valley below. It looked much the same as it had in the game.

River moved in close to him and stood stock still as they looked out over the lab and the overgrown graveyard slumbering at the back of the building.

"A lot more than three souls went missing from that place," she whispered, a catch in her voice.

CHAPTER **SEVENTEEN**

♦

It started to snow harder, fat flakes at first that drifted lazily, soon turning into wind-driven pellets of ice.

Hawk slung an arm around River's shoulders as she stood in silence, staring at the valley below them. Her blue eyes carefully assessed the layout of the laboratory slumbering at the base of the mountain.

She was looking for the graveyard.

Hawk, too, surveyed the landscape, although he was more interested in how they'd get inside the fence that surrounded the lab. Anticipation helped him forget the aches and pains from the long uphill hike. He was another step closer to home.

Hawk felt River tighten beneath his arm, her shoulders hitching upward against the cold, and his heart twisted. She was looking at the place where her parents had suffered for almost three decades. She'd seen their suffering firsthand only a few short days ago, and a few days before that, she'd felt it while still in her game. This had to be hard for her, and he didn't know how to make it right.

From the beginning he'd tried to protect her, but the truth was that she could look after herself. She'd survived a battering from the Dark Lord while trapped in her video game. She'd survived the truth of her heritage, her magic, and the death of her friends. She'd witnessed the dark side of humanity, yet she continued to believe in the good, not in the bad.

If anything happened to her now, he'd never forgive himself. It had nothing to do with her being Fae. It had everything to do with how much he loved her.

There was an attraction between them that he knew she felt as well, but he was thankful she didn't love him, too. She had never known him, not as himself. He could stand it if only he suffered loss when they were forced to part. He couldn't stand it if she were hurt by it, too.

Ignoring the others, he worked to steady his heart rate as he asked her, "You okay?"

"This place gives me the creeps." River's hand went to her stomach. "It's like a black hole is sucking the life from me."

The description was more accurate than she probably realized. It worried him. She'd likened the absence of souls in the subway station to a black hole.

Hawk thought about the black hole she now sensed and what it meant. His mouth went dry and he reached out and braced his hand on the nearest redwood tree.

He'd blanked out again.

"Hawk?" She sounded more anxious now, twisting to look up at him rather than into the valley.

He blinked, trying to clear his blurred vision. She had enough to occupy her mind as it was. He didn't want her to see him like this and he didn't want her to worry.

The sun was well into decline and the snow was falling more heavily. They needed to hurry.

Peters cleared his throat. He was watching Hawk, and it was obvious he knew something wasn't quite right with him. He didn't mention it.

"The Were and I will go in the front gate," Peters said instead. "You two can circle around and come in from the other side."

Since this had been their plan all along, Hawk wondered why he needed to repeat it.

"No way," interrupted the Were. His animal scent was exceptionally strong tonight, enhanced by the dampness of melting snow on his face and hair. Fear shone from the whites of his eyes. That didn't bode well. "I came this far. And this is as far as I go."

He bolted for the woods, disappearing into a swirl of white snow. Hawk grabbed for one of the MK16s, intending to shoot him down.

Peters gripped the barrel of the gun to stop him.

"Let him go," he said. "It doesn't change anything, other than that they won't be able to track me now. That gives me a bit more freedom to move around inside." He patted the pack of C4 he carried.

Hawk lowered the weapon, then slowly slung it over his shoulder. Peters had known all along that the Were would run. He supposed Peters was right. Whoever was tracking the Were already knew where they were. It wouldn't be long before they showed up to uncover their identities as well.

At least now, he and River wouldn't have to waste time circling the grounds. And the snow would slow down whoever was tracking them.

Climbing off the bluff and into the valley was no easy effort either, made more difficult by the slickness of the snow on the rocky terrain.

By the time they reached the fence, darkness had fully descended and the snow had whipped into an actual storm.

Hawk scanned the building, counting the security cameras as best he could. It didn't really matter who saw them now, although the snow would make it difficult for anyone to tell who they were.

"Can you get us over the fence?" Hawk asked River.

She nodded and Hawk stepped back to give her room, pulling Peters with him. River concentrated, and within seconds, a young sapling had morphed into a full grown tree that draped over the top of the fence.

"Jesus," breathed Peters, then collected himself with a shake of his head. "That takes some getting used to."

Once they were on the other side of the fence, Peters took the pack of C4 from Hawk and handed one of the grenade launchers to him. Hawk took one of the MK16s from River but left her the other.

Peters showed Hawk how to rewind and load the grenade launcher. The cylinder didn't pop out, so the grenades had to be dropped into the chambers one at a time.

"Here's the safety switch, above the pistol grip," he said, tapping it with his finger. "Keep it on, no matter what, until you're ready to use it. That way if you drop it, it can't go off by accident."

"Where's Andy?" Hawk asked.

Peters lifted his shoulders. "I have no idea. She said she'd be here."

And the cop had believed her. Hawk's lips thinned. Funny. He hadn't seemed stupid, at least not until now.

"We might as well get out of this storm and wait inside the building to see if she shows up." Hawk had to admit, he really wanted to get a look at what the lab contained.

Whatever it was, it had cost a Fae and a Guardian their lives.

"She'll show up," River said. "I want to wait near the fence, like she asked."

"She didn't know there would be a storm," Peters pointed out. He looked at the sky. "The weather is going to slow everyone down. We can watch for her from inside."

River still looked uncertain, so Hawk seized her hand and left her no choice.

They ran to the front of the building. The doors were made of thick steel. They were also locked.

"Stand back," Peters said.

Hawk shielded River with his body, covering her head and her ears as Peters took aim with his grenade launcher. He chose the door frame, not the doors themselves, as his target.

When the smoke and dust cleared and Hawk's ears stopped ringing, he saw that the doors had buckled inward as a single unit, blown off the hinges on one side. Brick and mortar around the frame had given way, leaving barely enough space for them to enter.

Peters went through first, then River. Hawk took up the rear.

The building was dark inside except for the faint glow of the emergency lights.

A hulking man beast, more machine than mammal, peeled out of the shadows, gun cocked and aimed point blank at River. Lightning fast, River grabbed an MK16 by the barrel and swung the butt of it against the creature's head. It staggered backward, stunned by the unexpected assault.

Hawk's military training kicked in. Propping his MK16 on one hip, adrenaline pumping, he sprayed the bioengineered monstrosity with gunfire.

Two more closed in on River, coming at her from opposite angles. She clutched the assault rifle in her hands like a club, ready to swing again.

"Peters, your left!" Hawk shouted, protective instincts kicking into full force as he took down the beast approaching her from the right.

Peters dropped the grenade launcher and drew his service revolver in a smooth motion. A single shot to the head, execution style, took care of the third.

"Are there any more?" River asked as the echoes of gunfire died away.

"Why? Are you planning to beat them to death?" Hawk pried the rifle from her fingers and handed it to Peters, who stooped and retrieved the grenade launcher he'd dropped. Hawk crooked his elbow around River's neck and drew her in close to kiss the top of her head. "Tell you what. If anything else needs its ass kicked, it's yours."

"The only thing needing its ass kicked right now is you."

River sounded totally put out with him, and it made him grin. She wasn't a killer. He'd known that already. But she'd really nailed that thing, whatever it was, with the butt of the rifle.

He stooped for a closer look at it, and his heart sank. It was much the same as what Jake had shown him in the cave in the woods. How these things had managed to survive here on their own, he didn't care to think about.

"Could you people possibly make any more noise?"

Hawk turned, and Andy was standing directly behind him. He could smell the magic on her, and it put him on the defensive.

She pushed back the hood of her fur-lined parka and with a cry of welcome, River started toward her.

Hawk caught River's arm to hold her back.

"That's going to take some getting used to as well," Peters muttered under his breath. Hawk assumed he meant Andy's unusual method of travel. Peters had been facing in that direction.

Through the broken doors, the purr of an engine could be heard over the howl of the wind.

Everyone tensed.

"If you want to start planting the C4," Hawk said to Peters, passing him the pack of explosives he carried, "I'll hold them off."

"This isn't why we came here," River protested. Hawk read the beginnings of panic in her eyes, and knew she wasn't going to be put off any longer. "My parents come first."

"The C4 can wait," Peters said to Hawk. "I'll hold them off. But whatever you're going to do, do it fast." He looked at the dead creatures and shuddered. "Weres are bad enough. I don't want any more of these ugly bastards sneaking up behind me."

"Thank you," River said to him, her gratitude genuine, and Peters' harsh expression softened. He positioned himself by the doors.

"Follow me," Andy said to River and Hawk.

She led them down a long corridor. Hawk would have liked to stop to examine some of the rooms, but neither woman slowed her pace and he'd be damned if he let Andy have any more time with River alone.

They reached another set of steel doors at the far end of the corridor. Andy paused with her hand on the bar that opened the doors. She frowned, a knot of worry between her brows.

To Hawk, that wasn't a good sign.

"Your mother can be overprotective," Andy began, and Hawk's few remaining hopes took another nosedive. Things weren't going to go well. He'd expected this, so he didn't know why he should feel so surprised.

The grenade-launcher strap shifted and the weapon slipped off his shoulder. It distracted him for less than a second, but it was all the time River needed.

"I'll go first," she announced. She brushed past Andy and pushed on the doors. The tips of Hawk's fingers skimmed the back of her jacket, unable to make purchase and closing on empty air as the doors swung open and River stepped through them.

A thick wall of green sprang up in her wake.

Andy clapped a hand to her mouth in dismay. "That wasn't supposed to happen."

Of course not. The Wizard had everything so carefully planned.

Hawk wondered if he could shoot his way through the tangle of vines without hitting River by accident on the other side.

"Is there a reason why you can't simply strike up a normal conversation with a person when you want them to know something?" he asked her, although he was mindful of the fact that the last time he'd argued with her, she'd melted his gun. But this wasn't a game, and this time, his gun was real.

Melt that, bitch.

"Because I want only one person to know it, not the entire universe," she said, impatience with him making her sharp. To give her credit, she looked as frantic as he felt. "I need to get in there," she added. "River can convince her mother to let go of this world, but I'm the only one who can untie her magic from it."

"Can't you use your magic and blast your way in?"

Apparently not, because if she could blast anything, the look she gave him would have turned him to a lump of charcoal. "I used the last of my magic to get here."

"You're a Dark Lord." Hawk's spine turned to a sliver of ice. He'd thought so all along, but to have it confirmed turned a thought to a reality. The reality was scarier than shit. He frowned. "But Dark Lords are male."

"Dark Lords are nothing but Guardian imagination," she said dismissively. "Magic is magic. How the possessor uses it is what makes them who they are. I'm an immortal. That doesn't make me inherently evil."

Hawk had spent months at the mercy of a Dark Lord. He couldn't dismiss them so easily. Neither could he ignore what she was, no matter what she wanted to call herself. His lip curled in distaste. "You draw your magic from the souls of others." An ugly thought touched him. "You own Peters' soul. That's why he's helping you."

Andy looked at him, her green eyes filled with pity. "I take nothing that's not freely offered, and I always give something in return. James Peters is a decent man who wanted a chance to make up for his past. I've given him that. I have no hold over him."

"What about River?" His eyes narrowed. "You have some sort of hold over her."

"You're wrong," Andy said softly. "She has a hold over *me*. She gave me a soul. She grew it from something inside me that was there, but had never developed. She already owns mine. I can never own hers. All I can do is to ask for her help."

His head ached and he wanted nothing more than to believe her, but he was too close to the finish line to lose everything now. "No one can grow souls."

"River can."

From the front of the lab, Peters fired a shot. "That was just a warning," he called over his shoulder to Hawk. "They'll want to stay in their car for a while." Hawk heard him swear. "On second thought, they're going to back up out of range. That means they'll try to sneak in through the fence." He fired another shot. "At least they're going to be backing up on a flat tire."

"What do you want River to do?" Hawk asked Andy.

She hesitated. "I want her to convince her mother to give me her magic."

That would never happen. River's mother had no reason to trust Andy. Hawk didn't trust her either.

But that wasn't really the problem Hawk suddenly faced. The problem was whether or not he trusted River enough to make decisions he might not agree with.

Did she understand what it meant to be Fae?

♦ ♦

River pinched her eyes shut and opened them again, unable to see anything as her pupils worked to adjust to the pitch black. With no sense of where she now was, she reached her hand out to gather her bearings.

One palm cut through the cold dark air in front of her and came up empty.

"Hawk?" she whispered, wondering what the hell had just happened. One second she was with him, the next she was gone.

Maybe she'd jumped.

She shook the buzz from her head and drew in fresh air, catching a warm, familiar scent on the cold, icy wind.

Her eyes adjusted to the dim light. She was inside the graveyard.

She turned around in a slow circle, trying to orient herself to her new surroundings. Despite the chill in the mountain air, her flesh began to tingle when she found a towering wall of green behind her, across what had once been the exterior door to the building. She locked her knees to keep her upright.

She couldn't go backward.

Which meant she had no choice but to move forward.

Alone.

Hawk would have to take care of himself. This might be her last chance to help her parents find peace. She dipped her chin and stepped to the side, putting distance between herself and the row of headstones. She prayed the monsters buried in those shallow graves stayed where they were until she figured out how to free her parents.

Her pulse hammered but slowed slightly as the warm scent of sage drifted past her nostrils and propelled her into action. Dead leaves, slippery from the snowfall, crunched beneath her boots as she stepped forward. The sound of the outside world fell silent behind her, drowned out by the pounding of her heart.

And then, a gentle soul called out to her.

Guided by instinct, and drawn to her mother's presence, she walked unerringly to an unmarked grave, so achingly familiar to her that her insides twisted like a knotted root. She stood over it, not sure what she felt, although something about the last of the autumn's green grass still lush and green with life gave River a measure of comfort.

The grave was her father's. The presence that guarded it belonged to her mother. In life, the Guardians protected the Fae. In death, the Fae watched over them in return.

She dropped to her knees on the snow-slickened ground. An invisible band tightened around her heart as a million questions raced through her head.

She focused on one and whispered quietly into the night: "What is your name?"

A long moment of silence followed and then in the softest, most gentle voice she heard her mother say, *Annia*.

River's chest fluttered as raw emotions ripped through her. She struggled to steady her breathing. Her mother's name was Annia. How beautiful.

"I'm River," she said in response.

Something that felt like a palm touched her cheek and River had the sense that her mother was smiling at her. Eyes stinging, River grappled for control. If there was ever a time that she needed to think clearly, now was it. Taking a deep breath, she collected herself before asking, "Please. How can I help you?"

I want to know you, came her mother's reply, her hushed voice floating over the graveyard and warming everything it touched. The storm that lingered over the mountains did not reach this spot.

River drew back in awe. Hawk was mistaken. *This* was what it was like to be touched by a Fae.

"I'd really like for you to know me." River placed her palm over the warm spot on her cheek, released a long, slow breath, and let down all of her defenses. "I'd like to know you, too."

The second she opened herself, heat flared inside her and River gasped in response. Never in her life had she felt anything quite like this. Her head began spinning, and her heart crashed against her chest. River braced her hands on the cold ground to center herself as her mother's soul wrapped itself tightly around hers.

Memories flooded her. River's fingers dug into the dirt as those memories played out like an old VHS movie on fast forward in her mind's eye.

Time seemed suspended, and the world to slow, as she learned more about her biological parents. When she felt the love between her Fae mother and her Guardian father, and the love they still felt for their lost child, her heart skipped several beats. In return, River showed them that she'd been well loved by the parents who'd raised her, and that this world was her home. She wanted for nothing.

As her mother's soul continued to wrap around

hers, hugging tighter and tighter, River felt something else. She felt her mother's worry, her concern
for River's future, and her fear for the world River
loved.

"I'm okay," she whispered into the darkness, trying
to erase her mother's worries.

You're where you belong.

River thought her mother was sending some sort of
warning, except right now she didn't have time to dis-
sect it. "But you're not," she replied, briefly shutting
her eyes. A tear slipped from her closed eyelids, then
she blinked her eyes open, feeling stronger than she'd
ever felt before. "How do I free you?"

A sudden explosion knocked River to her stomach
on the damp ground. The acrid scent of sulfur and
gasoline stung her nostrils and she quickly scrambled
to her feet and spun around, prepared for a fight, until
she realized what had happened.

Hawk had tried to blast his way through with a grenade.

Instead, the green wall of foliage grew thicker and
higher until it formed an impenetrable wall around
the entire graveyard, protecting her.

River could hear Hawk swearing on the other side
of the green fence and Andy trying to calm him. It
might have been funny, except at the sound of their
voices, her mother retreated.

"No!" River spun back around, but it was too late.
She no longer felt her mother's soul wrapped around
hers. "Tell me how to free you!" she cried out.

When her plea met with no response, fear cut through

her and she ran to the door of the building, but the wall of green prevented her from reaching Hawk and Andy on the other side.

She needed their help. River ran her hands over the foliage, trying to find an opening. "Hawk!"

"I can't get through," she heard Hawk respond, frustration roughening his voice.

River searched the wall from her side. "Is there any other way around?"

When Andy spoke, her voice sounded much calmer than Hawk's. "Try calling the magic to you, River."

River had never called magic before. She didn't know how.

"Hurry," Andy added.

She was going to have to learn quickly. River held her hands out, palms up against the wall, and called the magic to her. The lush green leaves began to darken and crumble beneath her fingertips. A little surprised by the new talent, and not really liking it but trusting Andy, River continued to call the magic to her until a gaping hole appeared in the wall.

When she stepped back, Andy came through it. Hawk quickly followed.

"Are you okay?" he demanded, his eyes raking over her.

River reached past him and released a bit of the magic back into the foliage. She touched the dead twigs and under her care, the stems thickened to the size of saplings. Roots continued to knot together, spreading onward and outward until the hole mended itself and re-formed a protective barrier.

She liked giving life much better than taking it. Taking it felt dirty. Greasy.

She wiped her palms on her jeans before stepping back to admire her work. She savored the sense of peace that healing gave her.

This was a much better feeling.

"I met my mother," she said to Hawk. The wonder of that fact continued to fill her. "But I don't know how to free her." She turned to Andy. "What do I do?"

Andy, with her kind, lovely face and gray-streaked dark hair, looked nervous and ready to bolt. River didn't fully understand the hostility toward Andy she now sensed from her mother. Only River's acceptance of the other woman as someone she loved kept her mother from striking her.

This was terrible. River knew in her heart that violence had somehow damaged her gentle Fae mother. She hoped that by setting her free, she would help her find peace.

She wanted both of her parents to be at rest.

Andy, her beautiful emerald green eyes solemn, kept her voice soft and apologetic. "I gave souls to the bioengineered animals Amos Kaye was creating to try to humanize them. Until you gave me a soul, I swear, I didn't understand that what I was doing was wrong. I wanted to give them a conscience. I was a sci-entist." Andy was speaking to River, but River knew the apology was meant for her mother. "The night your parents were killed, things went terribly wrong. Your mother's soul came back to try to protect your father. Somehow, my magic got tied up and tangled with hers. Your mother is holding it now, and until she re-leases it back to me, I can't untangle it, and she can't be freed."

"What do I do?" River asked.

Andy looked deep into her eyes. Regret for the past clung to her like a shroud. "I'm sorry, River. I'm sorry for what I've done. Can you convince your mother to release her magic to me?"

"You aren't to blame for things that happened in another lifetime." River searched for her mother. "Andy wants to do the right thing," River said to her. "What's in the past needs to be laid to rest."

On the heels of River's acceptance came her mother's. River felt her mother release the magic. Andy gasped and drew it in.

"River, no!" Hawk shouted. His hands went to his head and she felt a tug on her soul as he dropped to his knees. "Don't—"

As Andy used magic to untie the souls, River dropped to her knees beside Hawk. A blast sounded in the distance and the wall of green shook. It occurred to River that she and Andy had little time left.

Hawk had none.

One minute he was beside her, the next he was gone.

Down on her hands and knees, cradling his still form in her arms, River's breath rushed from her lungs. Her mother's soul brushed against hers one more time before her presence disappeared.

Two holes joined the others. She'd taken River's father's soul with her.

River placed her hand on Hawk's cheek. Her heart ached, knowing she could try to draw him back, but if keeping him here longer didn't kill him, it would be a temporary reunion at best. He needed to return to his body.

"River, I know how to defeat the Dark Lord but I'll need your magic to do it."

The urgency in Andy's voice drew her attention from Hawk. River didn't understand at first what Andy was talking about. Then she remembered Hawk hadn't been alone in his head.

When she returned her attention to him, the eyes staring at her intently were no longer his.

They were Nick's.

CHAPTER EIGHTEEN

♦

Naked, wet, and shivering, Hawk rolled from the incubator to his hands and knees on the floor of the cryonics lab despite the hands trying to restrain him.

The smooth, hard tiles, the headache threatening to blow the lid off his brain, plus Spence clucking at him like an old mother hen, assured him more than anything else that he was home.

The fact that the timing couldn't be any fucking worse convinced him as well. He shook his head in an attempt to focus his eyes and happened to glance down past his navel.

Those were his boys dangling there, all right.

He tried to climb to his feet and fell flat on his face. A cry of protest rang out from the boys.

"Be careful, Colonel Hawkins," a woman's voice cautioned. A beautiful blonde's face swam into focus beside him as he turned his head. All he could think was that the face wasn't River's. "We pulled you from stasis a little too quickly. It will be a few hours before you regain enough motor control to sit, let alone stand."

A few hours. River might not have that much time. Desperation had him once again struggling to get his feet underneath him. Again, he sprawled gasping to the floor. Fire licked at his lungs as he sucked in his first breaths of air.

"Send me back," he ordered, except it came out more as a garbled, croaking noise with no resemblance to speech. The fire in his lungs turned to a roaring inferno.

"It will be awhile before you can speak, too," he heard Spence add. "And it's going to hurt like a son of a bitch because you've got warm air hitting thawing tissue."

No shit.

Then Spence, too, was on his knees beside him, trying to help lift him up. Since Hawk outweighed the elderly scientist by at least 110 pounds, he'd prefer being left on the floor, because chances were good Spence would drop him and his head already felt like it had cracked. Another good blow should split it wide open.

"Get me a stretcher," Spence barked at the woman. "We've got to get him out of here before we're discovered."

What in the name of the Mother was going on? Why would Spence not want anyone to see them?

What was happening to River?

The warm, comforting presence of her soul against his was gone, and for a few moments, Hawk went insane. He had no control over his body. He couldn't speak, he could barely see. The claustrophobic sense of being trapped in his own body was far worse than any of the torture he'd experienced to date. Physical pain, he could handle. Worry for River and this awful state of helplessness were too much for his mind to absorb.

"He's going into cardiac arrest!" Spence said sharply.

Hawk was flipped to his back, and then a thousand needles of excruciating pain shot through his chest to his fingertips as Spence jump-started his heart.

The associated pain brought him back to his senses. Losing his mind wouldn't help River. Neither would losing hope. She could take care of herself. That was what he needed to remember.

But once he was back on his feet, he would tear the universe apart if he had to in order to find his way back to her.

"This is no good, Shana," Spence was saying. He was breathing hard and Hawk realized the old man sounded distressed. "I'm going to have to sedate him. He's too agitated. We need Achala."

Hawk didn't want to be sedated. He tried to say so, but the proper formation of words continued to elude him. A sharp prick on his arm, then a cold, spreading tingle that ran up his shoulder and into his neck told him it was too late to protest.

"Dr. Jennings, someone's coming!"

Again, Hawk wondered why that was so bad, but his head started to swim as the drugs took effect.

◆ ◆

River gasped.

"Miss me?" Nick asked, a cocky gleam in his gaze.

But that cocky gleam quickly dissolved as doubt moved in to take its place. Struggling, Nick blinked and River witnessed the battle going on inside him.

"What the—"

Doubt became panic, and then River wasn't staring into Nick's eyes.

She was staring into the Dark Lord's.

"Nick!" she shouted at him, trying to call him back, but his body stiffened. Unable to reach Nick, who was now trapped deep inside his own body, River jumped to her feet and sprang away as if stung.

Andy stepped to her side. "Do you want the Dark Lord defeated?"

"Yes!" River said, badly frightened. She'd never been able to do so herself. Even in her game, he'd had to beat her in order for her to win.

"Then give me your magic," Andy demanded.

River reacted instinctively to a command.

Andy grabbed her by the hand as she opened herself. Energy shifted inside River, building, increasing in strength. Then she felt it move down her arms, to her fingertips, and flow out into Andy.

Andy spoke softly under her breath but River couldn't understand what she was saying. The air changed and the wind picked up, blowing dirt and debris across her face. Another explosion rattled the ground beneath her.

Within seconds, the Dark Lord was on his feet, moving toward them. Andy pushed River to the side, her eyes darkening as she lifted her hands.

The Dark Lord let loose a bolt of lightning, striking Andy, but she shook it off easily and retaliated with a bolt of her own. The resulting clap of thunder sent River careening backward. She heard the snap of her wrist as she landed on the hard ground. Pain shot up her arm. She tried to clear her head, to heal her bone, but everything was happening so fast and she no longer had possession of her magic. A shot rang out on the other side of the enclosure.

Electricity charged the air, lifting her hair and setting her nerve endings on fire. She might have been standing in a glass bowl during a lightning storm.

The storm stopped. Nick, his face twisted in angry disbelief, crumpled and fell.

River spun around in time to see Andy begin to collapse as well. She rushed to her, gathering her into her arms and trying to keep her on her feet.

As long as she was standing, it meant she was fine.

Andy placed her palm on River's cheek and sent back the magic River had loaned her.

She was releasing what remained of her life to River, too.

"Stop it," River cried, grasping the magic and trying to heal the gaping hole in her friend's chest. "Don't do this to me."

"I'm so tired," Andy sighed.

River closed her hand over Andy's and could feel the magic, stronger than ever now, pour back into her soul as Andy released it to her. River's skin began to prickle.

"You could never have beaten him," Andy said. "Not as you are. Fae give life, they don't take it away." She struggled for breath. "I want you to be Fae. Don't start down a path not meant for you."

"If I give life, then let me give it to you." River tried to redirect the magic back into Andy, but again, nothing happened.

"You've already done that. Several times, in fact. This time I did what needed to be done. Let me be Fae, just this once." A lump lodged in River's throat when she realized her friend had given her life to save River's and was refusing to take it back.

"You can still save Nick." Andy's voice was thready now, and growing weaker. "He's worth saving. So is this world. They'll be coming for you, you know. When they do, this world will mean nothing to them."

That was the last thing River heard Andy say before her friend's lids fell shut and her gentle soul drifted away.

She turned to Nick on the ground nearby. Magic, recently ignited and still seeking release, raced through her body and boiled her blood, raising her internal temperature to dangerous levels.

Using that energy she held her palms out and centered her magic on Nick's chest. He emerged from the depths, his wild eyes locking on hers.

The Dark Lord was gone from them.

Nick cried out in pain as he gasped for breath. "What the hell are you doing?"

Giving you life, you bastard. She hoped Andy was right, and that he was worth it, because in reality, River was furious with him.

He sat up, incredulous, checking his body. He looked at her and parted his lips, but before he could vocalize anything, River punched him in the mouth, knocking him backward.

Nick let loose a round of curses as he spit out a mouthful of blood.

"That was for Hawk," she said.

Kaye's voice sounded on the other side of the wall and her rage redirected. She rose to her feet, and as darkness spread through her body, swamping her, she drew air into her lungs, lifted her hands, and gathered her magic.

She heard Peters yelling out to her, and she remembered the cue. She directed her magic to ignite the C4, then grabbed Nick and jumped before the graveyard exploded.

They landed on the top of the ridge, their limbs intertwined. Hot, violent energy erupted below as the building shattered from multiple explosions, the force of the blasts sending shards of glass sailing across the night sky, the deadly fragments glittering as smoke and flames shot upward.

River disentangled herself and climbed to her feet. She shot a glance at Nick, who looked shell-shocked and frightened. She breathed deep and closed her eyes to the chaos. After a long pause, she opened her eyes again and took in the destruction around her.

She saw Peters run from the wreckage, the grenade launcher still strapped to his back. He wiped dirt from his eyes as he strode up the mountain to join her.

"You good?" he asked, breathless by the time he joined them.

River sent out a thread in an attempt to locate Hawk, but felt nothing in response. Heaviness settled around her heart.

"We're good," she answered, and turned to Nick. She held a hand out to him, and he understood the implications. He accepted it, and a truce was formed.

"Where's Andy?" Peters asked.

River shook her head, unable to speak, and hoped her friend had finally found the peace she was seeking. As she recalled Andy's parting words, she took one more look at the wreckage below and knew Andy was right, River hadn't even begun to do what needed to be done. She owed it to her parents, all four of them, and she owed it to her friend.

Nick made a noise and she turned to him. His gaze scanned the ground before settling on her. They stared at each other for a long moment, then he broke the silence by asking, "Where do we go from here?"

She looked at the sky. The storm had passed, and stars now winked against a black velvet backdrop.

Hawk was gone. Their connection was broken, and the pain of it consumed her heart in a way she doubted would ever completely heal. She needed to accept that, because although he'd insisted she was Fae, he didn't fully understand what that meant. Now, thanks to Andy, she did.

Fae gave life, they didn't take it away. For him to ask her to walk away from her world was like asking her to abandon her soul.

And if he returned for her as he'd said he would, he wouldn't be returning alone.

She turned to Peters.

"We need to prepare. An army is coming."

EPILOGUE

Hawk waited impatiently outside the meeting chamber in the Hall of the Great Lords, although his impatience would have been apparent only to someone who knew him well.

There was only one person in the universe who knew him that well, and no matter what the result of this meeting with the Great Lords, he intended to find her. It had been two days now and he would not wait a third.

The one positive outcome was the return of his body. He'd never considered himself handsome, but now when he looked in the mirror, he wanted to kiss himself.

He wished he'd punched himself in the face at least once though, before he'd been yanked from Nick Sutton's body. He'd been too worried about River at the time to think of it.

"Colonel Hawkins?"

Hawk looked up at the sound of his name. A page had been sent to summon him, a young man with a faint scruff of beard meant to make him seem older. He looked like a child with a hormone problem.

Hawk followed him into the meeting chamber to face the row of men seated at a long table on the far side of the room.

Hawk understood the venue, as well as its purpose.
Anyone walking across that broad, empty space had
plenty of time to reflect on the importance of the hearing. The intent was to intimidate.

Intimidation was wasted on Hawk. He had survived
imprisonment with a Dark Lord. These men were
mortals. Nothing they could do or say would keep
him from searching for River. He had enough friends
in high places who owed him favors to see to it.

Spence was one of them, and the fact that Hawk
hadn't seen him since being pulled from stasis was a
cause for concern. He would raise that question with
the Great Lords as well.

"Colonel Hawkins, it's good to see you've rejoined
us," the First Lord greeted him. "You appear to be in
excellent health. Dr. Jess tells us you came through
cryonics with flying colors."

Hawk nodded his acknowledgment and waited.
Something about this debriefing didn't feel right to
him.

The First Lord cleared his throat in the silence. "Dr.
Jennings informed us you volunteered for the experiment."

"Yes." Hawk waited again.

"Perhaps you could tell us what you've encountered
over the past thirteen months."

Hawk still found it difficult to believe that he'd been
in stasis for more than a year. That was 231 days longer than anyone before him.

It was also thirty-five days longer than Spence had
considered safe. He didn't know whether to be pissed

or pleased that Spence had given him the extra time. He did know that something had made Spence pull him too fast, and that he hadn't seen the scientist since. If he wasn't so worried about River, he decided he'd be pissed. Something really was not right.

"I was captured and imprisoned by a Dark Lord," he said.

Hawk went on to explain how his consciousness had drifted too close to the forgotten virtual prison on the desert planet. He told how River had tapped into the prison through a game, and that they'd escaped together by working their way through its levels.

"Once you were free, why didn't you return to our world?" one of the Great Lords asked.

"Because River is Fae."

"Impossible."

"I'm afraid it isn't." Hawk turned to the Lord who had spoken. Hawk remembered the gray-haired and humorless man from his military career as a solid but unimpressive leader. "Nearly thirty years ago, a Fae and a Guardian were lost. They're dead now, but River is their daughter. She possesses Fae magic. She has a Fae soul."

Caution made Hawk tell the story of her parents as simply as he could. The Guardian had discovered what was happening to the lost souls. He'd died trying to protect the Fae and their unborn child from the ones who had stolen those souls, but the Fae hadn't survived and her soul had been captured. Their daughter had been raised by people who had no idea who or what she was. He left out any details of River, and also of Andy.

He had no idea what to think of Andy.

"River is Fae, and she's in danger. I have to go back for her," Hawk finished. "I need to bring her home." He'd had his face clenched so tightly to keep his emotions in check that a muscle in his jaw went into spasm. If River was dead, he'd make damned sure her soul was at peace. She wouldn't suffer the way her parents had for thirty years.

Dust motes fluttered and danced in the broad beams of light streaming in through the skylights. They wouldn't say no to him. They would never abandon a Fae.

"Well." The First Lord sank back in his seat, his palms pressed together so that his fingers steepled in front of his face and his two thumbs rested under his chin, giving him the appearance of a man deep in thought. "Dr. Jennings has gotten more from his experiment than he could have imagined."

"Where is Dr. Jennings?" Hawk asked, directing his question to the First Lord but sweeping his gaze across the panel to include them all. "As you pointed out, this was his experiment. He would want to learn the results."

The First Lord peered at Hawk over his fingertips. "Dr. Jennings resigned from his position and has gone into retirement."

Spence had retired before hearing the details of Hawk's travels? It was too far out of character to make any sense. Spencer Jennings was the nosiest man Hawk knew, although in a kind and well-intentioned way. Spence liked people.

And he loved research.

"You spoke of a Dark Lord," another one of the Great Lords interrupted, fracturing the uncomfortable silence that had greeted the news of Spence's unexpected and uncharacteristic retirement. "Is he dead?"

The bastard had been killed a couple of times now, so Hawk would never be sure. But Andy was an immortal as well, and she had River to help take him out. He hoped Nick Sutton got what was coming to him, too.

"He's an immortal," Hawk said, as if that explained it all. "Even though his program failed, Fae magic contained him. It shouldn't be assumed that he's dead." It could only be hoped for.

"This Fae you speak of," the First Lord pressed. "She tapped into a Guardian prison through a video game?" Hawk inclined his head in confirmation. "Doesn't that indicate to you that she has the abilities of her father as well?"

Nodding once again, Hawk worked hard to keep his expression neutral. They were wasting valuable time. They all knew what the outcome of this meeting would be. He should be traveling.

"It's unfortunate about the Fae and her Guardian," one of the Lords said to the others, speaking as if Hawk wasn't present. "Very sad. Without the last rites of the spiritual leaders to send the Fae's soul on its journey, that soul is now damaged. Corrupt. The Fae need to know of this."

Corrupt? Hawk thought of the shining soul that had lingered for nearly thirty years, protecting its loved ones. The Great Lords were wrong. But that was for the Fae to explain to them.

"What of the Fae who survives?" he asked. "She needs our protection." She needed *him*.

Something unspoken passed between the Great Lords. Cold premonition hit Hawk like an icy fist.

They weren't going to help her.

The First Lord spoke. "Give us a few moments, Colonel Hawkins."

Incredulous anger washed over him in fierce, fiery waves, dispelling the chill. He nodded, spun on his heel, and with steady steps walked from the hall as if inside, he wasn't about to explode. He had known this was a possibility. Deep down he hadn't believed it.

Waiting to be told River would be offered no help was the most difficult thing Hawk had done in the past thirteen months. He had no intentions of abiding by any decision that kept him from her. He would go after her. If that meant he could never return to his world, it was no longer a loss to him.

But a part of him continued to hold onto hope, and as hard as it was, he decided to wait for their final decision.

While it seemed like forever, it was no more than fifteen minutes before he was called back into the room and again stood in front of the Lords.

"Colonel Hawkins," the First Lord began, "before we go in search of this half-breed, there are a few things you need to understand. The first is where the Dark Lords came from. There is a reason why Guardians and Fae are forbidden to pair."

Hawk listened in angry disbelief as they told him that Dark Lords and half-breeds were one and the same.

"Dark Lords are male," he said, repeating what he'd always been taught, his insides twisting in denial.

"Males are stronger and more aggressive, therefore more likely to survive a confrontation," the First Lord replied. "And there's always confrontation when Dark Lords meet. That's why we'd thought all but the one imprisoned had died off."

They believed that River was a Dark Lord.

Hawk had suspected it of Andy. He still did, despite her assertion she was an immortal and not necessarily evil. So why wouldn't they believe it of River? The Great Lords didn't know her. They didn't know it couldn't be possible.

They were wrong.

"What else do I need to know?" he asked, his voice and expression carefully controlled. River was in more danger than he'd thought, and from the people he'd expected to protect her. He had no intention of not getting the assignment that was coming.

"The world where you found the half-breed has been corrupted by Dark Lords. We'd spared it in the past at the request of the Fae, and because the last of the Dark Lords had been captured and was considered no longer a threat. Now the Dark Lords are back, and from what you've told us, whether directly or not, most likely the cause of the missing Fae souls." The First Lord rested his weight on his forearms on the long table before him, his hands loosely clasped. "You asked for this assignment, and you will be offered it. You, Colonel Hawkins, are a demolition man. You will return to this world, and you will defuse it. It is no longer worth salvaging."

What of people like Peters? And River's brothers, Jake and Sam? Were they beyond salvage?

Inside, Hawk was reeling. Outwardly, he maintained his calm. He had to, for River's sake.

And then came the final blow.

"And as for the half-breed," the First Lord continued, "she must be destroyed as well. Based on your report, imprisonment is no longer an option. She cannot be allowed to come into her full magic. If she does, there will be no way to stop her." He fixed his eyes on Hawk, and in them, any pretense of mildness was gone.

"No world will be safe from her."

TOR
ROMANCE

Believe that love is magic

Please join us at the website below
for more information about this
author and other great romance
selections, and to sign up for our
monthly newsletter!

www.tor-forge.com